Twelve

Happy Reading!

Susan Bran

Twelve

by

Susan Brown

Yellow Farmhouse Publications

Twelve

ISBN Print Edition: 978-1-950402-02-1

Yellow Farmhouse Publications, Lake Stevens, WA, USA
Copyright © 2021
Publication Date: 2021
www.susanbrownwrites.com

This is a work of fiction. Names, characters, places and incidents are either the product of the author's imagination or are used fictitiously, and any resemblance to actual persons, living or dead, business establishments, events or locales is entirely coincidental.

Excerpt from Dragons of Frost and Fire 9781514161852
© 2015 by Susan Brown
Excerpt from The Nightmare and the Unicorn 9781950402038
© 2021 by Susan Brown

Cover and Interior Design: Heather McIntyre
Cover&Layout, www.coverandlayout.com

Cover Photography: Granite © Areeya Slangsing;
Marble © Vvoevale; Opal © Ruslan Minakryn;
Rhodochrosite © Ruslan Minakryn; Amber © Jazziel D;
Limestone © Johan Larson; Chalk, Peridot © vvoe;
Agate © Hubert Schwarz; Jade © Vladimirkarp;
Sandstone © Somnath C; Obsidian © Tyler Boyes;
Kronos © karlovserg

This book is dedicated to my family,
Bobby, Laurel, Heather, and Karen

who listened and encouraged
while I researched and struggled to
create this story. They embody all
the traits of humanity that formed
the backbone of this book.

Books by Susan Brown

www.susanbrownwrites.com

Fantasy:

The Nightmare and the Unicorn

Dragons of Earth, Sea, Fire, and Air series:

Dragons of Frost and Fire

Dragons of Desert and Dust

Dragons of Wind and Waves

A Thunder of Dragons

* New! Boxed Set includes *Dragons of Frost and Fire, Dragons of Desert and Dust, Dragons of Wind and Waves, A Thunder of Dragons* – Find it on Amazon!

3 Witches series:

Witch Magic

Witch Fire

The Adventure Books:

Hey, Chicken Man!

Pirates, Prowlers, and Cherry Pie

Sammy and the Devil Dog

Not Yet Summer

The Amber and Elliot Mysteries **with Anne Stephenson:**
Something's Fishy at Ash Lake
The Mad Hacker
The Secret of Ash Manor

Written with Anne Stephenson as Stephanie Browning:
Outbid by the Star
Undone by the Boss
Making Up is Hard to Do
The Boy She Left Behind, *An All American Boy Romance*

Short Story Collections:
Holiday Cheers: *Stories to Celebrate Your Year*
Romance in Pajama Pants: *Stories to Celebrate Your Happily Ever After*
Romance Sweet and Dark: *The Patchwork of Love*
Last Dance at the Polka Dot Restaurant: *And Other Travels Through Life*
Fantasy Shorts: *Stories to Tickle Your Wonder*

Twelve

Contents

Part II
Apple Tor Castle, Peaks District, England

Bodhhgaya, India

Transformation

At first Deirdre grips the six-year-old twins' hands tightly, and at first Jared and Meghan are happy to press close. Jared twists to look back at the hotel sign, and stares at the letters: Hotel Bodhgaya Ashok. He doesn't know what the last two words are. He doesn't know where he is, except this place is called India. Most of the buildings have signs, but the words are written in the curly-cues and slants that his mother says is Indian writing.

Jared can't make it out.

This city makes him afraid, with its hot, hot air. Dust rises in the streets, so that when the wind blows he can see nothing but a reddish cloud. The crowded, smelly train had frightened him. Everyone shouted and laughed and talked in words he couldn't understand. The bus after that was worse – more crowded and smellier.

When Deirdre pauses for a moment, Jared shuts his eyes and tries again to imagine the place that is green and safe with a pattern of pink flowers on the floor. But with a jab of fear, he remembers that even in the dream, there are shadows lurking in cupboards and behind stone walls. He opens his eyes again and looks at his twin, but she is busy staring at everything.

Meghan isn't afraid at all. Ever. She loves this hot, strange place and is determined to meet all the people and try all the food sold from roadside tents. She tugs her hand loose, and before Deirdre can stop her, darts away, disappearing into the crowd.

"Oh, drat her!" Deirdre exclaims. She stands Jared by a tree. "Don't move. Not one step!"

She runs in search of her daughter.

Jared looks in every direction. Kronos, The Man Who Watches is staring at them again. Jared can feel it. His mother won't notice him while she chases Meghan.

There. At the edge of the streaming crowd...Jared sees the burning eyes in the pale face. Despite the still air, Kronos' black hair looks like it has been thrashed by a storm. Jared knows that no one else in the pushing crowd sees Kronos. If they did, their shadowed eyes would open wide with fear and their muttering voices would rise into screams. Kronos raises a hand to Jared, beckoning, commanding. Sunlight glimmers on his golden mark.

Jared squeezes his eyes shut, breathing hard, fighting the urge to follow the beckoning hand. His Mama told him to stay put.

"Jared!" Deirdre grabs his hand. He opens his eyes with relief. "At least one of you will stand still." She glares at Meghan who laughs and tosses her fire-red hair.

"The grandpa was nice." Meghan holds up a small orange that a toothless old man has given her.

Jared looks back to Kronos. He is gone now. With his mother and sister, Jared joins the mass of people walking down the road to the temple.

"This is the holiest place in India," Deirdre tells them. "The monks know things we don't understand. I hope..." She bites her lip. "I think they might help us..."

The temple rises like a pointed ant hill. Low walls of carved pinky-red rock direct the flow of the crowd. Most people swarm along a walkway. It looks like a parade with all the flowers and fluttering silk scarves. Deirdre pulls them forward, down stone steps and past another stream of people walking round and round the temple. Jared nearly falls over a man lying on his stomach with his arms stretched out.

"Is he hurt?" He clutches his mother's hand more tightly.

"No, he's praying." She steers them past more people lying on their stomachs and over to a wall, out of the press of people. "Shoes off, kids. We can't wear them in the temple."

His mom puts their shoes in her bag, and then in sock feet, they rejoin the crowd.

People pour through the gate and towards a huge open door. Jared, Meghan and Deirdre are swept along with them into a cool, dim room. Everyone sits on the floor.

An old man in baggy yellow clothes with a red shawl over one shoulder is speaking to the seated people. Deirdre leans forward, hands twisting in her lap. Jared's eyes fix on a huge gold statue of a seated man. Buddha. Many of the people are bowing to the statue. Meghan elbows her twin and points around the room. Every wall and even the ceiling are decorated with vast pictures. While the old man talks and talks, Jared stares open-mouthed at the paintings of scenery, people, gods and demons. Some are happy; some are crying; some are writhing their many arms and showing fangs.

One picture draws his eyes. It is The Man Who Watches, riding a horse breathing fire from its mouth and striking flames from its hooves. Jared hears the hoof beats, smells the acrid smoke...

"No!" he whispers. The sounds and smells fade. He thinks the smiling statue of Buddha may have chased Kronos away.

The old man at the front stops talking. Their mother surges up from the pillows and taking each of them by hand, approaches a yellow-robed monk.

"Excuse me," she says, "I have an appointment to see His Holiness Lama Choedak Jamyang." She drops the twins' hands to pull a letter from her bag. Her voice trembles. "I was told he can help me."

The monk nods. "He expects you. Also, his Holiness Lama Satya asks permission to visit with your children."

Deirdre looks at them doubtfully. "I don't know..."

"I'm not going," Meghan grips her mother's hand. "I want to come with you, Mama, and give our presents to the llama."

The monk looks calmly at Jared.

"I'll go," Jared says. Why did he say that?

The monk bows, hands pressed together. Another young monk appears at his side. Deirdre and Meghan go with him. Nervously, Jared follows the older one along narrow corridors filled with weird smells and quiet footsteps.

"It is custom to bow three times when entering the presence of His Holiness," the monk whispers and opens a door. Jared steps into a room ablaze with color. Red walls are highlighted by yellow cloth that hangs like curtains or drapes across the furniture. A soccer ball lies under a table. On a raised platform, a boy about ten, sits cross-legged. He is dressed like the monks.

Jared stares, then says, "Hi." Behind him, the monk is bowing.

The boy smiles. "Hi, Jared," he replies. "Didn't Meghan come?"

Jared shakes his head. "She's with my mother."

The boy's expression becomes serious again and he jumps down from the platform. "I am sorry she is not here. I have something important to show you."

He heads out of the room and down the hallway. Not knowing what else to do, Jared follows. They walk down several more narrow corridors, all scented like smoky flowers, then come into the sunlight in an open courtyard. A large twisted tree grows in the center. Bits of gold glimmer on its trunk. Masses of flowers are strewn on the ground and white scarves tied to the branches lift and fall in the breeze.

Jared thinks the place should be full of people, but he and the boy are alone.

"It is under the ancestor of this fig tree that Buddha received enlightenment," the boy says. "And here," he leads Jared to a slab of brick-red stone, "is the stone on which he sat. It is the only stone strong enough to have held the world together when the transformation came. It is the center of the universe."

As though he had been told to do it, Jared steps forward and stands on the stone. Heat gathers in a pool, rises through his feet and floats up into his body, lifting him into the air.

"I'm flying!" he cries. "Can Meghan come and do this?"

The boy shakes his head. "There is only this one moment when the flow of time has stilled and she did not come. You alone are chosen."

Jared flaps his arms trying to rise higher.

The boy takes something from inside his robe – a stone, the same reddish color as the one Jared hovers over. He offers it. "I have guarded this for you through all my lifetimes. It is carved with the eyes of Buddha and holds the key to transformation and enlightenment."

"What's that?" Jared's hands close on the rock and his mind glows.

"The ancient gods cannot change. They are what they are. Neither love nor death nor suffering can transform their hearts and spirits. Only humans can become more than they were. One day people may become greater than the gods. They fear this."

"Jared!" Deirdre's voice pierces the air. Startled, Jared's feet touch the ground and he jumps off the stone. Like ghosts melting back into reality, people and chatter fill the courtyard. The stone is now covered in bright cloth, with oranges, money, and bowls of rice heaped over it. The boy smiles, then walks back into the temple.

Deirdre and Meghan run to Jared. "Thank goodness!" Deirdre hugs him. "None of the other monks spoke English. I thought I'd lost you."

"There wasn't a llama," Meghan complains as they put their shoes back on. "Just an old man with glasses. Did you see a llama?"

Jared shakes his head. "Just a boy. He gave me a stone."

For the first time Jared really looks at it. The eyes of Buddha look back. More of the curly writing he can't read has been carved into the stone.

"The old man gave me a handkerchief." Meghan displays a small square of white silk with a faded picture and the same curly writing.

"Well, at least you two got something out of this trip." Deirdre takes their hands and hauls them toward the gate. "Come on kids, we have hurry. If we're lucky, we can still make it to New York by next Friday. Pat has an audition set up for me."

"I thought we were staying," Jared protests.

"No," Deirdre says. "The Lama says he can't protect me from my demons. We have to keep going."

8   Susan Brown

Part I

Seattle, Washington

Chapter 1

The Song

March rain splattered down, cold and insistent, as fifteen-year-old Jared stepped off the San Francisco to Seattle bus and looked around. Another city, another bus station. He hefted his backpack onto his shoulders and took a couple of quick steps to catch up to his mom and Meghan. It had seemed like a miracle when this job came through – they'd been down to their last hundred dollars. If the job worked out, if they didn't have to run, the family might get a few dollars into a savings account again.

If they didn't have to run. Head down, eyelids slightly lowered, Jared scanned the milling crowds. A grandmother here, a homeless man there, a few kids running wild while their harassed parents groped through bags. Nothing to set the short hairs on his neck prickling. No hint of the hunters who never gave up, never seemed to rest.

Meghan and his mom had paused in front of a snack bar, Meghan clearly arguing to immediately make up for their missed lunch; his mom just as clearly urging for her to wait, to conserve their few remaining dollars. Jared swept his eyes over the crowd again. Everything ordinary. He let out his pent-up breath and eased through the jostling crowd of travelers.

And then...*the Song*. Jared stopped cold. He could feel sweat forming on his forehead and upper lip. He could hear it – the singing had started again.

He lifted his head like a dog to a scent. The singing was clear, very clear. This time... surely this time, he would be able to make out the words. Jared shook his head, tried to separate the unearthly melody from noises surrounding him – the growl of traffic, shouting passengers, and drumming rain. But there was too much confusion.

Over there...the singing came from the end of the station. He ran through the crowd, dodging bags, boxes and people. At an empty loading platform, he stopped and shut his eyes tightly. This time he would arrow himself to the source of the singing – finally hear all the words.

A picture crowded into his mind. He could hear everything in the bus terminal, but behind it, like a brightening movie screen, the thrumming began...

Noise of a heart beating too fast...beating in terror....
Fist clutching....

Behind...red eyes...the red-eared dogs of night... howling...closer...closer....hunting through the woods... baying for blood...

Heart throbbing...

But the last Guardian will follow the lines of power and sing the Song of Light...He begins the chanting melody...it lifts into the wind.

Jared can hear it now...it fills him again...he can sing with the old man...

A hard hand tugged his sleeve. "Hey kid, spare some change?"

The Song shattered. Jared blinked, confused. A raggedy teenager, only a couple of years older than himself, held out her hand. Her eyes were grey nuggets in a white face.

"What?"

"Change," the girl whined. "I got nowhere to sleep. Nothing to eat...you got some money? Something in your pack to help me out?"

Her hand inserted itself under the flap, fingers searching.

"No way," Jared twisted away. "Hey! What do you think you're doing?"

"I could trade," the girl whispered. "I got this to trade…"

She held up her fist, so close to Jared's face that he could scarcely make out the twisted shape of a tattoo above the knuckle of her middle finger. It seemed to be a distorted spider…shimmering in front of his eyes.

"Hey! Get away!" the girl shrieked.

A black and white dog pushed between Jared and the girl, growling deep in its throat. The girl faltered back, made shooing motions with her hands, then with a hoarse sob turned and ran. The dog's growling stopped, his head raised and with an air of all business taken care of, scratched his ear with a hind foot. Without a glance at Jared, he turned and trotted through the crowds.

"Now, that was weird," Jared muttered. Almost as weird, he thought, as trying to learn a Song that no one else could hear. Or as weird as carrying ten heavy rocks in his backpack and one more stone in his pocket as his family gypsied around the world. The Song was silent again. Slowly, he wove back through the thinning crowd to his mom and sister.

"Jared," his mom's voice rose over the hubbub. "Get the bags, hon."

His small family had not paid any attention to his dash through the crowd. Jared wasn't really surprised – he had long since become aware that the Song sometimes suppressed time, or memory, or just plain noticing. With a nod to his mom, he picked up two suitcases; Meghan dropped the bag she'd held to push back her long red hair with both hands.

"The rain's turning me into a frizzball." She pulled an elastic from her pocket and caught her hair into a fat ponytail. Like her brother, she carried a bulging, frayed backpack over her shoulders. Hers was weighted down with books, music and a flute; Jared's shoulders ached with the weight of his fist-sized rocks.

"Now, if you just turn left, Mrs. Singer," the ticket agent was telling their mother, "and go along Stewart about two blocks, there's the Regency Inn right there." He beamed at her. "It's a nice place. Better than that Carmen Hotel you were talking about."

"Thank you, so much." Deirdre smiled charmingly and turned back to her children.

"Another guy?" Meghan teased softly. She hoisted her bag higher on her shoulders.

"Oh, don't be silly," her mom shushed her. "He's just a nice person trying to be helpful." She picked up her own suitcase and led them toward the street.

Outside the station, an old man with a curling white beard sat with a sign:

Real Change, Seattle's Homeless Newspaper. Help the Homeless Help Themselves.

Jared eyed at the man's tattered clothes and turned his head away. His stomach knotted. Homeless came after broke. His family was awfully close to broke....

Meghan's gaze slid past the dirt and rips, up to the man's face. She smiled. "Wet today," she said.

His clear eyes sparkled. "Not so bad as yesterday. It'll come onto sun in a bit. Have a good afternoon."

"Thank you," she called back.

"Why'd you talk to him?" Jared hissed.

"Why didn't you?" she retorted. "He's broke. That's hard enough without being invisible, too."

Jared flushed and glanced back. The black and white dog stood with its front paws propped on the old man's knees. His master was talking to him and gently rubbing his ears.

The family trudged down Stewart Street, giving the Regency Inn only a brief look of regret. The Seattle Space Needle, built for the '62 World's Fair, towered in the distance.

Above, city crows wheeled and squawked. At Sixth Avenue they turned left, away from the Space Needle, and kept on walking. Expensive shops gave way to shabby stores. To his right, down a steep hill, Jared could see the rippling glint of Puget Sound.

"How far is it?" Meghan grunted.

"Another couple of blocks. It's very central – close to Pike Place Market and the historic part of town," Deirdre Singer said.

Jared and Meghan exchanged depressed glances. Historic always meant old and run-down when it came to their rooms.

Rain fell more heavily. Jared's dark hair slicked down and hung in his eyes. Despite the ponytail, Meghan's writhed into tight corkscrews. Finally, they cut through a parking lot to a grey hotel crouched behind an office building.

"Sweet," Meghan muttered.

The door squealed. Light barely penetrated the lobby. Behind the counter, a young man put down his phone, and stood to greet them with a wide smile.

Jared dropped the bags. An air of mildew and dust drifted upward from the threadbare carpet. An ancient elevator clanked open. No one got out.

"Ghosts," Meghan whispered.

Their mom headed to the desk.

"Welcome to The Carmen," the clerk said. "Marquis is my name, and I'm here to make your stay as comfortable as your favorite dream. Your name, please, Ma'am?"

"Deirdre Singer. My children and I have a reservation."

Marquis typed something into a computer.

"Yes, Ma'am, here it is." Marquis smiled widely again. "Six weeks. That's a long time to be sightseeing."

"I'll be working. I have a role in *The Phantom of the Opera* revival."

"No way!" Marquis exclaimed. "I thought they all was staying at the Warwick."

"The main players are. I have a small part a friend arranged for me."

"You sing then?"

"Whenever I can."

"Well, well!" Marquis rubbed his hands together. "A star staying at our hotel. I'll give you the best efficiency suite in the house. Big and at the back. None of that traffic noise. Fully equipped with a range top, fridge and dishes. And no extra charge!"

"Thank you." Mrs. Singer smiled. "We appreciate it."

"Yes, Ma'am. Comfortable as a dream. Take the elevator to sixth floor then turn right.

Corner room on your left."

The twins picked up the bags and followed their mom into the elevator.

"I think this dream's going to be a nightmare," Meghan said. The doors crashed shut, opened a couple of inches, and then banged shut again.

"At least there's a nice desk clerk," Mrs. Singer pointed out. "That makes it more pleasant."

"And the hotel's in a business area," Jared added. "We can go sightseeing without getting mugged."

Over the last few years, the hotels had gotten worse and worse as their mom struggled harder and harder for bit parts in the operas and traveling musical productions that supported them. Most big cities had their own opera companies and regular theater players. Deirdre picked up the leavings – this time taking a part in the chorus. The contracted actor had broken her leg.

That was the way it always was now. Sometimes a singer would get sick, or take time off for a baby, or quarrel with the director. The production company would frantically call the agents, and Pat, their mom's agent would call Deirdre, telling her what city she had to get to – right away.

"I fill in for disaster," Deirdre had said wryly.

The elevator clanged to a stop. The doors

squealed open.

A young man, unshaven with greasy hair, eyed them from the hall.

"Up or down?" he demanded.

"Up," Deirdre said.

He grunted. Deirdre pushed the "Close Door" button. Nothing happened. They stared at the man in the hall and he stared at them. His eyes slid over to Meghan and his expression changed. Jared stepped in front of his sister. She elbowed him.

"What floor..." Deirdre began to ask. The doors clanged shut.

"I know I'm going to just love this place," Meghan said.

"Only six weeks, sweetie. Seattle's a great city. When the weather clears we can rent a car and drive to the ocean beaches. They're spectacular."

A sudden memory of sound...pounding waves...pounding footsteps. Jared stiffened. The call was from a place by the ocean. But, how could his whole family have been maneuvered here from hundreds of miles away? Did the magic in the rocks completely control their lives?

Automatically, Jared closed his fingers around the rock in his pocket...remembering.

Athens, Greece

Hope

Seven years old. Alone with his sister in the hotel room on the outskirts of Athens. An ear infection aching like a stabbing spike. The thrumming starts. Must be the pain...

"Mama, it's calling me..." He'd forgotten...Mama is at rehearsal. Meghan is asleep.

Still in pajamas, he stumbles out of the seedy hotel.

"Kali mara!" calls a white-haired old man sitting by the front door. "That way, good playing for you...maybe you will find a treasure... "

"Thank you...Efharisto..." Jared mumbles. A few dirty streets. Some puzzled looks from residents. Then a parched pasture littered with broken stones.

In his head, voices are singing, then shouting and crying, piercing his mind. He claps his hands to his ears but that does not block out the shrieking.

"What do you want?" he cries. The skinny goat in the distance stares a moment and goes back to cropping the bare ground.

He turns, and a house, shining white and gold in the sunlight, rises before him. Where the field was dried up and brown, plants nod in the breeze and waterfalls gurgle from basins of gleaming white rock.

Jared goes up stone steps. All the doors and windows are open so he goes in, glad to be out of the sun and heat. In the center is a garden, cool and delicious smelling. A lady sits at a table with a stone vase in front of her. She stares at it, sometimes running her fingers over the surface. Shyly, Jared comes over.

"Hi!" he says.

The lady does not even look up. She just stares and stares at the vase, so Jared looks at it too. The stone is the color of rich blood and sunny clouds blended together. Streaks of pure white branch through it. A black lid seals the mouth.

"This vase must hold a treasure...or else why would the container be fashioned with such rare marble?" the woman says to herself. "And why should I not simply peek? I won't touch or take. The gods surely do not mean that I should not look. Other people perhaps...but I am Pandora and am blessed above other women. Their rule could not be intended for me...."

She stands, strokes the rich marble once more, and then smiling uses both hands to pull the stopper from the vase. It comes free with a hiss so loud Pandora drops it on the stone floor.

Crack! The lid shatters into a thousand thousand pieces.

Jared cries out. Smoke, the color of rotting flesh seeps out the top of the vase. The stench makes him want to throw up. The shrieking, crying, and shouting pierce his mind again.

Pandora screams. She tries to cover the top of the vase with her hands but the thick vapor oozes between her fingers.

"Help me," she cries out. "Great gods, mothers and fathers please help me! Someone help me!"

Jared falters back. He won't put his hands on the smoke. It is bad...

The smoke curls into shapes that weave back and forth in front of his eyes...sick people, dying animals, dead fields, fighting men, hungry children, empty, empty eyes. There is a sound now...laughing.

Jared screams and steps back again, but trips and falls.

Pandora pleads again and again with the gods. But there is no answer except the terrible laugh. The smoke crawls across the courtyard. It never seems to stop. The wind gusts in through the open windows and carries the smog out the doors and across the fields. Jared sees the beautiful garden wither and die.

Finally the jar is empty. Pandora lays her head on the table and sobs. The smoke has smudged her face and wrinkled her hands so that she is no longer beautiful. Jared sits on the flagstones trying not to cry. His ear throbs with pain.

The woman suddenly strikes out. The vase falls to the stone floor and shatters.

"Is there no help for us?" she whispers. The laughing fades away. Instead Jared hears a Song. It is the most beautiful Song he has ever heard, all joy and goodness. From the shards of the broken vase comes a whirring of soft wings. A pure white bird flutters to the table edge and perches a moment cooing softly to Pandora.

"Hope," she breathes.

The bird takes flight and soars through the open window. A feather drifts down to Jared's feet. When he touches it, Pandora and her house fade away.

He looks around. He is sitting in the prickly field. The goat still munches on dry grass. The feather is gone, but Jared spies a piece of the red and blue marble. When he touches it, it is so cool and smooth that he feels the pain drain from his ear. With his thumb he rubs away dirt and dead lichen. The marble is streaked with a white vein, shaped like the wing of a bird.

Chapter 2

Kronos

The elevator door clanked to another stop. They waited. The doors squealed open. Cautiously Meghan stuck out her head.

"Sixth floor," she announced. "We made it!"

They trudged out into the dim hall. The elevator doors banged shut. Jared just missed having his backpack caught in the crack.

"Six-Ten, Six-O-Eight..." Deirdre read off the numbers as they walked down the corridor. "Here we are, six hundred."

She unlocked the door and pushed it open. As always, the stale-disinfected-other-people smell bubbled out. Jared wrinkled his nose.

They trooped inside. Jared strode forward and pulled back the heavy curtains. It seemed that the clouds parted at the same time. Light flooded through the dusty window, highlighting the crammed furniture – double bed, shabby sofa-bed and chipped table and chairs.

"I'm glad they didn't give us a small room," Meghan said. "There wouldn't have been room for a bed."

Deirdre dropped her purse on the miniature counter beside a two-burner range top, and stooped to inspect the tiny fridge below.

"It makes ice," she announced with satisfaction.

"I bet it freezes everything," Meghan replied.

Jared wriggled his shoulders and shed the backpack. At practically the same time Meghan stepped toward him. The bag landed square on her toe.

"*Yeow!* Can't you at least keep those rocks out of the way?" She hobbled past him and yanked open the window. City smells and sounds flooded in, mingling with the odor of disinfectant and distant clang of the elevator. Over everything echoed the clamor of a school bell, and then children's shouts and laughter.

"Look." Meghan pointed. Through a gap in the office buildings, they could just make out a whipping flag in front of a school. Trees and small apartment buildings flowed up the hill behind it.

"We could walk over there tomorrow," Jared said. "Check it out."

Meghan shrugged. "If there's nothing else to do."

They always did. In every city. The first day, they found the closest school and walked by. It had been a long time though since Meghan and Jared talked about what it would be like to have friends and a classroom and a teacher. To walk down a sidewalk in their own neighborhood. To have a key to a door that opened into their own home, with a bedroom for each of them. To have more belongings than could fit into a backpack and suitcase.

Once they had almost gone to school... hadn't they? Jared's mind seemed foggy... Maybe they hadn't...

A spider, disturbed by the opened window crawled across the sill. Jared stared, puzzled. The spider had something to do with going to school...with a man... Kronos...

With a wrench of fear, Jared groped for the First Rock. A tingling crept from the rock, up through his fingers, vibrating through his body, burning the mists from his memory. He had to remember!

Before the First Rock...their mom had found a job at a TV station. The family had started looking at apartments and had even gone to tour a couple of schools.

Jared remembered how the three of them had been walking away from the school, swinging hands, chattering about the kids and the artwork on the walls and the math lesson. A man with pale skin, black hair and burning eyes, wearing a steel grey business suit watched them leave the school, watched them stop for ice cream. When Jared stared at him, he came across the road toward them.

"Mrs. Singer? Perhaps you remember me? I'm Kronos. I'm here to help you." He smiled and held out his hand.

It hung in the air in front of six-year-old eyes. Like sunshine on an oil slick, a spidery tattoo glittered on the man's palm. Then the tattoo seemed to be alive, to be crawling through the air toward them. At the same instant as Meghan screamed, Jared smashed the man's hand away from his mother. The trance shattered.

"Run! *Run!*" Deirdre cried.

They ran. Like all howling hell was after them. They never even went back to the hotel. Just tore onto a bus. Found a connection to a train station. At the next city, they took a shuttle to an airport.

They had flown to Calcutta, without any of them ever talking about Kronos or why they had run. And even now, Jared thought, the incident was like a nightmare, vividly remembered and somehow forgotten, too.

As though the memory had been hidden by a mist that oozed into their minds.

"Do you remember the time we almost went to school?" he asked Meghan.

Meghan frowned. "We've never been inside a school. Don't start that again."

In his pocket, Jared's hand held fast to the rock with Buddha's eyes. "We were little. Around six, and there was this guy who scared us."

"It never happened, Jared." Meghan turned away, face flushed. "And I don't know why you keep talking about it. Just don't get weird on me, okay?" She went into the bathroom and shut the door.

"Mom," Jared tried again. "Remember when you took that TV job and this weird guy named Kronos scared us all."

Deirdre frowned and paused in the middle of hanging up a skirt. "I remember my friend, Ian, tried to arrange a job like that for me," she said. "But it never materialized. Jared, it's not good for you, sweetie, to cling to the might-have-beens back when you were small. I've never met anyone named...what was it? Cracken?"

She turned away and hung up the skirt.

Jared gripped the rock so tightly that his fingers ached. Something cold and sickly had made his mother and sister forget. Only the First Rock carved with Buddha's eyes, kept his own memory strong – let him see clearly. He had to remember everything. Forgetting would let the evil in. Most of all, he had to remember the slick, spidery mark on the palm of Kronos' hand.

With a start he realized he'd seen it again. Today, tattooed on the street girl's knuckle.

"Jared, honey," his mom called. "We're going to need some provisions."

Jared sighed. Kronos and the rocks would have to wait. The usual, settling-in routine and purchase of something for dinner took precedence. Jared checked his pocket for money and left the room.

At the corner mini-mart, he chose a box of mac and cheese, a loaf of bread, a quart of milk and a very small package of butter. Jared eyed a wilted head of lettuce but passed it up. Tomorrow, he would find a real market and buy something better for less money.

When he got back to the room, the peanut butter and other non-perishables were in the cupboard. Their clothes were in the closet and Meghan was helping their mom pick out what to wear for her meeting with the director.

"Maybe this time, you'll get the lead," Meghan told her mother. "This time they'll figure out that you have the most amazing voice on stage and they'll make you an offer you can't give up!"

She twirled around with their mom's best sweater held up against her.

Deirdre shook her head. "It won't happen, sweetie."

"Why not?" Meghan demanded. "When you sing to us, your music is like magic. It is so gloriously perfect it cuts through my heart. But when you audition, all that comes out is a little voice that never gets you more than the smallest part. It's not right!"

"Stage fright." Deirdre turned back to the closet and pulled out a long black skirt. "What about this?"

Meghan threw herself back in the chair. "What difference does it make if you don't try?"

"Meghan, no one gets to be a star unless she wants it more than anything. I don't care about it enough."

"Is there anything you do care about enough?"

Deirdre smiled at her. "Oh, yes."

"Well, if it isn't a chance to sing where it matters, I don't know what it is. I'd fight for that chance." Meghan slapped her hands against the arms of the chair. "I'd give up anything for it."

"I used to feel that way," Deirdre said.

"And you gave up," Meghan exclaimed. "When I get my chance, and I *will* get my chance, I won't throw it away. I'm going to be a star with a big house, and friends, and a lot of money. I'm sick of this third-rate life."

Their mom's lips pressed together and she turned away from them. Meghan glared out the window.

Jared knew enough to stay out of it, to avoid the questions Deirdre would never answer. Instead, he picked up a book of legends he'd unofficially borrowed from a library. He'd tried everything else. Maybe there would be some answers here.

Beijing, China

Mercy

Running...breath tearing at his lungs...Meghan falling...
Eight-year-old Jared grabs her arm and pulls her to her feet.
He looks behind. The Chinese police pour from cars, leap
low fences, and teem from shaded buildings, all shouting.
Street vendors erupt into a flood of fleeing bodies. The tourists
at Tiananmen Square stare open-mouthed at the police raid
on the horde of unlicensed vendors.

"Run!" Jared cries.

Meghan takes a deep breath like a sob and they dart
between cars and bicycles, tearing down a narrow street.
People sitting in the shade of crumbling brick walls and
leafy trees stare, but no one tries to stop them.

They turn another corner and another and another. In
the distance they can still hear the police. They twist down
one last lane, and at the end a gate opens. A tall Chinese
lady dressed in bright silk, stands beside it as though waiting
for them. A breeze lifts a light veil draped over the hair piled
high on her head. Her face is calm and gentle. Desperate,
the children stumble to a stop.

"Help us!" Meghan cries. "Please, help us."

"Don't let them put us in jail!" Jared pants.

"I will help you," the lady says. "The police will not come into my garden. Come with me."

They follow her inside. Graceful plants fringe a stone-paved courtyard. Small statues peek between them. The top of the wall is molded to imitate the curves of dragon bodies, with the heads resting at the top of the gate. The lady leads them across a small bridge that arches over a pond where gold and white fish swirl in calm water. Pink edged flowers drift on wide lily pads. Even the buzz of insects seems peaceful here. She takes the children into a red-roofed, open-walled building beside the pond. The breeze cools the air.

The lady sits on a carved wooden chair and gestures for the children to sit on pillows at her feet. On a table beside her, wait a small teapot and three small cups. She pours tea into the small cups and offers one to each twin. Jared sniffs it hesitantly, but Meghan takes a deep sip, then sighs with pleasure.

"It tastes just like flowers smell," she announces.

Jared grips the cup tightly. The lady is being so nice. "Please..." He feels his face go hot. "We didn't do anything bad..."

"Honest, we didn't," Meghan interrupts. "We just tried to sell things from the hotel so we could buy puppets at the gift shop. It was the stuff hotel *gives* away. We weren't *stealing* it. Our mom is singing at the American embassy. I'm Meghan and this is my brother, Jared. We're twins. And I don't know why they chased us. May I have more tea, please?"

The woman smiles and pours Meghan more tea. "All children who are hurt or frightened are welcome in my house. My name is Kwan Yin. To pass the time until you go back to your mother, I will tell you a story. It is a story about my sister."

The twins wriggle themselves comfortable and Kwan Yin begins...

In the time that came after time was born, a poor farmer wished for a wife. All he had in the world was his small house, his small field and a small water buffalo.

This water buffalo was really a good spirit in disguise. Because the farmer was a kind man, the water buffalo said to him, "Master, if you go down to the river, you will see a maiden bathing. Take her robe and hide it in a safe place. I promise you will get a perfect wife."

The farmer did as the water buffalo advised. When the robe was hidden, he sat down and waited. Soon, a knock came at his door. A beautiful young woman stood before him.

"I am searching for my robe," she said.

"I have it, but I will not return it," said the farmer.

"Then what shall I do? Where shall I go?" the woman cried.

"Marry me," begged the farmer. "I will make you happy."

She agreed. They married the next day. In time they had two beautiful children.

The young woman was not an ordinary woman. She was Chih-Nii, the youngest daughter of the god,

Twelve   35

Jade. She had been bored with her life and so had come to swim in the river like a mortal girl. Without her robe, Chih-Nii could not fly back to the heavens.

For a long time she was happy with her family and life on earth, but little by little she began to miss her old home in the skies.

"Please give me back my robe," she begged.

"Whatever you wish, I will give you," the farmer replied, for now he only wanted her to be happy. He fetched the robe from its hiding place. As soon as Chih-Nii put it on, she floated up to the heavens.

Her husband and children cried miserably in their loneliness.

The water buffalo then said, "Master, if you and your children climb onto my back, I will take you to your wife."

The farmer did as the water buffalo told him, and before long he was standing before the great god, Jade.

Jade said, "You cannot be married to my daughter unless you too become a god."

The farmer agreed and so Jade turned him into a deity.

"And now," Jade said, "you must be punished for tricking my daughter." Jade ordered the farmer to be the god of a distant western star, while Chih-Nii stayed in the east.

The couple wept bitterly, but Jade would not change his mind. The farmer god was sent to the distant star. Chih-Nii pleaded with her father to release *her husband. Again and again, Jade refused. At last however, the weeping of his daughter and grandchildren softened his heart, and he said, "I will show you mercy. You may meet with your husband for one day each year on the seventh day of the seventh month."*

And so it was. Each year, magpies build a footbridge across the sky for the couple. It almost always rains on the seventh day of the seventh month because Chih-Nii and the farmer weep for joy as they embrace each other again. Their tears are so many that they fall to Earth."

Kwan Yin stands and goes to the edge of the gazebo.

"And you see," she says, "it is the seventh day of the seventh month, and my sister's joyful tears fall down upon the just and the unjust, blessing us all."

The children go and stand beside her, watching rain fall on the quiet water of the pond. The water flowers shine even more brightly with the droplets shimmering on their petals. She turns back to the children. "Your mother is back in the hotel. If you go out the front gate of my garden and turn right at the first street, you will see your hotel in front of you. As you leave, you may each take one thing from my garden."

As they step into the soft rain, Meghan looks up at Kwan Yin. "May I have a flower for my mother?"

The lady leans over the edge of the pond to break off a flower. "You may have a lotus for her."

Jared's eye is caught by a single rock shining in the

earth, so he picks it up. It ripples in his hand, shimmering white like the flower's reflection in the green pond. On one side there is a carving of a lotus with seven drops of water clinging to its petals. And it sings like the soft patter of rain. Listening, he follows Meghan out the garden gate. Remembering his manners, he looks back to thank Kwan Yin.

But the house is gone and only an old apartment building stands in its place.

Chapter 3

Thief!

The next morning, their mom was up and out early – extra rehearsal and costume fittings. She roused Jared and Meghan just before she left.

"Are we okay for cash?" she asked her son. "I've got a ten dollar bill and a sandwich in my purse, but I don't know what the cast will be doing."

Jared forced his sleepy mind to focus. Money. He'd been handling their money for a couple of years now. "Don't spend it if you don't have to," he advised.

Deirdre quirked a smile. "Do I ever?"

"Yes." Jared smiled at her and she brushed the hair back from his eyes.

"See you around four. I'll expect to see at least two lessons done from each subject – exams in three weeks, you know."

Jared groaned. He and Meghan had gotten seriously behind in their studies from the correspondence school. "Right," he muttered.

"Time to get up, Meghan," Deirdre called. "Have a good day, you two." And she was gone.

Jared threw his legs out of bed and sat up. He wriggled his back and shoulders – this was one of the worst beds ever. Meghan was sinking back into sleep already, an arm flung over her face to blot out the day. He'd get her up later, *after* he got his own shower and some peace in the bathroom.

In half an hour, Jared slathered peanut butter on toast while Meghan crawled out of bed.

"Coffee?" he asked. Meghan nodded and lurched into the bathroom. Jared took down a mug, then poured a bit of milk into a pan to heat. Too bad there was no microwave, but the range worked and the coffee pot was still half full.

He could hear the shower clank as it turned on. In about ten minutes Meghan would emerge, almost human. Methodically, Jared drew back the curtains, cleared the small table, then searched out their assignment pages. He turned on their ancient laptop, searched out the wi fi connection and found the education site they used. Meghan was nearly a year ahead of him in math and French, but he was way beyond her in literature and history. That was because of the rocks. He'd once thought that if he read enough, he'd find someone else, somewhere, who had seen or heard the same things he had.

It hadn't happened.

The pipes squealed as the shower turned off. Jared poured the waiting mug half full of coffee and then filled it with heated milk and two spoonfuls of sugar.

The bathroom door opened in a cloud of fragrant steam. Meghan, her hair twisted into a wildly frizzing ponytail on top of her head, emerged. She accepted the mug Jared offered and took a long, rapturous sip.

"Ahhhh…. thank you!"

He let her have a couple more long draughts of coffee before trying to talk to her. She was *not* a morning person.

"So what's the plan?" he asked when her eyes seemed to be more or less open.

"Mom said we had to study," she mumbled.

"Never put off 'til later what you can ignore altogether." Jared grinned. "How about a tour of Pike Place Market? It's been years since we've been in Seattle. Do you remember those juggling sticks I got from a street vendor?"

Meghan winced. "I have a horrible memory of a flight attendant taking them away from you for bopping all the passengers – and me – on the head."

Jared laughed. "I was just getting good. If I can find another set, you'll be amazed."

"Spare me." She put down the empty mug, grabbed a sweater and pulled it over her T-shirt. "Let's go."

They clattered down the stairs and with a wave at Marquis at the desk, headed out the front door. The morning was cloudy but pleasant. Meghan squinted up at the sky. "Think it will rain?"

Jared shrugged. "This is Seattle. Who knows?"

Then, without another word they turned toward the low hills.

The Saturday morning schoolyard was empty except for a young mother pushing a toddler on a tire swing. Jared and Meghan circled the flat-roofed building peering in the windows. Jared wished he could read the kids' stories and poems stapled to the classroom walls. In one room, living luxuriously in a large cage below a crayoned mobile, a rusty orange guinea pig peered up through the window at them. His little mouth twitched as he leaned his front paws up on the side of the cage and squealed his starvation, despite a full food dish and his very plump body.

Meghan laughed. "That looks like one spoiled little pig."

They made another round of the playground, climbed the big toys, slid down the corkscrew slide, and did flips on the monkey bars. After a while, they walked away from the school and headed back toward the businesses and market.

The shops were interesting – a blend of tourist fare and fashion. Meghan paused in front of a window where hand-crafted Native American silver necklaces, bracelets and ear rings were draped over jade and soapstone carvings.

"I sure wish we were rich," she said.

Jared waited until she was done wishing and then they ran, laughing and dodging pedestrians, down to Pike Place Market overlooking the salt water of Puget Sound. For awhile they watched clerks huckstering seafood in the fish market. With all the other tourists they laughed when one clerk picked up a salmon as long as his arm and hurled it like a javelin to another clerk to be packaged.

"Sockeye flying at you!" he yelled. The other clerk caught it deftly. A moment later a bag of oysters was tossed and caught as well.

The twins moved past stall after stall of hand-crafted goods – everything from carved wood to tie-dyed baby clothes to home-made jams and jellies. Jared examined the fresh vegetables, choosing a bunch of baby lettuce and a half-dozen apples while Meghan lingered in front of huge bouquets of vibrant flowers.

"Ten dollars!" an elderly Asian woman coaxed.

Meghan shook her head and they went on. At a stall of brightly painted juggling sticks, Jared stared for a long time.

"We can't event think about affording those," Meghan reminded him.

"I know...but they're only eight dollars. Maybe I miscounted how much we have." Without much hope, Jared took out his wallet. What if there was a stray ten dollar bill he'd forgotten about. Nope. $82. Barely food money until their mom got paid. One of their two credit cards wouldn't accept any more charges. The other was nearly maxed out, too.

Even if he had found a forgotten $10 or $20, he couldn't spend it on juggling sticks.

Jared was sliding the wallet back into his pocket when it happened. He felt a jolt against his arm. The wallet was wrenched from his hand. The teenage girl took to her heels, weaving between the shoppers.

"Stop her!" Jared yelled.

Meghan, five stalls up, turned her head sharply at her twin's voice.

"She stole our wallet!" He was running full out, but the girl had too much of a head start. She didn't count on Meghan.

Dropping the bracelet she'd been fingering, Meghan launched herself at the thief in a full body tackle. The girl went down, Meghan on top of her.

A woman in the crowd screamed. The girl writhed from beneath Meghan, but Jared grabbed the thief by both arms and hauled her, twisting and swearing, to her feet.

"Meghan! You okay?"

"Fine," his sister said, getting up and rubbing the greasy dirt from her elbows and jeans. The girl hunched back, scowling. "What's the big idea?" Enraged, Meghan waved her fist in the girl's face. "Don't you ever think you can swipe our money! When you don't have much, you fight to keep it. Understand!"

"Ah, I'm so scared," the thief sneered back. Her voice was curiously flat. With a shock, Jared recognized her as the girl in the bus station, the one who had interrupted his attempt to get control of the Song that was haunting him. The one with the tattoo on her knuckle.

"What's going on?" A police officer towered over them.

"It's a fight, officer," the screaming woman cried. "These teenagers!"

"This witch stole our wallet," Meghan retorted. She snatched the leather billfold from the girl's hand and held it up. "This is our grocery money and she just whammed into my brother and yanked it out of his hand. She ran toward me so I tackled her."

"Really?" the police officer said. "And so you two got into a fight?"

"You think?" Meghan handed the wallet to Jared. "Maybe I should point out that it's your job, not mine, to tackle thieves."

"And what if she'd had a knife?"

"Then you really should have hurried up, instead of leaving it to us."

"Meghan, cool it!" Jared hissed.

But the officer seemed to be amused by Meghan. "I'm here now."

Meghan smiled sunnily. "Then why don't you take her away to jail or something?"

Until now the girl had been glaring sullenly at the police officer. Abruptly, she began to swear at them. The words were hoarse, harsh words – more terrible for being uttered in such a flat voice.

The officer's face hardened, and he gripped her arm. "Watch your mouth," he ordered. "I've had my eye on you."

"You can't do nothin' to me." The girl smiled, but her eyes were as cold and lifeless as the thrown salmon's.

"I can at least get you off the street for a few days." The officer looked around at the staring crowd. "Show's over folks. Enjoy your shopping."

Jared's eyes had riveted to the girl's blank face. She wasn't that old...seventeen maybe. Why were her eyes so dead, like the life had been sucked out?

"We need our money," Meghan was still lecturing the girl. "You've got no right to rip people off. I don't care how broke you are – you aren't the only one."

As Jared watched, the girl's eyes changed. The dead look was replaced by fear...terror. As the officer groped for his handcuffs, his grip loosened. The girl wrenched free and ran. But Jared was ready. She hadn't gotten more than fifteen feet before he had her again, caught by both arms. She twisted frantically.

"Let me go...let me go..." she panted. Abruptly she froze, body quivering. Jared followed her line of sight. A tall, elegant woman moved gracefully toward them.

"Now, Emma," she chided. "This isn't what we agreed to, is it?"

Emma cowered back against Jared. Her mouth opened and closed without sound. The woman carelessly patted the girl's cheek. Jared felt a shudder run through her body.

The woman went to the police officer, and half turned, gesturing sadly toward the culprit. Light glinted on the large broach pinned to her suit. The ornament was a curious design, shaped like a twisting spider.

"I'm Rhea," she told the policeman, "Emma's parole officer. This morning I'm afraid I didn't do a very effective job of supervising her. If you'll release her into my custody, I guarantee she won't trouble you again."

"Release her!" Meghan interrupted. "She should have her butt hauled off to jail!"

The adults paid no attention. The police officer seemed mesmerized by the woman's words. "I'll release her to your custody, Miss Rhea," he repeated. "She won't bother us..."

The girl uttered an animal cry of despair. Jared looked down at her, still angry. Meghan was right. Let her get everything she deserved!

"Please..." the girl's flat voice cracked with fear.

"I'll take her off your hands," the woman murmured. The officer nodded mutely. The sky darkened.

"What? Are you all nuts?" Meghan demanded.

It began to rain, gentle drops that lay on the girl's cheeks like tears.

Jared looked back at Rhea. The spider broach seemed to glow dully. A shimmering mist oozed into the air. Its fingers coiled around Meghan's angry face, and stretched toward Jared and his captive. Evil...

With a gasp, he released the girl's arms and gave her a push. "Run," he hissed. "Run!"

She darted a look of wonder at him and then took to her heels, disappearing into the crowd.

A shiver of dread crawled over Jared. They had to get away. He edged toward Meghan, avoiding the misty tendrils. He took her arm and squeezed it meaningfully.

"Ow..." She looked sharply at him, then without another word followed him into the crowd. Before they turned the corner away from the market, Jared steeled himself to look back. Rhea's eyes followed him. Even from this distance, he could see the glint of the spider broach.

"Why'd you let that little jerk get away," Meghan demanded. "You know she deserved everything she'd get."

"It was that woman," Jared said. "There was something really bad about her."

"What woman?"

Jared stopped in dismay. "Rhea!"

"Who?" Meghan looked bewildered.

"The woman who said she was that girl's parole officer. She had this broach..."

"Oh," Meghan puzzled. "I didn't see any broaches. But I did see these really sweet earrings. Silver! Nineteen dollars! Is there *any* way we can afford them?"

"No," Jared forced out, "even though our money wasn't stolen."

"What are you talking about?" Meghan demanded with a toss of her head. "Who'd bother to rip *us* off? We don't have coffee money hardly." She started walking quickly up the hill. "C'mon Jared. We've got time for more window shopping before we absolutely positively, have to go back to the room and study."

Jared followed. Above, the clouds thickened and the drops fell faster and faster. While Meghan hungrily eyed the goods in the store windows, Jared held out his hand and watched the rain roll over his skin like teardrops on a lotus petal.

Edge of the Australian Bush

Wonder

"This is so cool," eleven-year-old Meghan declares when the jeep pulls up to Camp Karora. As they unload their gear, they see children swimming and sailing small boats in the man-made lake. The rustic buildings are freshly painted. Sounds of laughter ripple through the Australian afternoon.

"Do you think Bart is making a play for Mom?" Jared whispers as he hauls his bag from the vehicle.

"Yeah!" Meghan rolls her eyes. "But do you really think she'll fall for him?"

Jared recalls the man's booming voice, frequent trips to the bar, and habit of slapping the behinds of the chorus girls in the production. His shoulders relax as he returns Meghan's grin. "Not a chance."

Bart Logan, Australian producer of Cats, says he doesn't think children should be shuttled between hotels and theaters. The twins figure he wants them out of the way while he makes up to Deirdre. But they're willing to play along when he sets up a three week vacation at his brother's very expensive, outdoor education camp.

Camp Karora lies on the fringe of the settled region

of the continent. Under clear blue skies the children ride horses, swim, sail, learn camp craft, and hike to remote spots to view Australian wildlife. The days drift by. They are blissfully happy. They try not to think of when the treat will end.

Two days before they are due to leave, Jared's eyes fly open. Groping for his watch, he sees it's just 5 a.m. An hour to dawn. He flops back, closes his eyes...then stiffens. It's the Song. He's sure the music flows from an aboriginal didgeridoo. The earthy tones thrum in his mind. In the pre-dawn light he looks around the cabin. The other boys are all asleep. No one else hears the music.

But who is playing the Song? Jared quietly dresses, laces up his hiking boots, fills his canteen with water, and sets out toward the source of the music – the bush.

Trees thin as he hikes the trail. Before long the music beckons him away from the marked path.

"This is stupid," he whispers, but plunges into the scrub. The air hums with the music of the ancient land. The scent of honeysuckle fills the air. Birds whirl and whirp in the scrub. He catches sight of native animals, wallabies and sugar squirrels, seemingly unafraid of him today. Jared feels himself melting into oneness with the bush.

Near a stream, his foot slides in the mud. His arms flail and he falls backwards. He has no memory of hitting his head, but he is numb, sleepy, spread-eagled in mud. Perhaps he is paralyzed, because only his head will move.

The humming of the didgeridoo becomes louder, swelling into his mind, filling him until he barely remembers who he is. A bandicoot waddles out from the grasses and climbs onto his body, claws digging into Jared's flesh. Jared stares into the black, glossy eyes of the long-faced creature. It leans forward and breaths on him, its breath scented with wind, dust and honeysuckle. Jared tries to call out, but he has lost his voice. Flower petals drift up from his mouth, catch on the breeze and flutter around him. Where they light, small plants begin to grow. The scent of flowers fills the air.

The bandicoot scrabbles with its powerful front claws and Jared's shirt hangs in tatters. His skin is not cut. He takes a deep breath and giggles as tiny mice, possums and other small creatures scamper from his navel. With pleasure, he watches them grow to life size as they scurry to dig burrows and make nests in the grasses around him. They nibble the new plants' petals, fruits and seeds.

Jared drifts in and out of awareness although the bandicoot's eyes still stare into his own. He dreams a hundred dreams of creatures being born, living their lives and dying. From his armpits he feels the rustle of animals growing to life. Kangaroos, koalas, cuscuses and a hundred others stream from his body, small as ants but growing to full size as he dreamily watches them multiply outwards across the land.

At last the music of the didgeridoo fades and is gone. The bandicoot huffs its warm breath on Jared's face again, and then waddles away into the brush. Jared sleeps. He is awoken when he hears a woman calling him.

"Boy...boy..."

Jared opens his eyes. His head and whole body ache. An aboriginal woman is crouched beside him. A cloth, wet from the stream has been laid on his forehead. Feebly, Jared struggles to a sitting position, the woman helping him.

She supports him back to the camp. The counselors temper scolding with concern for the sunburn and lump on his head. Only later, as he changes his clothing, does he find the egg-shaped limestone in his pocket. Over the rock's tiny fossilized imprints of ancient life are carved three circles, each one within the other. Jared holds it up to his nostrils, and once again sniffs the scent of honeysuckle.

Chapter 4

Dogs of Night

Jared and Meghan were bent over their textbooks when Deirdre whooshed into the room.

"Guess what, kids!" She sparkled with pleasure. "No rehearsal tomorrow – it's the director's wife's birthday. And he repaid me for our bus fare and gave me a two week advance on my salary. We are solvent!"

Meghan slammed her history text shut. "Let's celebrate!"

"We will," Deirdre assured her. She leaned over and reopened the text. "Tomorrow – after you've finished those assignments."

Jared grinned. "Nice try."

"But mom!" Meghan wailed. "How can I concentrate when I'm so excited?"

"Force yourself. Your incentive is that I splurged and rented a car for 8 a.m. so that we can catch the 9:30 ferry to Whidbey Island. Langley is a great little town and I remember there's a lovely beach not far from there that is practically deserted."

"What about a bonfire?" Jared asked.

Deirdre opened her purse, and with the air of a magician, pulled out a large bag of marshmallows. "But we don't go unless you two have finished a lesson in all your subjects."

"Mom..." Meghan tried again.

Deirdre smiled and brushed her daughter's hair back from her forehead. "Being on the road is no excuse for being ignorant."

"If we got a better computer instead of lugging texts around, we could be less ignorant," Meghan grumbled. But she picked up her pen, and began taking notes again.

Jared bent his head back over his math book. He loved evenings like the one that stretched before them. He and Meghan would keep working on their school assignments at the chipped table, the way he imagined thousands of other kids did at thousands of other kitchen tables. If they got stuck, their mom would try and help them out. He could almost imagine they had a life and a family like other people did. He could almost imagine he never heard a whisper and a melody from something or somewhere that no one else ever heard.

*   *   *

The next morning dawned clear and beautiful. Even Meghan didn't complain about rolling out of bed. Jared made pancakes and fried eggs (definitely a luxury) while Meghan steamed herself awake in the bathroom.

The family was on the road by 8:30. All the way out of Seattle, they sang. Jared noted with pride that his voice was settling into a clear tenor. Maybe he would be good again. As the city fell away, they gazed up at sweeps of tall trees and admired the ridge of mountains rising in the distance. Deirdre slowed the car as much as she dared as they passed Boeing's plant where huge commercial airplanes were built. Seven were parked on the tarmac near the road, getting their final paint jobs.

At Mukilteo, they lined up with the parade of other cars waiting their turn on the bulky state ferry.

"Will there be room?" Meghan asked, eyeing the line ahead.

"We'll get on," Deirdre promised.

Their car was second from the last to load onto the ferry. Jared held his breath while his mom maneuvered it across the clanging gangplank and onto the crammed vehicle deck.

They climbed the echoing stairs to the passenger level, and while their mom bought coffee, Jared and Meghan went out to the small open deck to scan the choppy waters for dolphins, seals or killer whales.

Then it began.

At first Jared thought it was the vibration from the engine. But the whispers grew louder, sang through his mind, and swept over him like a blast of cold water. He was *there...*

"No!" he gasped.

"*Jared!*" Meghan cried, but her voice slipped into nothingness.

He spun backwards in time, over years... decades...centuries. The ferry faded. The passengers, his mother and sister, gone like ghosts. Jared stood on the top of a wild golden bluff, overlooking grey sea. Waves crashed below; crows screamed above.

He was there and not there. Didn't know where this was. The music's tempo changed and a sound like howling wolves rose behind it. Jared turned. His heart pounded in the rhythm of the terrible Song. An Indian man, grey haired, streaming sweat and blood ran doggedly toward him. A hundred yards behind, a slathering pack of red-eared dogs raced from the trees, hunting.

The man ran toward the bluff. Jared held up his arms, but like a ghost, the man ran through him.

"*No!*" The cry spun Jared away, back through months and years of time to the ferry. He shook, blinked and looked around. Everything was the same as before. He drew a sobbing breath.

"Earth to Jared!" Meghan poked him in the side and then scanned his face. Her usual cheerful expression faded. "*No!* Not again!"

She grabbed his arm and propelled him to the deserted bow. The wind slammed into them, whipping their hair and catching their voices. Jared fingered the first rock in his jacket pocket. The other ten were wrapped in T-shirts in his backpack in the trunk of the car.

"So?" Meghan shouted.

"A rock is calling me." He had to shout too.

"So don't answer." She leaned her elbows on the railing and stared at the tossing water.

"I wish." Jared slapped his hands on the cold metal. "Once it gets to me, I can't stop it."

"Yeah, right."

He didn't even look at her. They'd had this argument before. Ten times. Once for each rock since the first. It was the only thing they ever did argue about. Jared gazed at the deep green of the approaching island. It was there! The rock was there, waiting for him. He felt a thrill of expectation. He would hear the Song again.

"We're getting close to it, Meghan," he said. "I'm supposed to find it."

"Just don't, okay!" She punched his arm, hard, and then stalked back inside.

Jared stayed where he was until the PA system crackled on. *The ferry will be docking at Whidbey Island in five minutes. All passengers please return to your cars.*

Jared found his mom and Meghan in the jostling line heading down to the car deck. Meghan refused to meet his eyes and hurried ahead. At the car, she took the front seat beside their mom, leaving Jared to clambered into the back.

A few minutes later they had driven off the ferry and were zipping along the highway.

"Where to?" Deirdre said. "Where is adventure awaiting us?"

"Langley, first" Meghan said. "I want to see those cool shops."

"Sure thing. Would a couple of hours of shopping be okay, Jared?" Deirdre looked back via the rear view mirror.

Jared had a flashing vision of the golden bluff with waves foaming below. The rock waited. "There are great beaches on the west side of the island," he said. "I really want to go there, too."

"Absolutely." Their mom patted her bag. "We're equipped with marshmallows, don't forget."

Meghan twisted around in her seat to look at her twin. "How do you know about the beaches?"

"He's the details man," Deirdre said. "That's why we can't manage without him. Isn't that right, Jar?" Reaching her arm over the seat, she touched his cheek with her fingertips. She yanked her hand back as a car swerved to miss them.

"Mom!" Meghan shrieked. "Watch the road!"

Deirdre laughed. "Sorry! Out of practice!"

They found the turn-off to Langley, parked, and then spent considerably more than two hours looking at the shops. For a while Jared enjoyed the funky gift and antique shops that lined the wide main street, but with no money to spend, he soon became bored and restless.

"I'm going to get our dinner," he told his mom. She and Meghan were engrossed in trying out the effects of a combination of feather boas and hand woven shawls.

"Great," Deirdre replied. "Meet you in, oh, say and hour at the statue?"

Jared found a grocery and bought food for a picnic. Then he went to the metal statue of a boy and dog overlooking the ocean and sat and waited, drowsing in the sun. When he met his mom and sister, they presented him with a dripping blackberry ice cream cone.

Once the cones were finished they got back in the car.

"I'm just about certain the beach is this way," Deirdre said a few minutes later. She turned the car down a narrow road that appeared to lead to an old farm house. Jared settled back. The rocks would guide their mother to the right beach – whether she wanted to go or not.

*   *   *

As Jared's foot groped for support, the sandstone gave way and he skidded a few feet down the steep slope. He scrabbled for balance. A blackberry cane raked his hand, but then his foot found a jutting rock. Panting, feeling for hand holds, he pressed himself against the hill.

"You okay?" Meghan leaned over the top of the bank.

"Yeah," Jared grunted. He didn't look up at his sister or down at the rocky beach twenty feet below. He was sure either movement would make him fall.

"Most people take the path to the shore." Meghan said. "Right over there. There's even a railing for the steep part."

Jared shrugged his backpack into a more comfortable position and braced his left foot.

He risked grinning up at her. "But this is the right way."

Meghan's head withdrew. "You take the right way," floated down. "I'm taking the smart way."

Jared bit a blackberry thorn out of his hand and sucked off the blood. Metallic. Like the rock humming in his pocket. Like the ten others inside his backpack, weighing him down.

The bluff was only thirty feet high, but the loose golden soil and blackberries made it a tough descent. Taking a deep breath, Jared started the downward scramble again.

Decorated with skinned knees, scraped hands, and blackberry scratches, Jared made it to the shore. The water rushed toward him in long, endless rolls, each iced with a thick white fringe. Where the waves hit rocks they slapped upward into dancing sprays. His mom and sister were already standing at the water's edge, laughing at a screaming colony of loons and gulls as they strutted across drifting seaweed rafts. Jared rubbed his stinging palms on his shirt, leaving a smear of dirt.

Which way now?

He stared north then turned toward the south. Nothing. The pungent air whipped off the ocean and rushed into his mouth.

"I can fly!" Meghan's copper hair swept up with the wind like the wings of a bird. She raised her arms and began to sing, a simple trill of pure song rising on the wind and waves.

Their mom laughed and began a counterpoint of sound. Her voice had all the depth and range that Meghan was just reaching. It rippled with the elegance of years of training.

Jared watched and listened, wanting to open his mouth and sing too, but the rocks were humming again. South. Jared started slowly, like a dog waiting for the scent to trickle into his nostrils. His sister's song ended on a high clear note. Flushed with pleasure, she turned to him.

"Hey! Want to climb?" Meghan pointed toward the wave-worn monoliths rising from the ocean. The receding tide had exposed a wet path, littered with clams, barnacles and sea stars.

Their mom eyed the huge rock. "Is it safe?"

"*Mom!*" Meghan groaned.

"Later." Jared called. He turned his eyes back to the thousands – make that millions – of stones jumbled over the shingle beach.

Meghan picked her way over to him. "The tide will come in and we won't be able to reach the stack."

"The rocks are singing..." The summons washed over him like the ocean's salty spray. His family faded as the sounds spun him back through centuries.

66   Susan Brown

Whidbey Island, U.S.A.

Compassion

Jared stands at the foot of the golden bluff, overlooking the stormy grey sea. Waves are hurled to shore by the sudden cold wind. Gulls and crows scream above. The Song is faint.

He hears the howling, wants to run, but his feet don't move. The old Native American man, streaked in sweat and blood tops the bluff and with a cry of despair slides and tumbles to the base. He lies almost at Jared's feet.

"Get up! Run!" Jared urges, but there is no sound from his lips. The red-eared dogs are scrabbling at the top of the cliff. Desperate, Jared reaches down and grabs the old man's hand, but his fingers slide through like those of a ghost. But something has changed. Jared's heartbeat meshes with the runner's and he is trapped...

Must not stop...too late to hide...They have my scent. Do not look back! Get up! Run ...must hide the gift. NO! Don't look...! They are closing. The hunt is nearly over...

Pain...arm broken...must not stop...get up...run over the stones...do not think of the pain...the gift must be saved from Them.

Guide my arm, Changer! Yes! The rock spins, shines with the light of the sun, the splash to cleanse the scent...and now it lies among the millions of stones. They will not find it now.

I will lead them away. The hounds will follow the scent of my blood. Run. Keep running. Through the spray. The hounds! The hounds! I will not run now.

Here I am...I sing the Song of light...

Jared smells the breath of the wild dogs, feels their teeth close on his throat, sinks down and down...

A hand grabs him, pulls him from the dogs. They spin and fade.

"I am so sick of this," Meghan yanks his arm.

In a rush of gratitude, Jared recognizes the sunny beach of his own afternoon. But the whispered Song in his ear is still summoning him. Barely aware that his sister follows, Jared leaps onto a driftwood log and runs lightly to the base. He feels rather than sees the rock's golden glow amid a tangle of silvery roots.

Jared drops to his knees and digs, not caring that he jams his fingers against a litter of pebbles. With a sound of irritation, Meghan kneels and digs too.

Then he has it. Larger than usual – twice the size of his fist. An agate. Golden orange, sparkling with sand and its own translucence.

"Now that's cool," Meghan breathes.

Jared turns the rock over and over, pleased by the wave-smoothed shape and the warm color. A depression in the surface has filled with sand. Jared rubs it clean with his thumb. It's a figure, etched into the stone.

"Looks like one of those Indian carvings," Meghan says. "Except in rock instead of wood."

Jared hefts the stone from hand to hand. It's cool from the wet beach, but warming in the sun.

Last rock...

Susan Brown

Chapter 5

Circle of Rocks

Meghan sat back, wiggling her bottom to find a comfortable spot on the shifting stones and sand. "Mom's going to have a fit. Our bags are getting really heavy."

She didn't say anything about the books she'd left behind last month in the hotel in Singapore, saying she could download what she wanted from the Internet. The weight limit on international airlines was strict. Jared had already abandoned everything he could – books, music, extra shoes, everything, just to keep the rocks.

"I can't leave them. They're important."

"That's what you keep telling me." Meghan chewed on a glinting strand of hair.

Jared grinned. "Maybe we can ditch our textbooks?"

Meghan giggled. "Now that's an idea. I'm three assignments behind on History of the Middle East anyway."

"I could sacrifice math. I'm allergic to algebra." He swung the backpack off his shoulders and stowed the rock inside. The everyday world shifted back into focus.

"Then Mom would sacrifice us." They both stared down the beach where she walked along the shore. Deirdre Singer's arms were folded tightly across her chest but her dark coppery hair and the silk scarf that had bound it, lifted and blew in the breeze.

"She is so beautiful and talented and nice," Meghan said angrily. "Why does she mess everything up! Look at her! She's worrying again. I just know it."

"Any idea what's bugging her?" Jared asked.

"Whatever it is, she'll say, '*Kids, we're in a rut. We need a change of scene!*'"

Jared couldn't help but smile at Meghan's exact mimicry of their mom's determinedly cheerful announcements. No matter how bad it got, their mom always tried to make it sound like an adventure – like it was all part of the plan. When they were little, they believed her completely. It was a lot harder now.

"There's no way she'd pack us up and move on now." Meghan tossed a chunk of driftwood into a tide pool. "This is the best part she's had in months. There's a six week run with eight more cities booked after that. The other actor's leg will take ages to heal, don't you think?"

"Sure." But Jared didn't remind his sister that there had been other great jobs, but still their mom had quit and moved them on. "Do you ever wonder if we'll see our faces posted somewhere, some time?" Jared finally asked. "You know, '*Have you seen these children?*' and it will be us?"

"You mean like our father looking for us?" Meghan asked scornfully.

"I don't see why we move all the time," Jared insisted. "Other actors and singers have homes where they live when they're not on the road. Why are we always on busses and trains and airplanes? Meghan..." He looked at her searchingly. "Do you remember a time when we weren't on the road? I think I do. A little. Just snatches of things – like a dog I played with and a rug with big pink flowers and sunlight through funny windows...I just wondered if we did have a home and maybe we have a father looking for us."

"I don't remember anything at all and those memories could be from anywhere." Meghan rubbed his shoulder comfortingly. "But I asked mom on the bus last week about our father."

"And?"

"Waste of time. I should have learned that by now."

"Same answer?"

"Oh yes." Meghan wrapped her arms around her knees and dropped her forehead on them. "He's a very good man but his work makes having a family impossible. No name, no place of residence, and no way of us ever finding out who he is."

Jared nodded. "I suppose if he wanted anything to do with us, he'd make an appearance. You know... a Christmas card... "

"... or a birthday present on the wrong date."

"He's probably lost the address... "

"He's probably masterminding a corporate merger..."

"He's probably touring Tibet... "

"He probably doesn't speak English... "

Meghan laughed and turned her head to share a wry smile with her twin.

He probably doesn't even know we exist, Jared thought. *And that means Mom didn't want him to know.* He stared down the beach at the slender figure of their mother. She was kind and cheerful and full of love for them. If she didn't want them to know their father, there had to be a really good reason....Didn't there?

"Race you to the stack!" He leapt up, dropping the backpack. The rocks would stay quiet now. He could leave them.

"Jared, you rat!" Meghan surged to her feet, and laughing, tore along behind him.

Together, they spent the next hour shouting and clambering over slippery rocks while their mom alternately laughed and urged them to be careful.

Ham sandwiches and deli salad did for dinner. As the sun bled into the horizon, they collected driftwood into a great spiky pile. Tongue gripped between her teeth, Deirdre dropped burning matches into a clump of dried grass until it caught, smoldered, and then danced into life.

"Dessert!" Deirdre produced the package of marshmallows.

"Yes!" Jared shouted.

"What about sticks?" Meghan demanded.

Their mom began to laugh. "I forgot!"

It took a lot of giggling, shrieking and stumbling around in the dark to find willow saplings. Later, stuffed and sticky, they lounged back against driftwood logs. A huge full moon lit sea and shingle, frosting them with silver.

"This place looks totally magicked," Meghan murmured.

Deirdre got up restlessly. "I'm going for a walk."

"Mmm," Meghan muttered, half asleep.

Jared felt as restless as his mom. The rhythmic swash of waves had the same effect on him as the humming of his stones. He pulled the First Rock from his pocket and held it to the light of the fire.

Reddish brown and ordinary looking. Like a million billion others. But different.

He turned it this way and that in his hand, lovingly feeling the carved edges of Buddha's eyes. The curly cue writing he still didn't know how to read. Beside him, Meghan murmured in her sleep.

Twelve rocks, twelve symbols. Were there more scattered about the world? He had never thought before about how many. Funny – he should have.

Jared felt a prickling in the back of his neck. The voices began, wisping on the breeze, softly chanting, singing the memories of a thousand lifetimes.

"Shut up!" Jared shook his head, breaking his mind free from the chant. The siren songs wouldn't call him any more!

Feeling suddenly liberated, Jared relaxed and made a quick check around. His mom had wandered farther down the beach, a shadow against the silver light. The sound rumbling from Meghan's open mouth was definitely snoring. Jared grinned. Too bad he didn't have anything to record her with. Blackmail could always come in handy.

He brushed aside the pebbles in front of him, leaving a clear circle of sand, and then put the First Rock in the middle. Inside the backpack, swathed in T-shirts and underwear, lay the rest of his rocks. One by one, Jared unwrapped them and set them on the sand.

India. Greece. China. Australia. England.... the curved slashes of a running horse carved into ancient chalk particularly intrigued him tonight. Firmly he put it down and reached again into his backpack.

Peru. Mexico. Tunisia. Germany. Hawaii... South Africa... It called. It always called.

Breathing hard, Jared used his thumb and one finger to lift the thin slice of black obsidian. Volcanic glass. Made in the molten core of the earth from raging heat and crushing pressure. This rock was different – it had come into his hand slick with blood.

Jared held it so the glow of the embers flickered over the glistening surface. If he hurled it away now, into the ocean, it would be gone forever.

"What are you doing?" Meghan asked suddenly.

Jared jumped. The rock jerked from his hand and landed with the others.

Twelve   77

"Stupid... "Jared grunted. He sucked the tip of his finger where a razor-sharp edge had sliced it.

"Don't you ever get tired of those things?" Meghan mumbled. She snuggled her chin down into her coat and her eyes drifted shut again.

Breathing hard, Jared glared at the black glass, hating it. He was afraid to touch it again. And what about the new rock? A good one, he was sure. Jared took the agate from his jacket pocket and laid it with the others. For a long while he stared at them. There was a feeling tonight that something was different. That something was happening... *Magicked*, Meghan had said.

With a finger tip, Jared rolled and nudged the rocks into a line around the black one. Then into a circle. Growing in him was a...*a feel* that this was right and not right. He rearranged the rocks from smallest to biggest.

Not yet.

He shut his eyes. Like a remembered refrain of music, he knew. Smiling, he nudged them one by one into their right places in the circle. The First Rock was the last.

Satisfied, knowing he'd gotten it right, he leaned back.

At first it was barely perceptible. The air above the circle slowly vibrated. Thrumming, soft then louder... tendrils of color and light rising from the rocks...circling above. Then faster... rising higher...crackling with energy... expanding outward. From above the whirling air, a stream of light shot downward piercing the heart of the circle.

Jared leapt back, tripping over Meghan.

"What???" She blinked her eyes hard. "Jared! What's happening?"

"I don't know!"

Crouching shoulder to shoulder, they watched as swirls of energy moved faster and faster, fading in and out, pulsing.

"Make it stop!"

"*How?*" Hunched over, Jared tried to reach the stones under the halo of energy. The light zapped his hand like bee stings. He yanked it back. The thrumming cleared like a radio dial slowly tuning to a station... singing... shouting... singing... screaming... tuning to the black rock.

He couldn't stand it! He could hear the gunfire again, ricocheting through his head. No...not guns...the screams were death.... howling...the red-eared dogs were hunting again.... hunting the scents of all the singers....

They were hunting him! They smelled the ancient blood on the rocks! Something half asleep awakened. Jared saw darkness swirling toward the circle of light...heard the baying of the hunters...They must not find him! Jared lurched forward into the swirl of energy. His hand closed over the First Rock and he yanked it from the circle.

It all ended abruptly, as if there had never been a corona of raw energy or thrumming or singing and screaming. The twins looked from the ordinary red stone in Jared's shaking hand to the others in the broken ring. The fire flickered gently. As Jared looked around he thought for a moment he saw lines of pale light shooting outward from the circle. Beyond that, nothing but shadow.

Above, the moon broke from a cloud and shone down on them.

Cape Town, South Africa

Fear

The South African road is hot and dusty; the smells and bird cries are exotic and scary. The people walking along here are black, and they look at him sideways.

"Boy!" A policeman touches his shoulder. "What are you doing?"

"Walking," twelve-year-old Jared stammers. He knows by now that no one else can hear the music that forces him along this road.

The policeman rubs his hand over his face, as if trying to clear his sight. "Not this way. Not today. There is badness in the air today. It feels like the air of the old days when wickedness happened here all the time. You go on to where you belong. This is not a good day for a walk." He points his stick back the way Jared came, toward the city. Not knowing what else to do, Jared mumbles a thanks and retreats.

Nightfall. The background sounds have shifted and so have the smells. Dressed in black, Jared trots along the edge of the road. Soldiers lounge against a truck pulled onto a side road. They don't notice him. The rocks thrum in his mind.

Ahead, policemen are patrolling in pairs, looking this way and that. A truck pulls up. More police jump out and begin setting up roadblocks. Jared slips behind the bushes that line the road, and keeps going.

The Singing is quickening, urgent. He freezes. Is that someone breathing? Or a wild animal? The rock's Song is confused – he can't find the direction. His shoe crunches on something and the smell of old smoke and charcoal puffs up.

Without warning, it starts. Crack! Cra-cra-cra-crack!

Gunfire.

Screaming.

Jared gasps like a landed fish. A few feet away a charred board explodes.

He dives into a ditch and cowers on his belly, arms over his head, silent and shaking, wondering if whoever is wielding the gun would shoot a twelve-year-old boy who's just staying for a week while his mom sings in a show.

Soldiers pound past.

Crack! Cra-cra-cra-crack!

Above him, a man bursts from the bushes, leaping across the trench.

Crack... cra-cra-crack...

He screams and twists as he falls into the ditch.

Jared cries out, an animal gasp of terror. The man's hair is grey and soft like the fleece of a lamb. His eyes are brown and rich, circled with white in the moonlight.

"You came ..." he whispers. His arm slides forward like a wounded bird's wing. He shoves the rock under Jared's palm.

"Run, boy," he says. "They be after you now."

Jared can't move. The man groans, stumbles to his feet, and staggers from the ditch. A brilliant beam catches him like a deer pinned by headlights. The hunters shout in triumph.

Crack! Cra-cra-cra-crack!

The man cries out in despair and pain, then somehow lurches off into the underbrush.

Jared's hand convulses over the rock. Panting, sobbing, he scuttles backward on his belly the length of the trench. His beating heart and gasping sobs are louder than gunfire.

Soldiers with rifles leap over the ditch where the man had gone down. In the roar of shouting, gunfire and grinding vehicles, Jared bolts back three miles to the shabby hotel. Meghan flings open the door.

In the distance, muffled now... Crack! Cra-crack!

"Tell me that's fireworks," she hisses.

Shaking too hard to speak, Jared shows her the rock. A glossy black wedge, with one edge razor sharp.

"Jared..." Deirdre mutters sleepily from across the room.

"Bad dream," Meghan calls. "Go back to sleep, Mom."

In the bathroom, Jared can't make his teeth stop chattering. Meghan has to uncurl his fingers from the rock. There's blood all over.

"You cut yourself," she snaps. Jared lets her hold his hand under the tap. Blood streams away – too much to have come from the gouge in his palm. And it's on his shirt too. The rock throbs like his own pulse.

Meghan holds it under the tap, and the blood and dirt stream away. Etched on the flat surface is the symbol of a sword with flames leaping from the blade. The sight of it makes Jared sick with fear.

All night he lies awake, shivering, feeling the pulse of the black rock.

The next day, on the way to the airport, Jared stares out the taxi window looking for the place, but he can't find it. The newspaper he snags makes brief mention of an incident on the edge of Khayelitsha township. A man was killed.

Chapter 6

Please Help!

Jared swept his arm across the sand, scattering the rocks.

"I hate these rocks." Meghan sat way back, arms wrapped around her knees. "They're... possessed or something. Why don't you just leave them here?"

"I can't."

Gingerly, he picked up each stone, wrapped it and stuffed it in his backpack. He slid the First Rock into his pocket as Deirdre walked up from the water's edge.

"Time to go, kids," she said. "It's late."

With almost no conversation the family doused the fire, picked up their litter, and made their way back to the car. Getting in, Jared bumped Meghan with the backpack.

"Keep them away from me," she hissed.

Jared kept the bag between his feet and stared out the window. He couldn't...*wouldn't* think about the rocks. But somehow, his hand crept into his pocket and he touched the First Rock, pulling reassurance from its cool surface. It was good. He knew it was good. Then his thoughts slid to the black obsidian. Jared swallowed. That was another story.

The car bumped and lurched onto the ferry back to the mainland. Deirdre turned off the engine. "I could use a coffee. Anyone else?"

"Sure!" Jared declared and scrambled out of the back seat so fast he tripped and nearly went flying.

"Klutz!" Meghan said.

"He's growing again." Deirdre smiled and ruffled his hair.

"*Mom!*"

"Sorry, kiddo. Mothers get carried away."

They trooped upstairs to the snack bar, got drinks and stood on the cold deck to watch the lights from Mukilteo get larger and brighter as the ferry churned through the black water.

It was close to midnight before they walked through the shabby hotel lobby. Once inside their cramped room, Jared wriggled his shoulders and with a sigh shed the backpack. The new rock felt like it had added about twenty pounds. Meghan grabbed her nightgown and headed into the bathroom. First as always.

"Please, Jared," Deirdre said, "put that backpack away. This room's crowded enough."

He nodded and pushed the pack into a corner. Deirdre stepped toward the window to pull the curtains; her toe rammed the bag.

"Yeow!" She blinked rapidly, eyes watering. "Jar...a rock collection is really a bad hobby for people who travel like we do. You have to get rid of them."

Jared picked up the backpack again. "Mom, I really need to keep these rocks. They're special."

Deirdre sighed and reached for her nightgown. "What about a compromise? Keep one or two and get rid of the others. It's not like they're little specimens. Okay?"

To avoid answering, Jared turned away. He wouldn't care if he never saw the black one again. But he couldn't give up his First Rock, or the chalk with the running horse, or today's rock.

Tonight had proved they were all linked. When one rock was taken from the circle, the magic disappeared. Getting rid of one – even the black one – would cancel out all the others. Maybe that would be a good thing, Jared thought. Maybe that would get him and his family closer to normal. Closer to a life that didn't blow them from one end of the earth to the other.

Meghan came out of the bathroom and his mom went in. His sister fell into bed. Jared edged his rocks out of her way.

"Night, Jar..." she mumbled.

"Night."

Deirdre came out of the bathroom and climbed into her side of the double bed. "Go to bed, kiddo."

"Sure." Jared eyed the sofa against the wall. It was a back breaker. Last night he'd tried sleeping on the floor, but the smell of ancient crud had been too close to his nose.

With a sigh, he stripped down to his underwear and arranged the blankets and pillow into a nest. He settled in, twisting this way and that, trying to get comfortable. Finally he propped himself up, pulled back the curtains and gazed out the window into the city.

The skyline blinked and glowed. Jared stared upward, through glare of the streetlights and neon, trying to spot some stars. Giving up he looked downward.

Two men hovered in the shadows of the alley below. Probably a drug deal going down. Jared had stayed in so many second-rate places in so many corners of the world, he'd developed an eye for trouble and an instinct for avoiding it.

Except for when the stones called him. Then he was lost.

*   *   *

"Did you take any messages for Deirdre Singer?" Mom said into the room's phone. "...I know, but this is important. Maybe you put it in the wrong box?....Oh, well, thanks anyway." Deirdre carefully replaced the receiver.

Jared and Meghan looked up from their math books. Three weeks had slipped by since they had gone to Whidbey Island, and their mother's carefree mood had become increasingly strained.

"What's up?" Meghan asked.

"Nothing. I'm just having a bit of trouble reaching Pat." Deirdre jumped up and tripped over the backpack. "Jared! I thought we made an agreement about these rocks!" She managed to glare while half-hopping to rub her bruised foot.

Jared quickly decided that reminding her he'd never agreed would be downright dumb. "I'll do something about them, Mom."

"Today?"

He nodded.

"Thank you." Deirdre picked up a sweater. "I've got a couple of things I need look after. I'll be back later. "

The door closed behind her with a snap.

"She's been trying to call Pat for over a week." Meghan shut her book. "Let's get out of here."

"The sooner the better," Jared agreed. They grabbed their jackets, headed out, and then stopped. Deirdre was just standing by the elevator. The kids walked over slowly.

"You didn't push the button," Meghan leaned over and pressed the knob.

Deirdre startled and tried to summon a smile. "Oh, silly me... "

"Mom?" Meghan coaxed. The elevator thunked above them.

Deirdre bit her lip and jabbed the button twice more. "Last week, the director said the other actor's leg has healed faster than they expected. They're not going to need me after the 18th."

"That's four days from now!" Jared said.

"What's Pat lined up for you?" Meghan demanded.

The elevator swished open. An elderly couple was already on.

"Beautiful day," Deirdre smiled at the old people as their family stepped on. Meghan chewed on a strand of hair and Jared fingered the rock in his pocket.

The elevator bumped gently to the first floor. Jared held open the door while the old folks shuffled out.

"Are you going to call Pat again?" Meghan asked. Her mom always used the phones in the lobby to call her agent. That way she avoided the extra charges added on by the hotel. Or using up minutes on her burner phone.

Deirdre nodded. "I've already left about ten messages. But she has a new secretary, who doesn't seem to get who I am. Even so, Pat's bound to come up with a great part for me. Right, kids?"

The twins exchanged glances. "Right, Mom."

"Catch you later." Deirdre went across the lobby to the phones.

"What are we going to do?" Meghan's voice sounded as scared as Jared felt. If your agent didn't return your calls, it was the kiss of death in the theater world. They knew it had happened to other performers, but year after year, even when Deirdre had quit parts, Pat had always come through. She'd even loaned them money last summer when there hadn't been any jobs at all for two months.

Jared fingered the rock in his jeans pocket. "Pat's bound to come up with something."

"What if she doesn't?"

"She always has before, remember. And like Mom said, it's a new secretary."

Meghan gave a shaky laugh. "Right."

They headed out into the street. A block from the hotel, they passed by a raggedy woman crouched on the sidewalk holding a scrawled cardboard sign.

Have 2 kids.
Need $ for food and rent.
Please help!

Meghan dropped a dollar into her lap. Jared barely stopped himself from grabbing the money back. "Meghan, we can't afford to give money away."

"Don't be so stingy."

"We have to look out for ourselves. If Pat doesn't get Mom a job, we could be on the sidewalk too."

Meghan tossed her head. "Then I hope there's more people like me around than there are like you."

She stomped away. Jared sank down on a bench and did some quick calculations in his head. Scary. Two weeks – three, if they ate a lot of tuna and peanut butter. Then the hotel would give them the old heave ho.

They had no family to go to, no home to hunker down in – no real friends who might help them in a bad spot. Mom hadn't even stayed with one company the way a lot of performers did. It was as though she got a rock call too, Jared realized, but never found the right one.

London, England

Sacrifice

The noise of the big machines almost drowns the thrumming. Nine-year-old Jared circles the construction site, whacking the chain-link fence with his palm, darting between onlookers. There...he spots a gap by the northeast corner, behind the workmen's shed. He edges between the boards and the curling fence. The rocks are thrumming unbearably. It's thirty feet down and very steep. He trembles with fear. He won't go down there.

But the rocks won't stop.

"It'll kill me!" he yells. Dragging off his pack, he hurls it down into the pit. The keening tears through him, but he runs away.

Soon there's no more thrumming. Triumphant, he stops to buy a soda. But now he feels all empty – like the last curtain on the last night of the show, when they're already pulling down the sets. When all the beauty is over, and the darkness begins to close in. When you remember how small and unimportant you are.

So slowly, kicking at pebbles in the street, he goes back.

At the gap in the fence, he can barely make out his green backpack in the shadows below. He hangs around. One by one, the machines are turned off. The workmen shout goodnight to each other. The rocks are silent.

Taking a deep breath, Jared slides through the chain-link. It's a long way down. A few rocks jut out from the earth like handholds. Even though he's so afraid he can hardly breathe, he starts climbing, several times nearly slipping. At the bottom, Jared picks up the backpack. Underneath is a chunk of muddy chalk.

As he touches it, the sounds of London fade. The greyish dirt melts away. He is standing in a crowd of tribesmen. Their roughly braided hair and hide clothing ripple in the stiff breeze. Before them is a long escarpment. Carved through the turf to the white chalk below, hundreds of feet long, is a horse, all curves and flowing lines. The brave beauty of it catches Jared's breath. He walks like a ghost through the crowd of warriors until he stands at the foot of the hill. Far above him, a giant of a man with golden hair and a gold torque around his neck, obviously a chief or king, paces the perimeter of the great white horse. Behind him walks another man, wrapped in a red cloak, making precise movements with his hands and chanting.

A few yards in front of Jared, a small, dark-haired man squats on the turf. His eyes are lowered to something he holds concealed in his hands. Everything about him proclaims his weariness.

At last the golden warrior walks back to the dark-haired man, who stands and waits quietly.

"It is well made," the chief says. "You honor the gods."

"I honor my people who have died beneath the weapons of your warriors," the tired man says.

"Our priest guided us to this place. It is the will of the gods that it becomes our home now," the chief says.

"Talking may weaken the magic," the red-cloaked priest hisses.

Jared steps back. The priest's eyes are dead looking. An intricate gold broach, shaped like a distorted spider fastens the red cloak at his shoulder.

"Nothing will weaken the spirits of my people," the tired man says, "for we are bound to the bones of the earth."

"As will be my people," the chief says. "Those of your tribe who still live, will become children of my clan. The life you gave to your work binds us."

"There is the last binding," says the red-cloaked priest.

The three walk to the great head of the horse. Jared, as though pulled by a string, follows. The tired man kneels by the wide trench that forms the horse's eye. The priest pulls a bronze knife from his belt, and steps toward the kneeling man. But the chief gestures him aside and takes a knife from his own belt. The kneeling man looks up at the blue sky, as the chief slices the knife across his throat. The man's blood spurts across the white eye of the horse, staining it red.

Jared screams and screams, but his cries are drowned out by the shouting warriors below.

The priest smiles. The chief crouches by the body of the artist. "I would have liked to call him brother," he says.

The red-cloak shrugs. "It is done. Now our people will have their magic. That is what matters."

"So you say, priest," the chief says.

Sobbing, Jared stares at the fallen man. From his slackened grip, a stone falls into the eye of the horse. A stream of pure white light channels from the sky through the stone and into the eye of the horse. No one seems to notice the light, but the chieftain scoops up the stone. Without the priest noticing, he slips it into a leather pouch at his side. As Jared watches, the warriors, the chief, the priest, the fallen man, and even the great horse on the hillside fade away. All that remains is the stone, stained with browning blood.

No, it isn't blood...just mud from the excavation. Breathing quickly, Jared scoops up the rounded stone. With his thumb he rubs off centuries of mud. The white horse gleams, carved deeply into chalk taken from the great hill.

"What the...!" shouts a watchman. "What're you doin' down there!"

They haul him up on a long ladder, then march him back to the hotel.

"This lad's got problems," the watchman informs Deirdre.

"As if he would know," she grumbles when he leaves. "Do you think you two can stay out of trouble?" Meghan and Jared nod. Deirdre kisses them, then hurries off to dinner with Ian.

"Do you think I've gone loony?" Jared spreads the rocks across the rug. There are four now.

Meghan picks up the horse-carved chalk. She turns it this way and that, then licks it, a quick flick of pink and dampness. Making a face, she puts it down.

"I don't feel anything."

"Then I am crazy."

"Maybe. But who cares." Meghan whirls around like a dancer, face fiery and eyes intense. "If it's what you feel and it feels okay, then go with the flow."

"That doesn't make any sense."

Meghan grins, waggles her tongue and makes a rude gesture she'd picked up from a stage hand. "That's our life for you."

Chapter 7

Fake It

The key grated in the lock. Jared slipped the good luck rock back into his jeans pocket and took his feet off the table. Meghan put down her flute.

"You two still up?" Their mom gave them a bright smile. For a few seconds she fluttered around the room, apparently tidying. The twins looked at each other. Meghan raised her eyebrows.

"How was the show?" Jared asked.

Deirdre shrugged. "So so. The house was full, but they weren't very enthusiastic."

"Did you get through to Pat?" Meghan prompted.

Their mom nodded. "Oh, yes.... Live productions aren't doing well...the economy and all...."

"The part's a dud," Meghan interrupted. "Boy, Pat's got a lot of nerve – with your talent and experience...."

"No, Meggie." Deirdre fiddled with her silk scarf, running it through her hands. "There's no part. Not even as the maid to the heroine in a podunk touring company. Pat suggested I try another agent."

Jared just sat there. He hated living in hotel rooms – living on the street would be worse.

"Oh Mom!" Meghan flew across the room and put her arms around Deirdre. "Pat's a jerk. She doesn't know how to showcase your talent – I mean, how long has it been since she got you the lead?"

"It's not her fault. " Deirdre sunk onto the bed. "She's been carrying me for a long time. I knew it would fall apart sooner or later." She hugged Meghan. "I just hoped you would be older."

"Why?" Jared asked. "Why does us being older matter?"

Deirdre looked at him for a long minute. "It's because...it's a tough world out there."

"That isn't what you were going to say."

Deirdre turned away and drew the curtains shut. "I don't have anything else to say, Jared. It's hard out there and there are things... things and people, I don't want you to have to know about."

Jared gestured around the room. "We haven't exactly been sheltered. You should trust us."

"I wish trust was what I worried about," Deirdre said tightly.

"Then what *are* you worried about?" Jared got up and faced her. Their eyes were on the same level now. "We live like we're running away from something. What? You have to tell us!"

"Jared!" Meghan exclaimed.

"There's nothing...." Deirdre's eyes looked desperate. "I'm just not very good at making a living. That's all. Isn't that enough?"

"No!" Jared insisted. "Tell me the truth!"

Meghan stepped in front of him. "Back off," she hissed. "Just back off and leave Mom alone! She's trying and she's got enough trouble now without you getting paranoid or something."

"It's okay, Meggie," their mom said.

Jared saw tears sparking on his mom's lashes. That silenced him as Meghan hadn't. His mom never cried.

"I'm sorry," he said awkwardly. He put his arms around her and hugged, then Meghan put her arms around them both.

"Family hug!" she said.

They laughed, broke apart and began the routine of going to bed. Later, when all was quiet, Jared lay staring at the dingy ceiling. He knew his mom was hiding something. He *knew* it. But what?

*   *   *

For two weeks since the last day of their mom's job, the family had been crammed into the hotel room. Jared had gone for a lot of walks. Sometimes Meghan came with him and sometimes she stayed with their mom, fixing hair, talking, listening while Deirdre phoned agents, theater companies and acquaintances, hunting desperately for leads. Nothing. Every door slammed in Deirdre's face.

"When my luck's out, it's really out," she sighed.

"It'll change, Mom," Meghan replied with one of her quick hugs.

"Isn't there anyone you can call?" Jared asked. "A cousin, or an old, old friend, or someone who cares about you – maybe someone from a long time ago, when we were little? Sometimes I think I remember…"

Deirdre plunked in a chair and rested her head in her hands. "No…not them…"

"Who, them?" Meghan demanded.

Their mother looked startled. "No one. Never mind, kids. I'll figure out something." She got up, grabbed her handbag and left.

Jared stared after her.

"There is a them," Meghan said. "Relatives, do you think?"

Jared shrugged in frustration. "She won't tell us so it doesn't matter. I'm going to the Laundromat." He threw the laundry bag over his shoulder and left. When he returned two hours later, Meghan was in the throes of another beauty makeover.

He'd just dumped the bag of hot, clean clothes onto the bed when the door opened and Deirdre came in.

"Well?" Meghan looked up from painting her toenails, hand suspended in the air. Jared kept on folding the warm clothes. He figured if they were turned out onto the street they may as well start clean.

Deirdre plunked down on the bed, bouncing the neat stacks. Jared steadied them.

"Do you remember Ian Parker, the BBC producer I know in London?"

Meghan nodded, eyes suddenly sparkling. Whenever they'd been in London, Ian had come around. He'd roar up in an expensive car, offer Deirdre extravagant bouquets of flowers, then pass out handfuls of candy when the twins were little and intriguing toys when they were older. Jared had compared the man's dark hair and blue eyes to his own. They were alike. Ian could...perhaps...maybe...be his father.

Wanting so much for Ian to like him, Jared used to grow hot in the face, mutter answers, drop dishes, and generally make such a fool of himself, that he had always wanted to run within ten minutes of the man's arrival. Ian never seemed to notice. Meghan thought he was wonderful. It hadn't mattered a whole lot though, Jared remembered. Ian had never stayed more than a few minutes before he whisked their mom away to a party, play or dinner, leaving them alone.

"I couldn't let you down, kids, not after all this," Deirdre continued. "So, in absolute desperation I called Ian, and he gave me a terrific lead. Practically worked the whole thing out for me on the phone."

"Which is?" Meghan demanded.

"Edward Simon is in Victoria, Canada on vacation – a mere 50 miles from here. Apparently he bought a boat out here and is spending the week sightseeing."

"Who's Edward Simon?" Jared asked.

"Don't you pay attention to anything important?" Meghan demanded. "He's only the hottest director of musical stage productions in North America."

Jared shrugged and kept folding.

"Don't forget Europe, too." Deirdre added. "He'll be in Victoria one more day, and then he's off to London to begin packaging a summer production of *Madame Butterfly* for the BBC. Ian said I could use his name for a reference. Kids, how'd you like to take a trip across Puget Sound?"

"Can we have High Tea at the Empress Hotel?" Meghan demanded.

Jared groaned. "Mom, we're short of money. Seriously short."

"Don't remind me." Deirdre was raking through her closet, examining outfits. "What do you think of this, Meggie? I need to look professional and casual and above all, like I don't need the job."

"Mom, how are we going to get there?" Jared interrupted.

"Oh...there a catamaran service – the Victoria Clipper. Ian knew all about it. We can leave first thing in the morning and then he said we could catch the evening return. There and back in a day."

Meghan walked across the floor like a penguin, toes up, to keep from smearing the polish. "Try the grey silk jacket over a black sweater and black slacks."

"You think so?" Deirdre pulled them out too.

"Absolutely," Meghan assured her.

"Mom!" Jared said loudly. "We can't afford it!"

"Don't be a dork," Meghan retorted. "Victoria's great. And this is Mom's chance!"

Jared ignored her and turned to their mom. "The savings are wiped out. We only have four hundred and eighty-three dollars – enough to pay the hotel and eat for about a week, if we're really careful."

"And then what?" Deirdre laid the clothes down on the bed. "I've got to get a job."

"What about a regular job," he blurted out. "And we could just stay here?"

"I wish...but no, it wouldn't work..." Deirdre busied herself with her clothes and didn't meet his eyes."

"We wouldn't have to move around all the time."

"Not that again!" Meghan waved her fingernails in the air.

"Jared, I'm a singer. I may not be a great one, but it's what I am."

"Even singers have homes," Jared retorted.

Deirdre grimaced. "Well, unless I get this job we aren't even going to have a crummy hotel room. Meghan, what about a silk blouse and my leather skirt?"

*   *   *

They left the hotel at seven the next morning. His mom had changed clothes three times before finally settling on the first outfit.

This was so unlike her, that Jared and Meghan both caught the edgy feel.

"You okay?" Meghan asked.

Their mom forced a smile. "I feel like bad luck is breathing down my neck," she confessed. "And last night, I thought I saw..."

"Who?" Meghan demanded.

"Someone...someone who hurt me a lot, once.... I'd nearly forgotten, somehow. But it couldn't have been him, because he lives a long way from here," Deirdre said. "And he's probably forgotten I ever existed. Right?"

"Sure," Megan agreed quickly. But when Deirdre wasn't looking, she shot a look at her brother. Jared shrugged – he didn't get it either.

At the Victoria Clipper offices, Jared went to the ticket booth while Deirdre and Meghan bought coffee. Jared paid for one fare with their last credit card and used cash for the other two.

Tickets in his pocket, he wandered down the wharf, breathing in salty air and listening to the screaming of gulls. Green water lapped at the pylons of the huge docks. If he turned his back to the city and stared out at the water, he could almost imagine he had been carried to a deserted shore or an ancient seaport right out of the legends he loved to read.

"Jared," a husky voice said softly.

Rhea.

He turned and stared up into her endless eyes. "You have interfered with me. I will not allow that." She pursed her lips and gently blew her breath toward him.

Wind sprang up, driving him back toward the dock's edge, whipping his clothes and hair. The gusts came on harder and harder, pounding him back. Jared shouted but the wind tore away his breath. Water heaved upward, drenching the planks. Jared slipped and grabbed a pylon. He could hear screams as people were knocked over and belongings somersaulted down sidewalks. The gale dragged and buffeted him toward the cold water. Jared clawed the wood. Splinters sliced his skin. Clinging desperately, Jared saw that Rhea's scarf only fluttered gently. She laughed and her voice rolled with the howl of wind.

A policeman seated on a magnificent chestnut horse trotted up to Rhea. "This is not allowed," he said clearly.

Abruptly the wind dropped. Rhea glared up at the officer, who laughed hugely. He turned his horse and trotted to Jared sprawled and choking on the planks.

"Get up," he commanded. Shakily, Jared got to his hands and knees, and then using the pylon for support, stood upright. Aware that the man watched, he straightened his shoulders, lifted his chin and stared into the cold eyes.

"I will have what was mine," the man said. "If you find what I hunt for, you must give all to me, my boy. Only I can give you what you truly want."

Jared nodded dumbly. He looked over at Rhea, but all he could see was the flick of her scarf as she disappeared into the crowd. She should have towered over most people's heads, but Jared couldn't see her.

He turned back to the officer, meaning to ask what it was that had been stolen, but the man was gone too.

Meghan came charging up. "Are you okay? Have you ever seen anything like that wind? I nearly had the latté blown out of my hand."

"Did you see that woman?" Jared demanded shakily.

"What? Did something happen to someone?" Meghan's eyes were wide.

"No, it was Rhea!"

"Who?" Meghan sipped her coffee, eyes blank. Biting back the urge to yell at his sister, to force her to remember, Jared looked around him at the chaos. Meghan had forgotten the woman, just as she had forgotten their first trip to the school and the terror caused by Kronos. Jared's stomach dropped. Kronos. The policeman, the rider of the great red horse, had been Kronos.

He had said Jared had to give him something. What did he want? And what could Jared possibly have to do with the terrifying god?

Cuzco, Peru

Loyalty

With a rare bonus from the enthusiastic mayor of Lima, Deirdre recklessly signs them up for a tour of Cuzco, the once capital of the Inca empire. The town of Cuzco is warm and dry, with stone buildings gleaming golden in the sun. At the cathedral, Jared and Deirdre linger before the silver altars donated by the Spanish mine owners.

"You'd think it would bother them that the local Indian's slave labor mined all that silver," Deirdre whispers. Fourteen-year-old Meghan wanders outside and fakes a stone in her shoe to get a better look at a young man selling fruit. By the time the family finds each other, the tour has gone on without them.

"Now what?" Meghan asks in disgust. They stand helplessly in front of the cathedral when the old Indian man approaches them. At first they are inclined to ignore him, but he speaks quietly to them about the great building.

"Beneath this cathedral are the ruins of the Inca temples," he says. "This is the oldest city, one of the oldest in the world. It has stood for three thousand years."

Deirdre turns to him. "We've lost our tour group," she says. "Could we hire you to show us the best sights, Mr....?"

The man inclines his head. "Capac, Manco Capac is my name. I can indeed show you the wonders of my city."

They wander for hours looking at old buildings and ancient sites. Mr. Capac is full of vivid stories old and new, about the town. Distantly, Jared hears the Song played on native flutes. At each turn in the old, old town Jared expects to come upon the musicians, but they seem to be always just ahead of them.

"I'm ready to go back to the hotel." Meghan is limping on a blistered heel.

"One last stop," Mr. Capac insists. "The twelve sided stone."

"I'd like to see that," Jared says. Meghan opens her mouth to protest, sees the eager expression on Jared's face and shrugs.

"Let's go," she says.

They troop down a twist of old roads until they stand before a wall of inset stones. Jared is disappointed. The flute music is closer now, but this stone is just an oddly cut fieldstone made to set neatly in the wall.

Mr. Capac guides Jared's and Meghan's hands to touch the sun-warmed surface. "There is loyalty between you. Let me tell you an old story of loyalty between another sister and brother. It is the story of the Girl with the Stone Face..."

Once a chieftain had two children, a boy of great strength and cunning and a girl of unusual courage and intelligence. Since childhood, they had been devoted to each other.

In the next village lived a powerful chief who also had a fine son. In time, the girl was betrothed to the son of the neighboring chief and everyone was happy. Everyone, that is, but the chief's wife. This woman was a witch, a kalku, who used her magic for evil. She cared for no thing but power and no one except her son. When her husband announced the coming wedding, the witch beat the ground in rage and jealousy. She hated the girl's brother because he was as expert a hunter as her own son. She doubly hated the girl because her son was so delighted with his bride to be.

The witch decided to doom the marriage. She whispered evil words in her husband's ear, convincing him that the girl's brother was plotting to take over the village. Happy to have an excuse to conquer his prosperous neighbor, the chief led a war party to the next village, killed the chieftain and captured the girl's brother. The witch danced a wicked dance of triumph.

The warriors tried to drag the bound and bloody young man before the chief, but the girl grasped her brother's hand and would not let go.

"You cannot save him from death," snarled the witch.

"I will not release his hand, even to death!" cried the girl.

The warriors pulled with all their strength. The girl's hand slipped a little until only their little fingers were linked.

The witch took her knife and with magical strength,

chopped off the brother's finger. His blood spurted outward onto his sister's face. She screamed and dropped the finger.

"Kill him!" shouted the chief. His warriors thrust their lances into the boy, hacked his body into pieces and carried them away. All that was left was the finger lying in the dirt, and that, the witch stole.

The girl did not cry but she turned her face from her bridegroom. She refused the company of the maidens in the village, and slept in the bride hut alone.

The witch, believing the girl to be as evil as herself, made a potion from the ground up finger bone. When the girl slept, the wicked woman crept to her bed and rubbed the foul cream on the bride's face, mixing it with the blood she had not washed off. Hurrying back to her husband and son, she told them she had bathed the girl's face with a sweet potion that would show her true heart.

The next morning when the bride was brought out, everyone pulled back in horror. Her face had turned to blood red stone.

"You see!" cried the witch. "She has a heart of stone. She cannot love."

"No," whispered the girl. "When you killed my brother, grief turned my heart to stone. Where there was once great love both for him and my future husband, now there is only rock."

"Kill her!" hissed the witch.

But the son pleaded for her life. His father, however,

ordered the girl to be banished.

The girl went out into the jungle, living on berries, fruit and nuts. One morning as she reached to pick fruit from a tree, she saw a butterfly struggling in a spider's web. Remembering the ropes that had bound her brother, she freed the insect and set it on a flowering bush.

The butterfly fluttered its wings and soared upward. "Dig deep. Dig deep!" The rustle of its wings seemed to say.

The girl dug into the soil beneath the bush. There in the dirt she found the dry arm bones of a man. Every bone was there, but those of one finger. The girl gathered them up into a bag and carried them away with her.

The next morning as she walked by a lake, she saw a frog about to be swallowed by a snake. She remembered how the warriors had crept up and captured her brother unawares. She threw a stone at the snake and frightened it away. The frog dove for the safety of the water, croaking, "Dig deep. Dig deep!"

The girl pulled at the muck in the reeds and found the leg bones of a man. She put these bones into her bag with the others.

The next morning as she walked in a meadow, she came upon a young llama, pierced with lances and near to death. Remembering the weapons that had killed her brother, the girl gently washed the wounds of the llama.

It sprang up and rapped its feet on a stone. The tip tap seemed to say, "Dig deep. Dig deep!"

The girl dug beneath the stone, and sure enough,

there lay the bones of the body of a man. She added them to her bag and saw that all that was missing was the skull.

The next morning, the girl walked high into the mountains, where the sound of great roaring and whimpering caught her ears. Remembering the cries of her dying brother, the girl searched until she found a puma lying in its den biting at its foot and wailing in pain. Her stone heart could feel no fear and so the girl came up to the great cat. She saw that a huge thorn had driven into its paw. The wound bled like the blood her brother had lost.

Despite the cat's roars, the girl crouched down and pulled the thorn from the puma's paw. As the thorn came out, the blood spurted onto the girl's stone face. The puma limped to a nearby stream, and holding a vessel in its jaws, used it to scoop water and bring it to the girl. The girl splashed the water on her face. As she did, the stone mask fell, leaving her own face open to the sun.

She saw that the puma had brought her water in a man's skull. The girl added that too to her bag of bones. Now that the stone mask was gone, the girl wept at the memory of her brother. Her tears fell on the red stone mask at her feet and it instantly turned back into the bones of a man's finger.

The girl took the bones out of her bag, and laid them out into the full skeleton of a man. Last she put the finger bones in place. The second the skeleton was complete, her brother came back to life. Jumping up, he hugged his sister.

Together they and the puma went back through the jungle toward the chief's village. A butterfly flew down and lighted on the girl's shoulder.

"From the sky I saw the chief and his wife journeying on the next road," its wings rustled. "They have stopped for the night with their warriors."

A moment later, a little frog hopped by. "The witch can only die by drowning," it croaked. "I saw her admiring her reflection in my pond."

And then the young llama trotted up. "The chief is under a spell of safety made by his wife." The llama spat out a red stone arrowhead. "He can only be killed by this stone."

The brother quickly made a bow and bound the arrowhead to a straight shaft. As the animals predicted, they came upon the chief, his wife and warriors. The puma leapt upon the warriors and killed all those who had helped murder the girl's brother. As the chief raised his lance, the brother shot the magic arrow and pierced his heart, killing him instantly. A little way away, the girl came upon the witch admiring her reflection in a pool. The girl gave her a push and the witch, whose heart really was made of stone, sank to the bottom of the pond and drowned.

Then the brother and sister returned to the village. The girl's bridegroom shouted in joy at the return of the girl and her brother. The new chief and the girl were married that day. The two men ruled their villages wisely

and well to the end of their days. The girl became a great
machi, or good witch who could sometimes be seen
speaking to a butterfly, a frog and a llama, always with
her friend the puma at her side...

Mr. Capac stops speaking. The sun is slipping down
behind the buildings and a chill is stealing over the town.

"Your hotel is quite near," he says, "but I have a gift for
your loyal daughter."

He holds out a smooth, red stone to Meghan. She takes it
from him and turns it over. Engraved on one side is the Inca
figure of the puma. "Ancient Cuzco is laid out in the shape of
the puma. This stone from our hills holds our loyalty," he says.

Meghan meets his eyes. "Thank you," she says.

As they examine the carving, Mr. Capac walks away.

"Oh no," Deirdre says. "I didn't pay him."

Meghan puts the rock into Jared's hand. "From me to
you," she jokes. "Loyal to the end..."

Chapter 8

Big Mistakes and Other Specialties

After half an hour in *The Victoria Clipper*'s airplane style seats, Jared got up and headed for the stairs to the second level observation deck. His skin felt itchy, as though there were eyes everywhere, watching him. He wished the vessel wasn't enclosed – he'd have liked to feel the cold salt air whipping by. Remembering what Rhea had done with the wind, though, he decided maybe it was a good thing the catamaran had no open decks.

But the woman seemed to be gone. He sure hadn't seen her or Kronos on board. Just a full load of passengers and his mom and Meghan. With the family around constantly, he'd had no chance to handle his rocks or make the magic circle. What if he could call up that power any time? What if he could control it?

Control, whispered in his mind. *Be powerful... be rich. Never have to worry again. All the power...and the money that comes with power...he could see the house they would live in...and the clothes and gadgets and friends... Power and money...all the power would belong to him...*

"Hey, Jared!"

With a shock like cold water, his twin's voice broke the oozing dream.

"Meghan!" His voice was shaky.

"What? What's wrong?" She searched his face. "It's not those stupid rocks is it?"

He shook his head. "No...it's...it's the hunters...Not the rocks...." How could he make Meghan understand? "It's about that guy Kronos and the woman at Pike Place and that teenager who tried to rob us...I think they're following me!"

Meghan's face went stony. "Jar...you know those things didn't happen. You sound paranoid and you're really scaring me. So stop it!"

Jared grabbed her sleeve. "We should be scared. I don't know what's happening. I'm not imagining it and I don't think I'm going crazy." He could've winced at the expression on Meghan's face. "You think I'm hallucinating or something, don't you?"

"There's been a lot of stuff to stress you out – you know, like Mom worrying about her job and being short of cash."

He gripped his sister's arm tightly. "I need you to believe me. And I don't think I can fight them by myself. Promise me, Meghan, that you'll help me."

The expression on her face wavered, then got hard again. "Get rid of the rocks," Meghan said flatly. "They're making you crazy and we have enough problems." She shook her arm loose. "You know I'm right."

"Meghan, don't leave me alone on this."

"Have I ever?" She dropped her eyes then lifted them. "Did you bring the new rock?" She indicated the bulging backpack.

"What?"

"The agate with the Indian carving. You can check out the native artifacts in the museum in Victoria. Maybe that thing's valuable or something." She leaned casually against the window. "Jardy... do you think I look older than fifteen? Like maybe about eighteen or nineteen?"

"What are you up to?" Jardy was her baby name for him.

Meghan flushed. "Nothing. I just thought... maybe... Edward Simon would like to discover a new star. Someone young and terrifyingly talented. Like me." She lifted her chin defiantly.

"That's terrifying, all right." Jared forced a smile. Meghan jabbed him in the side and stalked off.

Jared stayed where he was until they announced docking.

"Ian says the name of Simon's boat is *The Aida*," Deirdre was telling Meghan. "Jared," she turned to her son, "you're the sailing nut."

"I'm what?"

"We have to find his boat," Deirdre explained patiently. "If you act as if you're enthusiastic about sailing it will give us an excuse to strike up a conversation."

"But I don't know anything about boats," Jared protested.

"Fake it," Meghan told him in a quiet hiss. "Or would you rather starve?"

Jared stomped ahead to the exit. Deirdre and Meghan, talking in low voices, followed behind. They stood in line with the other passengers, passed through Customs, and then were out on the wharf.

"Do you have a map?" Deirdre turned to him. Jared handed her the flyer he'd picked up from the brochure rack on the Clipper. She studied it a moment, then pointed south. "Public moorage is that way."

She and Meghan hurried along the sidewalk. Jared avoided looking at a bearded man who was lethargically panhandling as the tourists left the area.

Within ten minutes the family was strolling along the marina dock.

"Now that's a lovely vessel," Deirdre said enthusiastically, pointing to a sailboat bobbing at the quay. "Excuse me," she called to a woman tying down a sail. "What make is this?"

"It's a *C & C 26*," the woman replied.

"Beautiful," Meghan exclaimed.

They moved on again. Two or three times, Deirdre or Meghan stopped to chat with one of the boat owners. Jared kept his distance.

"You could at least try," Meghan told him.

"I'm saving it for the main performance," he snapped back.

"Well, get ready," Meghan retorted, "because there's *The Aida*. It's up to you, whether we sink or sail."

Jared knew he was about to make a complete fool of himself. He took a deep breath and sauntered toward *The Aida*.

"Say Jared," Deirdre exclaimed, "Isn't this an elegant boat."

"It's the kind I was showing you in *Sail Away* magazine," Jared said loudly. "Excuse me, sir," he called to the man winding a rope on the deck. "Sorry to bother you, but this is a customized vessel, isn't it?"

Edward Simon turned to stare at them. There was a moment of silence, powerful like the thrumming rocks. *He's going to snub us*, Jared thought. But the moment passed and the director smiled.

"Yes, it's a custom *Swan*," he said with a British accent. "Are you keen on sailing?"

Fingering the rock in his pocket, Jared said awkwardly, "I don't know much about it."

"Oh, a fairly recent interest?" He grinned and Jared found himself grinning back.

"I see you've named your boat *The Aida*," Deirdre interjected. "Are you a fan of opera?"

Mr. Simon turned to her politely. "As a matter of fact I am."

"What a coincidence," Deirdre said. "I sing professionally. Soprano."

"Really?" Mr. Simon's voice was noticeably less cordial. Despite the rising blush in her cheeks, Deirdre acted like she didn't notice. She sat casually on the edge of the dock, as if anticipating a delightful chat with a new-found friend.

Meghan leaned against a pylon. "I'm studying for a stage career, too," she said.

His part was done. He's set the bait and Jared didn't want to hang around for the hunt.

He took a few steps back. "Mom," he called, "I'm going over to the museum. Meet you at the Empress Hotel at five."

He didn't wait to hear her response. Whistling, he jogged along the sidewalk, past the tourist information office. He cut across the Empress Hotel's sweep of lawn and headed toward the museum.

Jared took the shallow steps two at a time, then paused in the courtyard to rub his hand over the totem poles in a gesture of respect and greeting. Inside the big wooden doors he paused. He'd forgotten about the admission fee. To buy time he turned into the gift shop.

This was almost as good as the museum. As well as the usual gift shop stuff, Native Canadian artwork was for sale. Jared spent a long time examining the displays of carved masks, lithographs and ceremonial gear. In the corner, he spotted a mask with a face like the carved figure on the agate. Taking the last rock from his backpack, Jared compared them. Similar, not identical.

"Excuse me," he said to a saleswoman. "I'd like to know about that mask."

She came over and looked up at it thoughtfully. "Bran Alfred is the sculptor."

"Oh," Jared said, disappointed. "I thought it would be a First Nations artist."

"He is," the woman smiled. "Kwakiutl tribe, I believe, although he works out of Seattle these days. He's a traditional artist, using the old symbols and art forms of the coastal tribes."

"What's that symbol? It's a traditional character isn't it?" Jared stared up at the geometric form, drawn as always to the mythology it represented.

The saleswoman frowned. "To tell you the truth, I don't know. We've had this mask around for months – it doesn't sell because customers can't recognize the symbols. I like it though."

"Yeah," Jared agreed. "But I'm trying to identify a figure that's like that."

"Try the books," she suggested.

Jared thanked her and followed her pointing finger to an alcove where the racks of books were kept. He chose a couple, then sat down cross-legged on the carpet with the agate between his folded legs. He'd been flipping through pages for twenty minutes when he heard a voice at his elbow.

"Hi!" Meghan crouched down beside him.

"Get the part?" Jared asked.

Meghan shook her head. "Not likely."

"Your voice is better than any we've ever heard even on stage," Jared comforted her. "You know it'll happen sometime."

Meghan smiled ruefully. "Sometime seems forever."

"How's Mom doing?"

Meghan flipped the pages of the book. "Not great, but still plugging. If nothing else, Mom has guts." She closed the book. "What about you? Found anything?"

"Nope. Just a similar mask by a Seattle-based artist."

"Let's check out the museum." Without waiting, Meghan left the gift shop.

Jared replaced the books on the rack and caught up. "We can't afford the admission fee," he said quietly.

Meghan grinned. "My specialty."

She walked confidently to the reception desk. "Excuse me," she said. "My brother and I have an appointment with the curator of the Native Art exhibit. Where is his office, please?"

The woman looked surprised. "Mr. Malik?" she asked.

"Mr. Malik. That's right."

"The entrance to the administrative wing's at the back of the lobby. Shall I ring through and tell him you're here, Miss... ?"

"No, I wouldn't want to trouble you. Thank you!" Meghan walked swiftly toward the back. Face hot, Jared hurried after her.

"Now what?" he demanded as they turned the corner. "I wanted to look at the exhibits."

"Well," Meghan said, "maybe there's a stairway from here. Besides, why don't we just ask this Mr. Malik about your rock?"

"He's probably too busy to talk to a couple of kids."

Meghan shrugged. "Then we won't see him. Besides, for all you know, that rock might be an archaeological find."

"I doubt it," Jared muttered, but Meghan had already pulled open the wooden door marked *Administration*. In the pit of his stomach, Jared was sure this was a mistake – a big one.

"We hate to bother him," Meghan was saying to the next receptionist, "but we've found a really ancient Native carving."

When Meghan turned on her smile, the assistant, like most people, was charmed. She put through a call to Mr. Malik. "Go on in," she said. "He has a meeting with the administrator shortly, but he'll spare you a few minutes. Second door on your right."

"Thanks!" Meghan replied. Jared tried to force a smile and look confident as they headed down the hallway, and Meghan rapped on the office door.

Malik's office looked like a storehouse.

Everywhere, on the walls and on top of the packed bookcases, Native art was displayed. Some of it was so old it was crumbling. The expression on some of the masks made Jared want to avert his eyes. Their evil faces made the room seem crowded with bad memories. He left the door open behind them.

In the middle of the room stood a chipped wooden desk. Behind it, watching them, sat a smallish man with thinning hair. He reminded Jared of a pale spring spider – skinny and skittery and desperately hungry. Not yet big and fat and bloated, but wanting with all its being to get that way.

"Mr. Malik?" Meghan crossed the room. "I'm Meghan Singer, and this is my brother Jared."

Mr. Malik gestured them into two wooden chairs facing the desk. "What can I do for you?"

Jared held the backpack in his lap, unwilling to take out the rock. Meghan nudged him. "Show him!"

Feeling like an idiot, Jared undid the flaps. Even in the murky room the agate glistened. Meghan grabbed it from him and handed it over to Malik. Jared tensed.

The curator stared at the rock, expression flickering. "Quite interesting," he said after a moment. "Where did you find it?"

"On a beach." Jared held out his hand for the stone, but Malik swiveled his chair, pulled back the drapes and held the stone up to the light of the window. It gleamed even more strongly. Jared's feeling of hungry ghosts grew.

"I don't know if it's really a find," Malik said, swiveling back. He was smiling now, friendly. "But on the chance it is, I could give you, say, a hundred dollars."

"All right!" Grinning, Meghan leaned across the desk, offering to shake hands with the curator. "We'll take it!"

Hawaii

Reverence

"This is fabulous," thirteen-year-old Meghan breathes. The Hawaiian sun shines down on her coppery hair like the fire of a volcano. Jared shoves his hands in the pockets of his shorts and surveys the beach. Maybe four minutes until a bunch of randy teenage boys discover Meghan's bikini-clad presence. As the brother, he'll be unwelcome to everyone, including his twin.

"I'm going for a walk," he says. Meghan nods, without even looking at him. He heads along the beach, kicking puffs of hot sand as he goes. When his feet feel burned, he runs to the water's edge. It's there, with cool water sucking his toes, that he hears it...the Song, tugging at his mind.

He glances back at Meghan. Sure enough, three beach boys are clustered around her and she's laughing, head tilted in major flirt mode. Jared walks toward the Song. Ahead looms a jumble of lava rock. Spray flashes against it.

Jared stops, bewildered. The Song is gone.

A boy about his own age, working on some old fishing nets, waves to him.

"Hey," Jared says.

The boy grins. "You've been a long time coming," he says. "I've been watching you walk along the beach. I thought my song would bring you quicker."

Jared's head snaps up, but the boy has turned away. "You ever been snorkeling?" he asks.

Jared shakes his head. "No...it costs too much. I..." Then he sees the boy is holding up snorkeling gear – enough for two people.

"I am Atua; it's a very old Hawaiian name – though not as old as my mother Hina or my father Ira-Waru. I am going to show you the world under the water."

"I don't know how to swim," Jared confesses.

Atua laughs. "Don't worry. I can teach anyone who is willing to learn." He hands the gear to Jared. "We will see beautiful things. The fish, the squid, and many other creatures – all that I love. But beware of Mamoa, the Shark Chief. He and his followers kill and bite even when they're not hungry. They do not observe tapu. Be watchful, my friend."

Jared nods. Together, he and Atua wade into the warm water, and somehow with his new friend's teaching, Jared finds he can snorkel and swim as though he's done it for years. They weave through waves, and swim with schools of fish. They cling to the back of a giant sea turtle and glide out toward the surf-frothed reefs.

It seems to go on for hours, the swash of waves, the undulating rhythms of plants and creatures, the bubbling sound of their own breathing that slides into the patterns of the Song. Jared drifts with the beauty of it. The Song gets louder and louder washing over and through him; he hears its call clearly now, then feels Atua's fist grab his arm. The boy points.

"Mamoa!"

A monster shark swishes toward them, mouth gaping showing rows and rows of teeth. Frantic, Jared kicks back. Horrified he sees Atua dive forward, a knife gripped in his hand.

The shark lunges. Red blood clouds the water. Jared tries to scream and surfaces coughing and choking. He has to get help! The beach is empty. What has happened to everyone?

Jared ducks back under the water again. Atua's knife lies on the sand beneath him. Jared kicks down and grabs it, hunting desperately for a sight of Atua...And Mamoa, the Shark Chief.

There! Atua's body lies trapped in a tangle of old cables and debris. Jared shoots down, frantically hacking with the knife and pulling away the garbage. He puts his arm around Atua and kicks toward the surface. A shape blocks the sun.

Shark!

Jared freezes. His lungs are bursting. He kicks upward, clutching the knife in his hand, trying to hold on to his friend with the other. The shark circles. From beneath, Jared strikes desperately, ripping a long gash in the shark's belly. More blood stains the water. Shark's blood. Jared surfaces, gasping. He shakes Atua and screams his name. The boy's eyes flutter open and he smiles.

Fins break the surface around them, diving and slashing.

"Swim slowly toward shore," Atua murmurs. "Sharks have no reverence even for each other. They are feasting on the Shark Chief once again."

Nearly dead with terror, Jared strokes toward shore. Atua swims effortlessly beside him. Too tired, to wonder how that could be, Jared just keeps going, staring at the beach getting nearer and nearer. He can see crowds of people now. Where had they been before? His hand grips the knife, hoping the sharks won't return.

When his feet touch bottom, he staggers to shore and falls into the sand. He lies there for long minutes, gasping. Atua! Where is his friend?

Only sunbathers lie on the beach. The surface of the water is unbroken.

"Atua!" Jared shouts. He sloshes, half stumbles into the water. He looks down at the knife still in his hand, but it is gone. Instead he holds a fist-sized rock – green as the seaweed, clear as crystal water, rounded from the wash of waves. As he turns it in his hand, he finds the shape of a shell, rounded and fluted against the smooth rock.

"Keep this safe, my friend," Atua's voice whispers across the waves. "Long ago, when the Shark Chief, Mamoa, was still a man, the people had to give him so many fish that they often went hungry. They sang many prayers for help and so the god Ira-Waru and his wife Hina, came to live among the people on the Island of Maui. They disguised themselves as man and woman and there I, Atua was born.

Ira-Waru and Hina taught the people to fish and find rock crab and shrimp, and they taught them tapu – to take only what they need and to show reverence for the sea and earth. But in time the people became cruel and greedy like Mamoa, taking much more than they needed. So, to punish them, Hina and Ira-Waru emptied the sea. But a few of the people did not follow Mamoa. They poured their love for the beauty of the world into this shell. With it, I brought back the fish, squid and rock crab. For them, I have kept the seas rich for a thousand years. Now the gift is yours."

Jared holds the rock up to the sun. Light shines through it like sunbeams shine through water. With a smile, he slides the stone in his pocket and slogs through the sand to his twin who is alone in the shade of a palm tree.

"What happened to the gorgeous guys?" Jared squats down beside her.

Meghan shrugs. "They laughed when one of them used a stick to spear a little gecko." She shakes her head and blinks hard. "And it was so beautiful here."

Chapter 9

Spider Webs

"No!" Jared shouted. He jumped up, thrusting his chair back. It grated on the bare floor. The ravenous greed in the room grew more insistent, pressing against him. He shook his head, as though a fog was filtering into his mind. "I won't sell the stone," he said doggedly.

Mr. Malik's expression didn't change, but Jared had a sense of numbing fingers stretching from the man toward him.

"Jared!" Meghan shot him a furious look, then cooled her voice to address the curator. "This rock means a lot to my brother. He wouldn't part with it for a mere hundred dollars."

A small smile flickered over Malik's mouth. "A hundred and fifteen then?"

"No!" Jared repeated. Breathing hard, he held out his hand. "It's not for sale. Could I have my rock back, please?" More and more

Malik reminded Jared of a spider, and his stone was caught in the web.

"Jared, it's a lot of money," Meghan hissed.

"It's not for sale," he repeated. It was becoming hard to think...to remember. "My rock. Give me back my rock..."

Malik didn't move, but abruptly his expression shifted. Jared heard quick footsteps behind him.

"George, your zeal in obtaining artifacts is admirable but a tad aggressive," a woman's voice said. The dark fog suddenly evaporated and the room was just an office again. Jared took a deep breath.

"It's nothing too special, Zoe." Malik smiled, the dislike in his eyes obvious. "Just doing a favor for these kids."

"Good of you." The woman, middle-aged and smartly tailored, nodded to the twins. "I'm Zoe Williamson, the Museum's administrator. Show it to me, George." She held out her hand.

Malik hesitated a fraction of an instant, then handed over the stone. She looked at the rock first one way and then another. "Unusual for a rock to be carved in these native symbols, I should think. But this isn't my area of expertise."

She handed the agate back to Jared, who gratefully stowed it in his backpack.

"Thanks," he muttered, already backing toward the door.

Meghan shot him a furious look, then with lifted chin, followed.

"You are such a dork!" she fumed at Jared as soon as they left the museum.

"Shut up!" he yelled. "What were you thinking? You tried to sell my rock! To them! In that place!"

"What place? It's a museum, you idiot!" she shouted back. "You're the one that's always going on about how broke we are. You should be grateful! I was on a roll in there. I could have gotten Malik up to a hundred and fifty!"

Jared grabbed her arm. "Meghan, that room was full of evil. Couldn't you feel it? And this rock's special. I'm not selling it for a thousand dollars! Get it?"

"Evil! Yeah, I get it." Meghan jerked back her arm and shoved him. "Get a grip. You're so righteous about Mom and me, but when you have a chance to help out like today at the boat, you take off. You could have made money for the family, but you blew that too. I'm sick of you and I'm sick of our second-rate life!"

She whirled around and ran down the street. Furious, Jared headed in the other direction. How did the whole family disaster become his fault? Why couldn't Meghan see how important the rock was?

And why couldn't she feel the danger that lurked just beyond their sight?

*   *   *

At five sharp, Jared walked into the Empress lobby. Meghan was there already, slumped in an overstuffed chair. He went to the opposite side of the room and stared out the window. For about ten minutes he waited without acknowledging his sister. But they had to get to the Clipper by six forty five.

Very stiff, he went over to her. "Where's Mom?"

"In the lounge," she said, barely audible.

Jared swallowed.

When they were little, Mom had gotten really drunk at some of the fancy parties Ian took her to. Once she'd left them alone in the hotel room for a long, long time. When she came back and found them so scared, she'd promised not to drink any more. And she'd kept her word. Until now.

"I'll get her," Jared said.

The entrance to the lounge was decorated with jungle safari motifs, complete with mounted skins. Jared didn't like it at all. Deirdre sat at a window table, absently stirring a drink around and around with a red swizzle stick.

Jared slid into the chair opposite. "Mom, we have to go or we'll miss the boat."

"I think I did that twelve years ago." She glanced at his stricken face. "Don't worry, Jar." She patted his cheek gently. "The cocktail's a Shirley Temple. No alcohol."

"Was it really bad?"

"We didn't fool him with the fake boat routine. Mr. Simon knew who I am. Even with Ian's recommendation, there are no parts around – for me. He said I'd gotten a reputation for being undependable – here today and gone tomorrow."

Jared swore softly. "It's not fair."

Deirdre smiled. "It's okay, Jared. He didn't tell me anything I didn't know. I just kept hoping nobody else would notice. He was very nice about it. But very final."

"What do we do now?"

She stood up. "Something I've been avoiding for such a long time."

That was all she would say, then or on the trip back to Seattle. Meghan remained furiously silent. If it wasn't so grim, Jared thought as he stared out the window, it would be funny.

By the time they reached the city the night had turned dark and drizzly. They stood glumly in line at Customs, declared with near hysterical finality that they had brought nothing back with them, and then walked silently through the terminal to the street.

Streetlights blurred in the haze of rain. Taxi doors slammed and roared off into the night. The family stood staring this way and that, hoping a cab would miraculously pull up in front of them and an eager driver would throw open a door.

"Our luck is holding," Deirdre said after ten minutes. "We may as well walk as stand here and get wet."

They set out through the dripping night. Skirting careening cars and stumbling over old railroad tracks, they tramped in the general direction of the downtown city lights. They hadn't counted on the steep hill of deserted buildings and empty parking lots between them and the city center. Deirdre walked stolidly, head down against the rain.

Nervously, Jared peered ahead into the blurred shadows. For a busy city, this area was frighteningly silent.

"Do you hear something?" Meghan clutched his arm. "Footsteps?"

Jared shook his head, then froze. Was there movement ahead? A drunk lurched from an alley. Jared and Meghan yelped together.

"Spare some change, lady?" he mumbled.

Deirdre shook her head and walked faster. The drunk stood head-down, swaying.

"Here." Meghan fished some change from her pocket and dropped it into his grimy hand. "Good luck."

The man sank down beside the building, indifferent to the rain running through his matted hair and down his face. A dime slipped from his hand and lay shining like a small moon on the sidewalk.

"He looked hungry," she said defensively to Jared. "At least we aren't hungry."

"I know," Jared said. They walked on shoulder to shoulder. Deirdre turned the corner.

"Why isn't she waiting?" Meghan demanded. "Jared, what's happening?"

The rain seemed to be thickening, fogging up the street. An acrid smell clouded the air.

"The fog's turning black," Jared grunted. "Must be a fire somewhere."

"But there aren't any sirens," Meghan argued. "And I still hear footsteps. At least, I think they're footsteps."

They stopped. Jared could hear the sound, too. Not footsteps...hoof beats! Ahead, in the smoky fog. Coming toward them...

"Back!" Jared shouted. "Run back!"

They whirled around and tore down the hill toward the terminal.

The drunk had disappeared, but the dime still shone on the wet sidewalk. A man stepped from the alley. Tall and hulking, with dead, grey eyes. Flashing a knife.

They stumbled to a stop. The sounds had faded away.

"Whatcha got, kids?" The man stepped closer.

"Nothing," Jared hoped his voice didn't quiver. "We haven't got any money."

"Yeah, right," growled the man. "I'll take the backpack."

"Do you always rob kids?" demanded Meghan furiously. "Like we're going to have a lot of money."

"I take what I can get," the man said. "Hand over the backpack, or I cut it off!" He waved the knife threateningly.

Face poker calm, thoughts raging, Jared slid the bag off his shoulders. No way *They* were going to rob him. Somewhere in the back of his mind, he was screaming in panic, but up front, he was furious. And he could feel the rocks thrumming.

"You want money?" demanded Meghan. "Here!"

She snatched the dime off the sidewalk and flicked it. Flashing silver, it flew through the air. As the mugger's eyes followed the coin, Jared swung the bag with all his strength. It *thunked* against the side of the man's head. With a sound between a yell and a groan, he sank to the sidewalk.

"*Run!*" Jared grabbed Meghan's arm. They raced back up the steep hill, hearts pounding, backpack and rocks thumping against Jared's legs. At the top of the hill, they turned toward the downtown.

"Fog's gone," Meghan panted. "Weird, huh?"

Deirdre was waiting on the corner of the next block. "Don't lag behind," she said. "It might not be safe."

"No kidding!" Meghan started.

Jared elbowed her hard and shook his head. The way he figured it, they'd managed fine, and his mom was worried enough already.

*   *   *

"Two, maybe three more days," Jared said, looking up from his notepad the next morning. "Providing we make our meals here." He gestured toward the tiny kitchenette.

Meghan threw herself backward onto the bed. "I am so sick of tuna melts and peanut butter sandwiches," she groaned. "Why can't we do it like the movies, just go into a restaurant and order a huge meal. Then someone charming and rich will rescue us and marry Mom."

The key turned in the lock and Deirdre came in. One look at her face and the twins knew the news wasn't good.

She was blinking hard, like there was something in her eyes. Within three steps she'd stumbled over Jared's backpack.

"Yeouch!" She hobbled over to the bed. "Jared, what have you got in there?"

"Rocks," Meghan retorted. "His stupid rocks! One of which he could have sold to the museum for a few hundred dollars."

"That's not true," Jared shouted.

"I don't care!" Deirdre snapped. "I want those things out of my way, now."

"I'll put them under the bed." Jared stood up to get his bag.

"Mom's and my suitcases are already there."

Jared started toward the closet.

"Look," Deirdre said, "I've had it with those rocks. We've carted them around the world about four times. I told you this before, and I mean it. Get rid of them. Go dump them in the alley."

"Mom," Jared started.

"Do it, Jared. I can't see us going to a homeless shelter with a backpack full of rocks, can you?"

Jared snapped his mouth shut, picked up the backpack and his jacket, and left the room. When the door slammed behind him, he leaned against the wall, so angry he was shaking. The First Rock was already in his jacket pocket. He took the agate from his pack and slipped it into his other pocket.

Determined, he rattled down the stairs to the lobby and went directly to the main desk. The clerk, Marquis, was leaning back in a chair, reading a car magazine.

"Hey there, Jared. What can I do for you?" the clerk asked.

Jared shifted the pack off his shoulders and onto the counter. "Marquis, I need to put this in the hotel safe."

The clerk's eyebrow's rose. "You in some kind of trouble?"

Jared shook his head. "No. I just need to keep this in a safe place. It's valuable."

The clerk put down his magazine, came to the counter and lifted the bag. "Feels like it's full of rocks."

Jared felt his face grow hot, but he said nothing. The clerk's brown eyes met his, then he smiled. "I'll keep it under the counter for you. Used to collect rocks myself."

Jared grinned. "Thanks, Marquis."

"Any time."

Turning away, Jared headed for the phones at the far end of the lobby. The museum woman had said Bran Alfred, the artist who had carved the mask, lived in Seattle. Jared wanted to talk to him – find out what the carving meant. Their computer was so old, he hadn't been able to do a search from it. None of the sites he tried would load, even when he was willing to wait.

Jared found an ancient phone book with its pages mostly intact, and flipped through until he found the listing. He hoped it was still good, but even if the sculptor had moved, maybe someone could tell him where. It was all he had to go on anyway. Should he try the number and ask for an appointment? Jared frowned. The address appeared to be about a mile from the hotel and even a short call would carry a charge on the hotel phone or minutes on the disposable one his mom had. Besides, he wanted to get out for a while and his legs worked just fine.

He swung the book shut and went toward the elevator. A man coming into the lobby glanced at him sharply and then quickly turned aside. Jared hurried past, hoping it wasn't someone wanting his mom to pay a forgotten bill. He so needed to get out of the hotel for awhile – to escape at least a few of the problems crowding in on his family. Jared longed for his mysterious rocks to bring some good luck, for once.

Mexico City

Creativity

"Don't you kids just love this place?" Deirdre takes a deep breath of the hot Mexican air. She swishes a colorful fan bought at one of the overflowing stalls. The square is packed with tourists and citizens celebrating the festival of La Vergen de Guatalupe. "Food, music, dancing and sun! It makes me feel alive all over!"

"Better than being in New York for December." Meghan flips the mantilla she bought over her fiery hair. For hours they have watched the pageants, delighted in the vibrant artwork, inhaled the cornucopia of smells, tasted the array of foods, and reveled in the music.

Jared says nothing. The warm sun is great, but he feels restless as though little electric currents are zapping him. While his sister and mother laugh and applaud the dancing, he scans the crowd. Everyone wears brightly colored clothing and costumes. Everyone shouts in Spanish, clapping and breaking into snatches of songs. The scene is bright, joyous and full of life.

"Jar," his mother says, "the tour guide we hired is over there. He's waving. Want to see if he's ready to start out?"

"Sure." Jared glances over the crowd to where his mother has pointed. The guide stands beside an ancient stone wall of a church, nearly unmoving, ignoring the crowds swirling around him. His stare nearly unnerves Jared.

"Boy, he's sure into the mood!" Jared tells his mother, but her attention has been caught by another colorful street performance. The guide wears the most colorful costume Jared has seen so far. A cape of green, red, and white feathers hangs from his shoulders. A mask in the shape of a snake rests above his extremely high forehead. He fixes his black eyes on Jared and beckons for him to follow.

Taking a deep breath, Jared shoulders his way through the crowd to reach him.

"This way, Jared." The man gestures away from the mass of celebrants toward an open hill. In his left hand, he flips two small grey sticks back and forth between his fingers.

"What about my mom and sister?" Jared asks, glancing back. They are still absorbed in the displays.

"They will meet us on Tepeyac Hill," he says, striding ahead.

"Wait!" Jared calls.

But the guide doesn't wait. Jared glances back again at his mom and sister. The performance has ended and they are moving through the crowd toward him, so Jared hurries after the guide, trying to keep him and his family in view.

The crowd finally thins. In the distance, Jared hears the songs sung in honor of the Virgin. A breeze ruffles his hair and tugs at his clothes, as though urgently pulling him elsewhere. The songs fade as Jared runs to catch up to his guide. The man trots ahead, not waiting.

"They will meet us on the Hill," the guide again calls back to Jared and speeds up his steps. Not sure what else to do, Jared runs after him, hoping his mother and sister will follow.

The hill is dry and dusty, dotted with brittle, winter-killed brush. Jared licks his lips. His head is thick feeling. The crowd's distant singing is blending into the Song.

An Indian woman waits at the top of the hill, and the guide joins her, standing just back within her shadow. Jared struggles up to them. It is like a dream. The woman gazes at him and Jared can only look back. She too, wears a bizarre costume – a head dress of feathers with bunches of corn above her ears. Her skirt is made of snakes – living snakes.

On the other side of the hill, away from the city, Jared sees a man in ragged clothing leave a cluster of huts and run panting up the steep slope. The boy shakes his head, trying to clear the picture of the twining serpents. The vision clears, and when he looks back at the wild woman, he sees with relief that she is dressed in a long robe embroidered with roses, much like the costumes of the people celebrating the holiday in the city.

The man struggles through the dead brush to reach them. "Lady...please...." He falls to his knees before her. "I cannot do what you wish. My uncle is dying and I must find the priest."

The woman blows into the air. A green feather catches in the breeze and flutters away to a cluster of huts below.

"You uncle is well, Juan Diego," the woman says. "I have cured him. Now go back to the bishop and tell him he must build my temple on this spot."

Diego looks everywhere except into the woman's face. He clasps his hands before him. "Bishop says he must have proof," he whispers.

"Then you must take him my flowers," she says. Again she purses her lips and blows softly.

Jared shakes his head again. A dry bush rattles in the breeze, then sprouts leaves and buds before his eyes. The buds burst open into fire red roses.

The woman helps Diego pick the flowers. With her own hands she wraps them in his serape. "Now go," she says, "and tell the bishop what he must do."

Diego bows several times then makes his way down the hill toward the city. Before he reaches the crowd, he vanishes from Jared's sight.

Jared swings his eyes back to the woman and guide. Once again she wears the head dress of feathers and corn and the skirt of snakes. Not knowing what else to do, Jared bows awkwardly. He hopes he isn't having a hallucination from bad water or too much sun.

"Life lies in the wheel of creation," she says. "Death becomes life. Old truth does not die but is reborn in a new form. An end becomes a beginning. And so the people who create and love art, music and beauty reach beyond death." She leans over and picks the last rose, but as she does so, a long thorn pierces her finger, making her cry out.

The guide flips the two small, grey sticks into the air. They fall onto the ground, so that one lies crossed over the other. To his horror, Jared sees the sticks are old bones, broken and grey with age.

The lady tosses the rose on top of the bones and holds out her hand so that a drop of blood falls on them. At the same moment, the guide spits. The blood and spittle touch the bones and rose at the same time.

The Song tugs at Jared's mind. He glances toward the town and sees his mother and sister climbing the hill toward him. When he looks back, the guide and the lady are gone. A puff of breeze, scented with corn and roses, riffles his hair. At his feet lies a white, four-cornered rock. In its center shimmers a red fire opal in the shape of a rose.

Jared smiles as he picks up the rock and slides it into his pocket.

"What are you doing, Jared?" Deirdre calls. "I send you to get our guide and the next thing I know you're up here on the hill." She flicks open her guide book. "Let's see....This is the first stop on the tour – the hill where Juan Diego saw the Virgin of Guadalupe in 1532. Isn't it amazing? Can't you just feel the history?"

Jared runs his fingers over the rock, caressing it. He grins. "I can just about see it all happening."

Chapter 10

Changer

When Jared returned to the hotel room after stashing his rocks with Marquis, his mom was just leaving.

"What's up?" he asked.

Deirdre shrugged, then gave him a small pinched smile. "There's a local production company here that's starting rehearsals for a musical. I'm going to muscle my way in and see if I can land some kind of part."

Jared patted her shoulder awkwardly. "Break a leg."

Deirdre smiled ruefully. "I probably will."

She walked determinedly down the hall and pushed the elevator button. Jared went into the room.

Meghan was pulling her hair into a twist on top of her head and softly singing an old ballad. Jared paused and listened. Even in the dingy hotel room, his sister's voice stirred a feeling of wind and sky and a sunrise about to burst out. There was her own kind of magic in it.

She finished her song, noticed he was watching, and grimaced. "Sorry. Mom says if I want a professional career I should forget folk songs."

Jared smiled. "I like them."

Meghan rolled her eyes. "I like them too, dummy, but they won't get me fame and fortune."

Jared flopped on the bed. "When you're a star, will you take a break now and then and sing some ballads for me?"

"Maybe. If you'll buy me a mocha," Meghan wheedled.

"We can't afford it!"

She grinned. "No mocha – no music."

On their way out, Jared checked his pocket for the key card, then pulled the door shut behind them. The lock clicked.

Outside, they walked along until they found a latté stand.

"Double tall mocha with whipped cream," Meghan ordered.

"Single short!" Jared protested. "No whipped cream!"

Meghan eyed him. "Single – with whipped cream."

Ignoring his sister's grin, Jared counted the price out in quarters, dimes and nickels.

While the espresso machine brewed the coffee and steamed the milk into foam, he told her that he had found Bran Alfred's address.

"I have to find out what the carving means," Jared said as they walked along. "Maybe then I'll understand what the stones are."

Meghan sipped her mocha. The whipped cream left a frothy white mustache on her upper lip. She swished it away with a flick of her tongue.

"Maybe then you'll dump those dumb rocks in the alley," she replied.

"I can't. They *chose* me."

"For what?" Meghan demanded scornfully. "Insanity?"

Jared scowled and searched his mind for some great insight. "I...I don't know," he finally admitted. "But I do know they're...important!"

"Maybe just cursed." Meghan faced him then, eyes flashing. "They're doing something to you, Jared. Taking you away from us! Even with our lives in a complete mess all you think about are those stupid rocks!"

Jared felt his face getting hot. "They aren't stupid!"

Meghan rolled her eyes. "Right."

They only make me sound stupid, Jared thought bitterly, as he and his sister walked several more blocks without speaking. They turned a corner into a narrow street, almost a laneway, and stopped in front of a red doorway squeezed between a pawnshop and a café. One of the four mailboxes screwed to the wall had a piece of masking tape on it with the penciled letters: *Alfred*.

"Go for it," Meghan said. She drained her coffee cup and tossed it in an overflowing garbage pail.

Jared hesitated and pushed the bell. It rasped deep within the building. A minute later, a stocky man in a paint-smeared T-shirt and jeans pulled open the door. He looked them over.

"I can't buy anything, kids," he said.

"Mr. Alfred...?"

The man nodded.

"We aren't selling anything, " Jared said quickly, hoping he wouldn't seem as stupid as Meghan thought he did. "I just wanted to ask you about something."

"Yeah, what?" the artist leaned against the edge of the door.

Jared took the agate from his coat pocket and held it out, carving side up. "This. You sculpted a mask that looks like this symbol."

The artist took the stone into his blunt hands and stepped out onto the sidewalk to catch the light. His expression barely changed, but his nostrils flared, and then he turned quickly and headed back inside. "Come on up," he called over his shoulder.

Jared and Meghan followed him up black painted stairs into a huge room on the second floor. Despite its size, the room was crowded with art supplies, propped up lithographs and paintings, and pieces of wood in various stages of carving. One corner of the room seemed to serve as a living area – there was a tiny kitchen, table and four chairs and a sofa with a pile of pillows and a blanket on it. The artist led the way to the table and sat in one of the chairs.

Jared and Meghan sat too. Alfred placed the agate in the very center of the table with the figure facing upward.

"Where did you get this?" he asked.

"I found it on a beach on Whidbey Island," Jared said cautiously.

"So, you were just playing around and this stone caught your eye because of the carving on it?"

Meghan and Jared exchanged glances. Do I make up something ordinary, Jared wondered. Or should I spill out the whole crazy. Meghan's taunt still stung, but when Jared looked back at the artist's square face, he decided he had to trust him. Had to trust someone who may have been called by the same magic...or felt its curse. Bran Alfred had carved symbols like the one on the rock. With a brief jolt of surprise, Jared realized this man was the only living person who seemed to be touched by the same symbols and their magic that pulled the strings of his own life.

He had to trust him. He had no choice...or he would become as crazy as Meghan thought he was.

"Rocks," Jared said slowly, "...special rocks call me sometimes. This one did a couple of weeks ago."

Alfred's eyes flew to his face. "You have more like this?" Alfred looked startled even as his fingers reached out to lightly touch the carved symbol.

Jared took a deep breath. "Eleven others – but each stone is different and they all came from different places."

The artist clasped his hands and rested his chin on them, gazing silently at the golden stone.

"Do you know what this is?" Meghan demanded. "Is it a valuable artifact? Or...is it some kind of...of creepy, ancient spell? Do you think Jared should get rid of it?"

She ignored the angry glance Jared shot at her.

The artist rubbed his hand over his chin. "I don't know if there's power in this rock, or if it holds any of the old magic. But the figure is Lummi – the Changer."

"The who?" Meghan asked.

"The Changer, son of the star people. Sometimes he is called Coyote or Raven." Bran Alfred smiled. He opened his arms, inviting them in, and his voice dropped into the tones of the traditional story-teller.

"Long ago when the earth was young, the people lived in misery and darkness and fear. They had no fire or weapons or medicines to heal their sick. Then the Changer came. He was kind to the people and taught them to make fire, to carve bows and spears and to gather herbs for healing.

Gods and animals do not change, but Lummi's gift made the people into more than they had been. The people became strong, full of joy and brotherhood. When he had done his work, Lummi jumped into the sky and became the moon, so that even at night, we would never again live in darkness."

Jared reached across the table and with his finger, outlined the figure carved in stone. Now that he had heard the story, it was as if he could feel the bright fire of kindness and compassion pouring from the yellow stone into his fingers, into the harsh world.

"The carving is in the old style," Alfred said. "Who knows how long it's been lost."

"So it's really old?" Meghan fixed her eyes on the artist. "Old enough to be worth a lot of money?"

Alfred shrugged. "This is a thing of power. Money is not the issue."

Meghan sat back. "Easy for you to say," she muttered.

"Do you know why the Changer would be carved on a stone?" Jared asked.

Bran Alfred shook his head. "No idea. Most Native artists work in wood – to carve a stone like this with old tools is almost impossible. There must have been an urgent reason for it."

He picked up the golden agate up with both hands and gave it to Jared. "The Changer has chosen you. Guard him carefully." He smiled. "Enough old stuff. You kids want a soft drink?"

Jared stowed the rock back in his jacket pocket and grinned. "Sure."

Meghan shrugged, apparently giving up for the moment. "Id love to hear something about your art," she said looking around. "It's gorgeous."

"Inspired by the old ones," Bran told them.

The twins spent the next couple of hours watching Bran work on a mask, carefully applying geometric swaths of red, black, and green to the stylized bear face. Finally as the sky turned dusky purple, they reluctantly told him they'd have to leave.

"Mom has a fit if we're wandering around at night," Meghan told him.

He clasped her shoulder. "Come back any time," he told them. "And please let me know if you find out anything more about Lummi."

They clattered down the narrow staircase to the street. Already the night was creeping in over the city, lying like a loose blanket above the street and auto lights. The kids huddled into their thin jackets as icy rain drizzled over them.

"If we stay here we're going to need new coats," Meghan muttered.

Jared hunched his shoulders. No money, he thought. No home and no money. Angrily he wondered why his mother had never settled anywhere – why didn't she *need* to belong somewhere? He ran his fingers over the smooth surface of the agate bulging in his pocket. This was a piece of the earth itself that belonged to him. The thought soothed him a little. Or maybe... he belonged to the rocks and they to the earth. He lifted his face to the sky and rain. That would be okay too, he decided, no matter what Meghan thought.

*   *   *

When the elevator doors opened, the twins could hear their mom's voice echoing down the hall. "I don't *care* that nothing was taken! What if my children had been here!"

Meghan and Jared exchanged scared glances, then together raced down the corridor. The door to their room was open. Marquis and the hotel manager stood just inside. Their mother stood in the center of a maelstrom, hands on hips, raging at the men.

"Ma'am," Marquis pleaded.

"Look, lady," the hotel manager had obviously lost his patience, "the door wasn't forced. Your kids left it open. End of story!"

"We did not leave the door open!" Meghan pushed past the men and looked around. Their belongings had been strewn everywhere. Jared sagged against the wall, grateful that he'd carried their meager supply of cash with him. Meghan faced the manager, her finger jabbing in the direction of his chest. "You're responsible."

"For what?" he snorted. "Nothing's been stolen."

"Damages!" Meghan announced. "We'll sue!"

"Oh, I'm worried." The manager turned away. "Check-out is 11 a.m. We don't need trouble-makers like you." He stormed past Jared.

Marquis looked at Jared helplessly, shrugged and left too.

"Oh, Meggie." Deirdre sat down on the side of the bed suddenly, as if her legs wouldn't support her. "I was so afraid something had happened to you."

"We went for a walk." Meghan threw herself on the sofa, scowling. "I'm sick of this crummy place."

"We didn't leave the door ajar," Jared said. "Why would someone break into our room?"

"Why not?" Meghan demanded.

"Because we're near the elevators and right in the middle of the hall. If the guy had a pass key, why not pick a room that's a little more secluded?"

"Oh, I know," Meghan snapped, "they must've been after your world-famous, extra special rocks."

"Why don't you just shut up!" Jared glared.

"Kids, don't start!" Deirdre begged. "My bad luck is still holding. I couldn't even get an audition."

"Oh, Mom.... " Meghan sat up. "It isn't fair!"

Jared swallowed and tried to think. The manager was tossing them out...they had no money for another hotel...their credit card was maxed. "What are we going to do?" He hoped his voice didn't sound as desperate as he felt.

Deirdre stood up. "Well, for starters, we'll clean up this mess."

"And then?" Jared forced himself to ask.

"And then, I'll think of something." Her lips tightened. "Don't worry. I won't let you down."

"Never crossed my mind," Meghan declared.

Jared bent over to pick up a suitcase that had been flung across the room. When the hotel bill was paid tomorrow there would be eighteen dollars left. Maybe he should have sold the rock to Mr. Malik after all. But a hundred would only last a couple of days anyway.

Meghan chattered breathlessly to Deirdre who responded brightly. Jared kept silent. He wished he had someplace quiet to look at his rocks. They were powerful – magic, if he believed in that stuff. With power comes money. The thought twined through his mind. What could be so wrong about wanting just to save his family? Maybe somehow he could use their power to get out of this.

When the room was more or less put back together, Jared straightened. "I'm going for a walk."

Before Deirdre could answer, he slipped out the door. He could hear the rocks. They were calling him. Something was happening.

Unwilling to wait for the elevator, Jared raced down the stairs. The First Rock and the agate, stuffed in his jacket pockets, thumped against his sides. Except for the desk clerk, the lobby was empty, but just the same Jared felt as if unfriendly watchers were everywhere. He went directly to the desk. Marquis was eating a sandwich, listening to music.

"Marquis," Jared said, "can I have my bag?"

"Sure thing." The clerk put his sandwich down and reached under the counter for the bag. "Jared, I sure am sorry about tonight."

"It's not your fault." Jared grabbed the bag and headed out the lobby door.

Outside, night had fallen. Jared took a deep breath of air – fresh now from the earlier rain. He needed someplace quiet and isolated. The rocks were thrumming in his mind, demanding...*something*. He shook his head, trying to clear his thoughts.

"Jared, isn't it?"

He whirled around. The glow from a streetlight highlighted the man's thinning hair. With a jolt Jared recognized the curator from the museum. Had his need for money drawn the man? Were the rocks manipulating both of them?

"Mr. Malik?" Jared stammered. "What are you doing here?"

"Me? Oh, just a few days vacation...." The man stepped forward and dropped his arm around the Jared's shoulders. Jared wanted to jerk away, but somehow he couldn't. Malik's voice went on, almost a sing-song. "How delightful to have run into you. Pleasant coincidence...lovely now that the rain has stopped...."

Jared found himself walking along the sidewalk with Malik. The halos of light from the street lamps looked hazy and distant. Vaguely he heard the rocks clamoring and shrilling, but he couldn't seem to do anything about it. His head felt thick and his thinking as sluggish as oozing mud.

And all the time Malik talked.

"...lovely girl, your sister...lucky to have a man like you to take care of her...."

"Take care...of Meghan?" Jared struggled with the words. "I...don't...." Somewhere, far away, the rocks were keening.

"Yes, of course...it's so important to you... and you need money for that...."

Their footsteps rang lightly on cobblestones as they walked into the shadowy park. A drunk saw them, stepped in their direction, then with a start of fear scuttled away.

"...so interested in your rock...so unique... gladly pay you for the stone...five hundred dollars each, if you have more...just let me see it now, Jared...I know you have it with you... show it to me...."

They stopped by a park bench. Cold waves of silence washed over Jared. He opened his backpack. Five hundred dollars...and everything would be fine.

The rocks cried out, but he couldn't stop. His hand reached into the bag, groping for a rock to give to Malik.

He would do this for Meghan, for his family. Everything would be fine.

170   Susan Brown

Near Sayda, Lebanon

Courage

The hot wind blows across the stony grey desert through the open windows of the ancient land rover, ruffling their light clothes but providing no relief.

Jared looks with concern at Meghan. His twin hunches over on the vehicle's seat, ghost-white from hours in the scorching heat. He shifts to allow the breeze to slide over her.

"I don't care what the problem is with your accursed car," Deirdre hisses at their driver. "You must find us some transportation back to Beirut or even Sayda before my daughter becomes even more ill. We have been sitting for two hours on this donkey path. I doubt you ever did know where these secret ruins are, but that is now beside the point..."

The driver tries to interrupt, to explain in his poor English that it is not his fault a rock has broken the radiator.

Deirdre talks over him. "Walk to the main road," she orders, "and find help."

"But my car..." he protests.

"This car isn't going anywhere," Deirdre retorts.

Cowed, the man stomps off toward the main road four miles away.

"I could have tried to walk," Meghan whispers. "It's just that my head is aching."

Jared meets his Mom's eyes. "I'm going to look over that way," he says. "I thought I saw a hut or something. Maybe there's some shade that's a little cooler."

Deirdre nods. She pours a bit of water from a plastic bottle onto her scarf and wipes Meghan's forehead, neck and wrists.

Jared steps out of the mild shade of the car. The blaze of heat and sunlight nearly knocks him over. Forcing himself to face into it, he climbs the rough escarpment to their right. Feet scrabbling on loose grey rock, he falls and skins his palms and knees.

"Climb two steps up; slide four steps back," he mutters. He glances back at the car and the shadows of his mother and sister. Then, taking a deep breath, he claws his way upward. When he tops the ridge there is nothing to see but more hills, stones and cracked earth. Yet he is sure he saw something this way...

Yes. There it is. An out-of-place regularity at the foot of the next hill. Jared slides down, scraping more skin. Limping, he makes his way to the shoulder-high stone and runs his hand along the rock's edge. It is weathered but squared. Inching behind, he can see a waist high opening. A cool draft of air smoothes past his face.

"Mom! Mom! I've found the ruins!" Jared yells. "It's cool in here!"

He would have loved to plunge inside, to finally cool off, but turns and scrabbles up the hill again. His mom will need help with Meghan.

They take the water, backpack, and flashlights, and leave a note on the windshield with an arrow pointing in the direction they're taking. Together, he and his mom support his near-fainting twin up the harsh ridge and then down again on the far side. Grey dust blows up and powders their face and clothes.

"I'm okay," Meghan protests weakly.

"We want you a little more okay," Deirdre replies.

It is easy to squeeze into the shelter. The entrance is clogged with loose rock and debris but within a few steps they can stand upright. Meghan sinks down on the cool stone floor. Deirdre crouches beside her.

Jared watches for a few minutes. At the back of his mind is an insistent hum.

"Mom, I'm going to go a little farther down the corridor," he says. "I'd like to see what's here."

Deirdre nods. "Just don't go far. I don't want to have to send out a search party for you."

"If you find jewels or anything," Meghan whispers, "I have dibs."

Jared grins. "You wish!"

A few feet from the entrance he snaps on his flashlight. The guidebook said ancient Phoenicians settled here five thousand years ago, that Sayda had been the greatest city in the empire until it was overrun by its enemies three thousand years ago.

At first the floor beneath Jared's feet is covered by rubble. The walls are rough and cracked. The Song hums louder and louder. Making him dizzy. He breathes deeply and closes his eyes. When he opens them again, the walls run straight and smooth and his vertigo has passed. He plays his light over murals painted into the plastered surfaces. They show warriors on chariots charging into battle, captives led before a king wearing a conical crown, and then the king making offerings of a two-handled golden goblet, sheaves of wheat, and ten cattle to a magnificent, curly-bearded god holding a thunderbolt.

Jared whistles softly. The colors are bright and perfect – like new.

He keeps walking, forgetting his mom and sister in the wonder of what he is finding. The Song throbs in the background. The cool air takes on a whiff of ancient flowers...incense. And the corridor is becoming brighter. Jared switches off his flashlight and turns a corner into blazing sunlight. He shades his eyes. Before him lies a wide courtyard, bathed in desert sun. Despite the dusty dryness of the air, Jared sniffs salt. They are near the sea.

Men and boys hurry everywhere, strapping supplies on horses, harnessing chariots, checking swords and spears.

Jared catches his breath. The humming in his mind is louder now, beating in time with weapons and armor. Everywhere is the smell of coming death.

Where is he? Where are Deirdre and Meghan?

Jared steps back. He has to get out of here...but the tunnel is gone. Jared shrinks back into shadow, hoping no one notices him. A flight of stone steps leads upward to an open corridor along the second floor.

"Soldiers or stairs," Jared mutters. He shrugs and runs up the steps. From this vantage point, he can see all the preparations below. They are obviously getting ready to fight a war. If they find him, will they think he is a spy?

He hurries along the corridor. At the end, a carved wooden door stands ajar.

Behind him, sandals tramp up the steps. Soldiers! Panic grips Jared. He dashes through the door and slams it tight behind him.

"You dare!" shouts a voice.

Jared whirls. A teenager, maybe only two or three years older than himself, rises from a tumble of linen on a couch. A conical cap like the one in the murals lies on the bed beside him. He is dressed like the soldiers, but with gold trim on his sword and leather armor, and rich purple on his clothes.

"Who are you, to enter my rooms?"

Despite his fierce voice, Jared sees the unmistakable streaks of tears on the boy's face. "Are you all right?" he asks.

The boy stiffens. "I am Kehret, son of El, ruler of sun and thunder, god and king of all Phoenicia. Who are you, slave?"

"None of your business." He frowns. "Besides, I am not sure I'm even born yet." He feels giddy with the events.

The boy blinks at him. "Your clothing...your speech...are you a vision sent by the gods?"

Jared feels a tingle in his spine. If this is ancient Phoenicia, then he is a vision for this boy king. "I suppose I am."

"Then you can help me," the boy whispers. "I have been praying for guidance."

"I don't know," Jared says. What does he know that could possibly help an ancient king? "What's the problem?"

"The enemy of my father, the lesser god Ba'al Kronos, has allied with our enemies. They have captured five of the outlying towns, cutting the kingdom in half. Stopping food supplies. The enemy god has brought fire from the ground to kill our crops and dry out our wells. Ba'al Kronos turns good land into desert."

Jared's mind fastened on the one word. Kronos. He is here. He is pursuing this boy-king, the way he pursues Jared's family.

Jared licks his lips. "What do you want me to do?"

The boy stares stonily out the latticed window. He wipes his forearm against his face. "I must lead my army against Ba'al Kronos and his allies the Zabulon and Koserite tribes. We are outnumbered and though he is mighty, our god El does not march with us. I...I don't think we can win..."

Jared stares at the boy. No wonder he was crying. Jared would cry too if he had to face an army helped by Kronos. "Run for it." He says flatly. "Take your army and leave."

The boy looks at him eagerly. "I could sail south...the queen is friendly to me...but...my kingdom..."

"What would happen?"

"They...our enemies will kill whoever is left. Enslave some. Burn the houses and crops...there would be no more kingdom. No one will be left of our people...only their cries and corpses..." There is silence.

Kehret looks at Jared. "You say you have not been born yet. Perhaps that is a sign that you will be my son – that El will watch over me and my people after all."

"I don't know," Jared says. "I don't know who my father is. I think it isn't you. I mean, I come from a long time ahead of now. Centuries..."

Kehret's eyes brighten. "Then I will begin a dynasty that will last for centuries."

"No. wait," Jared says. "What if you get killed? What if... what if they win? You could save yourself..."

Kehret's face hardens and he picks up the conical cap, placing it on his head. "I will not have the sons of my sons tell the story of how Kehret who was king ran from his enemies." He pauses. "Drink with me, son of a hundred children. Drink for the courage to fight a god."

He goes to a table and pours wine from a pitcher into a two-handled goblet. First he holds the cup upwards to the sunlight, then takes a deep gulp. He hands the cup to Jared. Squaring his shoulders, Jared lifts it to his lips. The wine is sour and strong. Some runs out the edges of his mouth and spatters onto his white shirt, like drops of blood.

The scene before him dims and swirls. He thinks he can hear the clangs and screams of a terrible battle, the roar of fire, the cries of wounded animals. He drops the cup.

He is in the corridor, standing in pitch dark.

"Jared!" Deirdre's voice echoes down the hollow space. "Come on! Our guide is back. He's found a ride for us!"

"Coming!" He switches on his flashlight. The panels are flaked, barely discernable. But the next panel of the mural shows the boy-king and his army fleeing, pursued by a horde led by a white-faced rider on a horse that breathes flame. Red spatters Kehret's shirt.

"Jared!" Deirdre calls.

Jared shines his light over the pictures. Over bodies of soldiers burned by flames. Over Kehret with an arrow in his shoulder, slinging a rock at Kronos. The last panel is badly damaged, but Jared thinks it shows the king sitting on a throne. A red-haired woman reclines beside him. Green hills and fruit trees decorate the background. A boy sits at their feet.

Jared plays his flashlight over the ground, hoping to find the goblet. The light flickers on gold. Eagerly, Jared scoops it up. The light glimmers through the golden glow of an amber rock. With his thumb, Jared feels the carved outline of a two-handled cup.

Chapter 11

They Be After You Now

"Stop!" A man's voice cried out.

Jared jerked his hand inside the backpack. Pain seared up his arm as his groping fingers were sliced by the black obsidian within. His mind thrashed with pain and memory.

Crack... cra...crack...thrumming...white-ringed eyes of the dying man....

"No!" In horror, Jared stared at Malik. The man's face contorted in rage and he leapt forward.

Clinging desperately to his pack with one hand, Jared dodged. "Leave me alone!"

"Give it to me!" Malik panted. "You don't even know what it is! Give it to me!"

"Not this time!" The producer, Edward Simon, stepped out of the shadows. "Are you all right, Jared?"

"This doesn't concern you!" Malik hissed. He sidled toward Jared, who stood panting, trying to clear the last fog from his mind. Trying to ignore the pain of his wounded hand.

Simon moved closer, cautious, as though approaching a wild animal. "Jared, come over by me. I'll keep you safe," he urged.

"He's lying," Malik hissed. "I'm trying to help your family. You need money, don't you? What did he do for you, except humiliate your mother?" Malik's voice was like a thick fog rolling toward him.

Panic growing, Jared forced himself to step back, away from both men.

"It couldn't be helped," Simon's voice was hoarse. "It's time. We have to get her back – all of you back – before it's too late."

Jared's eyes darted from one man to the other. The rocks were thrumming again. Crying...warning...

"I'm going to help you," Malik crooned.

"Help your master, you mean! Jared, you have to trust me!" Simon pleaded, holding out his hand.

"No!" Whirling around, Jared ran down the street, away from them both. Panting, gasping, he could hear them shout after him. The rocks thrummed, reverberating with the pounding of his heart, with the footsteps behind him.

Red-eared dogs hunting....

Mustn't stop....

Gulping for air, Jared dodged down alleyways, avoiding the glare of streetlights. Deep shadows waved from every side.

"No!" he cried.

Wave upon wave of dank fog rose from the distant water and rolled up the street. One by one, the lights hazed and disappeared. The Song rang in his head, out of tune.

"*Jared!*"

The summons came from behind. No... the side. Confused, Jared stopped, turned one way, then another. Which way? Fingers of mist curled around his face, draining his thoughts. They were going to catch him.

"Hey kid!' A voice hissed through the fog. A white face appeared beside him – the girl who'd tried to steal their money. "This way!"

The cries of the hunters were closer. She danced with fear and plucked Jared's sleeve. "Now, kid, or forget it!"

Desperate, Jared nodded. They set off at a run down more alleys. Sometimes, as the fog thickened, they felt their way along damp, crumbling walls. The girl's breathing was ragged.

A wind rose, pushing back the fog. The instant the gusts dropped, the fog rolled back toward them again.

"They're fighting," the girl whispered. "They want you bad." She paused look up and down the street ahead. "See that park?" Jared nodded. "There's a wild rose bush on the far side. Biggest you ever saw. There's a tunnel at the back, by that stone wall. They won't find you there." She gave him a push. "Get going."

"What about you?"

Suddenly, she smiled. "I got another place to go. I'm free of them now. See!" She held up her fist. The skin had been scraped away from her knuckle, leaving a raw scab where the tattoo had been. "They won't get me again."

She turned and trotted up a shadowy street, away from the rolling fog. Jared hesitated, then tore across to the park. He swerved past two homeless women sleeping on the grass, and ran for the stone wall. An opening in the bramble, like a small animal's lair was hidden at the back. Clutching his bag, Jared dove under the tangled branches. Thorns scratched his face and snagged his clothes but he wriggled deeper and deeper into the sweet smelling sanctuary. He lay still, face buried in his arms. Footsteps echoed, then faded.

Gradually his own heart stopped pounding and he peered around. A little farther over, the bushes hollowed into a tiny clearing. An old blanket was neatly folded to one side.

The moon shone down through a gap in the branches, forming a pool of light. Jared crawled toward it and pulled himself into a cross-legged position.

What was happening? Why were Malik and Simon chasing him? He felt ill at the memory of Malik's soft voice. It had hypnotized him, made him almost give up the rocks. And what about Simon? He had said something about his mother – getting her back. Jared shivered.

"Trust me!" Simon had said.

"Yeah, right," Jared whispered. Bitterly he remembered the pain the man had caused his mother.

His hand hurt excruciatingly. He held it up to moonlight. Blood dripped slowly from razor thin cuts on his palm and fingers. The black rock again. Malik had wanted the rocks, all of them. Why? What was their power?

Nursing his injured hand as best he could, Jared lifted the rocks from his backpack. This time he didn't hesitate over the order. Biting his lip, he forced himself to gingerly pick up the obsidian. It didn't seem to leap at him as it had before. Had enough blood for one night, Jared thought grimly.

But then suddenly, the memory of the black rock's finding seared across his mind.

"No!" Jared cried, but it was too late...

Crack! Cra-cra-cra-crack!

Gunfire.

Screaming.

Jared dives into a ditch and cowers on his belly, arms over his head, silent and shaking. Soldiers pound past.

Crack! Cra-cra-cra-crack!

Above him, a man bursts from the bushes, leaping across the trench.

Crack... cra-cra-crack...

He screams and twists as he falls into the ditch.

Jared cries out, an animal gasp of terror. The man's hair is grey and soft like the fleece of a lamb. His eyes are brown and rich, circled with white, flickering with bursts of reflected light from the battle around them.

"You came..." he whispers. His arm slides forward like a wounded bird's wing. He shoves the rock under Jared's palm.

"Run boy," he says. "They be after you now."

Shaking, Jared dropped the black obsidian. He should have given it to Malik, he thought savagely. Let him feel the pain and blood that drenched this rock. Why were the other rocks so good and this one so terrible?

Jared sat back on his heels. The moonlight shone over the wedge of glossy black, picking out the faint lines of the flaming sword. It always seemed to be this one, wanting to relive the terror again and again. Jared ground his teeth. Not if he could avoid it. The other rocks waited silently in their broken circle. Without the black one, they were incomplete.

Delaying contact with the black stone, Jared leaned over and turned each rock so that their symbols faced up to the moon.

Eyes of Buddha on red sandstone from India...
White Bird's Wing on red and blue marble from Greece...
Lotus Flower with seven drops of water on white jade from China...
Running Horse on grey-white chalk from England...
Red Rose on white fire opal from Mexico...
Three Concentric Circles on fossilized grey limestone from Australia...
Shell on wave green peridot from Hawaii...
Two-Handled Cup on golden amber from Lebanon...
Bread on black and white granite from Germany...
Puma on deep red rhodochrosite from Peru...
Face of Lummi on orange agate from Whidbey Island...

For a long while he studied the carvings, wondering what they meant. He had identified all the rocks from internet searches and library field guides. Some of the symbols he'd found on-line but a few had appeared only in fat books about ancient people and mythology. That hadn't meant any more to him than a painting in a museum. But Bran Alfred had said that that the agate had power right now, not just in some ancient religion.

Jared ran his finger tip over the face of Lummi. Every symbol must mean something. But what?

When the rocks and their symbols came together in a circle, they created some huge kind of power. Jared licked his lips – power that maybe he could use to rescue his family and fight whatever was stalking them. His hand hovered over the rocks then he pulled it back. What about the black rock? What if its power controlled him? What if the obsidian's shadow spread over the rocks? Called the hunt back to him and his family.

He couldn't risk it.

Defeated, Jared rewrapped the stones and one by one returned them to his backpack. The black rock with its fiery sword lay in its pool of shadow, almost invisible. A slice of darkness. Finally Jared scooped it up, and before the vision could sweep over him again, dropped it on top of the others. He zipped the bag shut and pushing it ahead, crawled out of the bushes.

The park was empty. The fog had disappeared. Jared took a deep breath and looked up at the moon.

Lummi, the son of the star people, jumped into the sky and became the moon so that even at night, we would never again live in darkness....

Jared slung the backpack over his shoulders and jogged in the direction of the hotel. The moonlight shone over the path ahead of him.

*   *   *

Jared looked at the bread frying in the pan and debated whether to throw in a little more butter. Live dangerously, he thought, and added another dollop. The door swung open and their mom came in.

Meghan roused herself from a cocoon of blankets. "Did the manager back down? Can we stay?"

Deirdre sank down on the bed and forced a smile. "Kids, I think it's time for a change anyway."

Across the room, Meghan and Jared exchanged glances.

"That's what we've been thinking," Meghan said. "Just look at this place. It's a dump."

"There have been a lot of dumps. But this is a little dumpier than most," Deirdre agreed. "I've tried everything and I can't get any kind of job. So I called someone...an old friend. We're flying to England tonight."

"England!" Meghan squealed. She struggled upright, jumped to her feet and hugged her mother. "Tonight! This is so fabulous!"

"How are we going to pay for this?" Jared asked.

Deirdre let go of Meghan, yanked open the top drawer of the dresser and began scooping out her neatly folded clothes. "John bought the tickets for us."

Jared asked slowly. "Who is John and how come we never heard about him before?"

"Actually, he's Ian's older brother."

"Yeah, so? Why is he buying us tickets?"

Deirdre smiled briefly, but there was no smile in her eyes. "You can't expect to hear all my secrets."

"Jared! It's obvious. He has a serious thing for Mom, but...but...Ian's always been in the way." Meghan danced across the room and flung open the closet. "Oh... I can't wait to go shopping in London again!"

Jared just stood there, fingering the First Rock in his pocket. This trip would get him away from Malik and Simon but the whole arrangement seemed weird. One look at his mom's closed face though, and he knew she wasn't about to tell them anything. So what else did he expect? She never did. Automatically, he turned off the heat under the pan and began gathering his own belongings.

Within two hours they were ready to leave. In a lot of ways it was no different than all the other moves they'd made. With practiced efficiency, they packed their bags. Jared flipped through the blankets and looked under the bed for stray socks. Meghan checked the bathroom and closets for dropped clothes. Deirdre called a taxi and went down to the lobby to pay the bill.

"That's it then," Jared said.

"Finally!" Meghan whirled around, posturing on her toes like a gawky ballerina. "I have a feeling that everything's going to change for the better."

"It could hardly get worse." Jared hesitated. "Meghan, something really weird happened to me last night."

"Tell me on the plane," she called over her shoulder. Bags gripped in her hands, she pushed her way out of the room.

"No, wait!"

Too late. Jared grabbed his own load, elbowed through the door and darted to elevator. The doors closed just as he reached it. By the time he caught up with Meghan, she was in the lobby, hovering by the door as their mom settled the bill.

"Jar," Meghan's eyes gleamed, "this guy, John, must have serious money to come up with airfare so fast. I'll bet he has a fabulous place – maybe one of those really cool row houses we saw in London. You know, the kind that cost about a million pounds and all have different colored doors. How long do you think we'll stay with him?"

Too long, Jared thought. But he knew that that wasn't the answer Meghan wanted. "A couple of weeks. A month at the most. You know Mom doesn't like to freeload."

Meghan elbowed him. "A visit to an old friend is not freeloading."

"This is freeloading, and don't forget he's getting us as well as Mom." Jared grinned. "Remember what happened in Australia. If the guy's got any subtlety he'll be really nice to us for about three days."

Meghan nodded. "And then for about a week he'll be great when Mom's around...."

"Then he'll think we're a pain in the butt and show it...."

"Then Mom will ditch him."

"Therefore," Jared said, "maximum time possible – two weeks. Less if the guy's a jerk."

"They're all jerks. But I can do some serious shopping in two weeks – especially if he tries to suck up to us with cash. Look, the taxi's here." Meghan pushed out of the door and hurried ahead.

Jared hefted the bag and followed after her. Maybe, somehow, this move would work out somehow. Maybe things would get better. Maybe even begin edging toward normal.

The rocks in his arms were completely silent, but they weighed a ton.

Dachau, Germany

Faith

When Deirdre gets the day off from her dinner theater job in Munich, she drags the fourteen-year-old twins to see Dachau, the Nazi concentration camp on the outskirts of the city.

"I don't want to go sightseeing where people were murdered," Meghan argues.

"I don't want you to grow up thinking it never happened," Deirdre replies. "Evil does exist. Only a fool tries to pretend it doesn't. You are old enough to know and see what happens when it rules in a civilized country."

The twins go with only occasional mutterings.

The city bus drops them off about a block from the camp. They walk past snug houses and small businesses, all surrounded by carefully tended yards and swaying, leafy trees. Jared had thought the death camp would be a stark ruin on a wasted plain, not a low roofed, fenced institutional building in a suburb. He swallows. From the outside, it looks city-normal.

"This is just a little scary," Meghan mutters.

At first the camp isn't what they expect either. A graveled square, hundreds of yards long and wide stretches to their right. A single white-washed barracks with open doors has visitors going in and out. The guidebook Deirdre refers to says the rest of the barracks have been demolished, but their outlines are preserved by cement curbs in the gravel – oblong, equidistant, one after another, stretching into the distance. Silently they turn left and walk into the museum.

This was not what they had expected either. The building is stark, cement-floored. The exhibits are mostly enlarged photos with descriptions of the Nazis' brutal rise to power.

"This was the intake area," Deirdre whispers, "where the prisoners were processed."

Jared pauses to look in a glass case of items that had been taken from the prisoners...letters, photos, pocketknives... the things an ordinary person keeps in his pocket.

"Look," Meghan points to a photo of a young man and woman grinning self-consciously into a camera. They have obviously been picnicking. "They were happy. And then they probably were dead. I hate knowing this," she says fiercely.

Jared nods. In the back of his mind he hears a soft whisper of Song...sung by hoarse voices over the years. He shakes his head to clear the sound, and for the moment it stops.

"Did you see?" Deirdre drifts back to them. "A lot of Catholic priests were killed here, the ones that ignored the Church's orders and tried to save the Jews in their parishes. The Nazis were equal opportunity murderers."

They go outside again, past the agonized iron memorial, past the rows of barracks markers to the chapels and memorials built by the churches of the people who had died. Then they walk toward a series of low buildings nestling in well-kept grounds.

"It looks like a park," Meghan murmurs. "Maybe we should have a picnic."

The horror is growing on Jared, not because the buildings look menacing, but because they look so normal. Inside are the brick and iron ovens where the bodies of the thousands who died were burned to ash. Obliterated from the earth. The family stands in a cement room that a photo shows had had starved bodies piled up along the walls, waiting for their turn to burned.

Jared hears the Song now, sung by thousands of despairing voices. He can't shake it clear any longer.

"I guess we should see the barracks," Deirdre says. Now her voice holds grim endurance.

They walk back along the ditches and barbed wire fence, see the iron entrance gates where the captives were unloaded from the trains. The iron is worked with a German slogan, "Work will set you free," Deirdre translates.

The barracks building is low and shadowy with wooden bed frames stacked nearly to the ceiling. The singing voices swell suddenly. Jared leans for support against the frame and it happens all at once. He stands in the barracks still. But this barracks is crammed with people sleeping in the bed frames, barely lit by predawn twilight. The stench of vomit, sweat and urine is overwhelming. Jared puts a hand over his nose and mouth to try and block it out. Impossible. Snores, sighs and whimpering moans drift in the stifling air.

Just below his own gripping hand, a boy, hardly older than himself, cries nearly silently into his folded arms.

Above him, Jared hears a soft intake of breath, and then one of the men slides awkwardly down from his sleeping place. His bearded face is starved to gauntness, greyish in the light. One of the lenses of his glasses is cracked like a broken windshield.

"Nathan," he whispers. "I'm here." He slides his arm over the boy's shoulders.

The boy stiffens, then swings himself upright. He wipes his eyes on his sleeves. "You don't have to worry about me, father," he whispers. But Jared sees his hand slip into the older man's. The priest sits beside him and puts his arm around the boy's shoulders again. Nathan huddles into the older man. "We're going to die," he whispers. "They're going to kill us. Like my father and...why?...I didn't do any bad things?"

"Shh...shh..." the priest hushes. "No, you didn't, Nathan. And with God's help you will live past this to do many good things...."

For a long time Jared watches them sitting together. "I have a bit of bread I saved," the priest murmurs. "You're a growing boy and need a lot of food. You need strength...."

"To do the good things?" It is a small joke.

"To do the good things." The priest pulls a dried-out chunk of bread from inside his shirt. He stares at the wall while Nathan wolfs down the bit of food, even to licking up the tiniest crumbs. Around them, other men are beginning to stir.

The priest sighs. "The sun's coming up. We are one day closer to God's deliverance from this evil. Will you pray with me for that day?"

"You know I'm Jewish," Nathan says.

The priest nods. "God is God. He goes to both churches and synagogues."

Jared watches as they kneel by the beds. In the soft light, many of the other men climb down and kneel with them.

The Lord is my Shepherd...
Yea though I walk through the valley of the shadow of
death,
I shall fear no evil
For Thou are with me...

Jared feels himself spinning forward into time. Meghan nudges him. "Are you coming? We still have the movie to watch. I'll bet it's a blast."

Numbly, Jared follows his mother and sister out into the yard. He is grateful that the coming twilight puts his face in shadow. He doesn't want them to see he has been crying.

He stumbles a little in the yard, kicking up a stone, a little larger than the rest. When he picks it up, he sees that the black and white speckled granite is carved with a tiny loaf of bread.

The movie is harsh. It shows death and despair, cruelty and the evil that lived. It shows starved and dying prisoners sobbing as the Allied forces free them. In the crowd, Jared sees Nathan. Thinner, a little older. The priest with the broken glasses is no longer beside him.

Chapter 12

John

The plane circled widely, angling toward London's Heathrow Airport. Jared craned his neck to see past his sister. At the pilot's instructions, they spotted Windsor Castle, larger than most of the fields around it. The inside courtyard was an immaculate, emerald green. The battlements shone in the bright light. No one moved. It was as clean as a new toy castle.

Then London sprawled below, a seemingly endless mass of old and new buildings with the Thames winding through, almost invisible from the shadows of the buildings.

The flight attendants streamed past the seats, putting up tray tables, insisting passengers put their chairs in upright positions and fasten their seat belts. The ear-popping descent to the runway ended with a bump, lurch and roar of engines as the plane touched down.

The morning light pierced Jared's eyes as the sun shone through the window. He felt slightly light-headed after the nine-hour flight. His body said it was three in the morning, but the British sun and clocks claimed it was 11 a.m. Meghan insisted on finding a restroom to brush her hair and put on some makeup.

"I should let Ian know we're here, too," Deirdre said and disappeared toward the pay phones. Jared stood bleary-eyed at the thumping baggage carousel and retrieved their suitcases. Meghan and his mom returned at the same time.

They whisked through Customs. They had nothing to declare, were on vacation, would be staying for a couple of weeks with friends.

Outside the customs area, loaded with bags, they ran the gauntlet of people waiting to meet passengers. Drivers held up name signs, grandparents cried out, friends waved and shouted. Deirdre craned her neck, looking anxiously back and forth.

"Is he here?" Meghan asked.

"I don't see him, but the plane was a few minutes early," Deirdre said. "And he doesn't like crowds. Let's wait over there."

They broke from the mob, and then Deirdre suddenly stood still. The twins followed her line of vision to a man waiting with folded arms, his back to one of the terminal's huge support columns.

"I guess that's John," Meghan whispered.

The man's hair was dark, grizzled with a bit of grey. He was not especially tall, but athletic looking just the same, dressed in a neat tweed jacket with black sweater and pants beneath it. His eyes, even at that distance, seemed as alive as stars in a night sky. Frowning, he didn't move toward them. Deirdre didn't move either.

The crowds passed around and through. Meghan looked from one to the other, then dropped her bags and strode forward, hand outstretched.

"Hi," she said, "I'm Meghan. You're John?"

He looked down at her, frowned briefly, and clasped her hand in both of his. Then he looked back at their mother. She seemed to come out of her trance, and came slowly forward. Jared trailed her.

"Hello, John." Her voice sounded strained. "And this is Jared. They've changed a lot since you last saw them."

"We've met you before?" Meghan removed her hand and stuck it behind her back.

John's eyes flashed at Deirdre but he spoke evenly. "Yes. I haven't seen you since you were three. It's been a long time. Hello, Jared." He extended his hand to shake. Jared took it. The clasp was warm and firm.

"Well, let's get you loaded up." Effortlessly, John took Deirdre's bags and led the way outside.

The day was sunny and bright, a little cool. "I love England," Meghan declared.

"You've been here often?" John asked. Their mother flushed but Meghan didn't notice.

"Oh yes," she confided. "Tons of times."

"Not that often," Jared interrupted. "Maybe when we were little, and then we were here for six months when we were nine, and then last year for a short run of a musical that bombed."

"Ian told me that he'd run into you four years ago, but you disappeared on him," John said.

Deirdre looked straight ahead. "How are things at the Castle?" she asked.

"Castle?" Meghan whispered, eyes wide. "Where exactly do you live?" she leaned forward to ask John.

"In the Peaks district," John told her. "About three hours drive to the door. I thought we'd lunch on the way." He looked at their mother. "The Hammond Cottage?"

Deirdre smiled. From the angle that she turned her head, Jared saw that this time, the smile reached his mother's eyes.

"Lovely," she said.

Meghan leaned forward farther. "Excuse

me. But what about London? What kind of shopping do you have where you live?"

John grinned and shrugged. "Sorry, Meghan. Mostly tourist shops. But we do have glorious scenery."

"Scenery?" Meghan sat back, arms folded. "This visit better not be a minute more than two weeks," she whispered to Jared. "I don't do scenery."

"It'll be a whole new experience for you," he teased. "Something gorgeous besides boys and clothes."

She punched his arm and maintained a dignified silence while he laughed.

John's car was sleek and narrow, hinting at power as he shifted gears to speed out of the packed lot at Heathrow. The sun shone brilliantly over the businesses, small houses and modern signs. As they sped onto the motorway, Jared watched as the trappings of a modern city fell away and the road became lined with fields and farms. The towns and villages were close together, but between them were stands of old trees, stunningly green fields polka dotted with powder puffs of sheep. Occasionally, ancient ruins stood like stony skeletons against the horizon.

In the front, John and his mom chatted like they had known each other forever, like they knew the same people and had visited the same places. But after a few minutes, Jared could tell they were talking so much that they were trying not to say anything about the one big thing on their minds – like on the really rare times he and Meghan had a serious fight they didn't know how to fix.

What was the big thing they weren't talking about?

After a couple of hours, John pulled into the gravel parking lot in front of an old, old stone house.

"This where you live?" Meghan muttered sleepily.

"No, this is a lunch stop," John replied as he turned off the engine.

"Oh," Deirdre breathed. "It hasn't changed."

"From what?" Meghan asked.

"Oh," their mom said vaguely, "we used to eat here years ago when we motored down to London."

"Motored?" Meghan whispered to Jared. She rolled her eyes, but their mother didn't notice.

Inside, the cottage was a maze of small rooms, each with a very few tables. They were seated in a small parlor overlooking a tangled garden of bright flowers. Jared and Meghan weren't entirely sure what to do with the white linen and silverware, but no one seemed to notice. The food was great and the conversation, what there was of it, was boring.

An hour later they were back on the road.

"We're getting into Derbyshire," John told them after a bit. "Only a half hour to the Castle on Apple Tor."

"Where does the name come from?" Jared asked.

"A tor is a mountain or hill," John replied. "We have a very old apple orchard attached to the castle. Written records of it go back hundreds of years; oral tradition says it goes back to the beginning of time."

Jared sat back and looked out at the scenery, imagining the roll of hills and deep forests of trees as they must have been in the nearly forgotten centuries. The hills before his eyes seemed to rise a little more steeply now and the valleys cleft deeper and wider. Few of the houses looked less than a couple of hundred years old. Perhaps it had been like this for centuries. Worn rocks cropped out in the fields, looking like sleeping grey sheep.

Jared ran his fingers over the shapes of the rocks in his bag, stroking them. Beneath his hands, through the canvas, they began to thrum. He stared down at the bag, bewildered.

"What's that sound?" John demanded sharply. Jared saw his fingers whiten on the wheel.

"What sound?" Deirdre asked.

Jared didn't move. No one else, not even Meghan, had ever heard the rocks. What was happening?

The thrumming increased, grew louder. Screaming. The rocks were screaming. Jared clutched the bag to his chest, then his eyes met John's in the rear view mirror.

He knows, Jared thought. *He knows.*

"Is there something wrong with the car?" Deirdre asked. "Should we pull over?"

"No," John said tersely. "We have to get back to the Castle, quickly." Eyes scanning the road, the cars, the fields, John forced down the accelerator. The car roared, trembled with speed. The rocks shrieked. Jared bit his lip to keep from howling. Terror rolled in like bitter fog.

The wind began, gusts bending trees nearly double. The blue sky faded as roiling clouds crowded out the afternoon sun. Through the window, silhouetted against the sky, a horseman galloped on a gleaming stallion, leaping fences and bushes as though flying. He seemed to go as fast as the car. Impossible.

Meghan grabbed her brother's arm. "What's John doing? He's crazy," she hissed.

Jared's eyes were fixed on the horseman. He couldn't speak.

The sky boiled with slate and green clouds, lightning shattered the building gloom, clotted flakes of wet snow thickened the air. The snow stuck to the windshield, clumping and mounding despite the wipers.

"I hate these sudden weather changes," Deirdre commented. "Shouldn't you slow down, John?"

He didn't answer.

The wind rose, howling and buffeting the car. Other motorists had pulled over, but John raced on. The car slid, skidded. He fought with the wheel and pulled the vehicle straight again.

Snow covered everything; the white sheep were hidden beneath the stifling blanket. All the green disappeared. Clouds of fog mushroomed around and ahead.

"John," Deirdre shrieked. "Pull over. You're going to kill us all!"

"Have to make it to the White Peak," John gasped. "Or *They* will kill us."

Slam!

A black car loomed beside them, dropped back, and then as Jared watched, raced forward and swerved into the side of their vehicle.

Their car spun on the slick pavement. John cranked the wheel. Jared dropped the backpack and grabbed Meghan as her door flew open. He held onto her in the vortex of grinding and crashing. The door swung back, slamming shut. Jared smashed down the lock.

Somehow, John kept the car on the road. Through the hail and fog, their car put on another burst of speed. Jared felt the motion upwards, heard the gears grind as they struggled up the hill. On either side, a row of upright stones stood like frozen warriors.

Crack! Cra-cra-cra-crack!

Hailstones splintered the window, shattering it outward into a spider web pattern of shards. Deirdre screamed. Through the wind, Jared was sure he heard dogs howling, snarling, fighting. He had a brief view of stone walls and an arched stone gate ahead. The car roared into the paved courtyard of a small castle, spun and died.

The noise stopped. Snow, fog and clouds disappeared. The sun shone clean and strong from a sky of forget-me-not blue. John eased the car out of gear, and for a moment rested his head on the steering wheel. A dribble of blood etched down from his hairline.

Jared felt Meghan shuddering as he held her, but abruptly she pulled herself upright. Her sleeve was torn and an ugly bruise was forming on her arm.

"Did you ever think of learning to drive?" she shrieked at John. "You nearly killed us! You crazy old man!"

Jared expected his mother to join the tirade, but she simply sat, looking out the window at the ivy covered stone walls.

John touched Deirdre's arm. "Are you all right?" he asked.

She moved her arm away and faced him. "It hasn't changed, has it?"

John rubbed his hand across his forehead, smearing the browning blood. "It's worse."

"Worse..." she repeated. "What have I done?"

210   Susan Brown

Part II

Apple Tor Castle
Peaks District, England

Chapter 13

The Castle

Like sleepwalkers escaping a nightmare, Jared and his family slowly got out of the car. John walked around, assessing the damage. The windshield was shattered, the fenders crumpled and one wheel leaned at an unnatural angle.

"It's really bad, isn't it?" Jared said.

John smiled grimly. "Not as bad as it could have been. It's only a car – though it was rather a nice one."

Meghan was simply standing, staring up at the massive building before them. The late afternoon sun shone golden white across the light grey stone. To Jared, it looked as though the light shone right through the stone to the heart of the mountain, then bubbled up and overflowed out again, spreading across the ground as far as he could see. It was glorious.

"This looks like something out of King Arthur," Meghan breathed.

"Welcome to Apple Tor," John said. "Actually, family history has it that the oldest parts of The Castle were built long before Arthur's time. It's all very old and very inconvenient, but my family has lived here time out of mind. And it's suitable for the work I do."

"What kind of work?" Jared asked.

A look passed between his mother and John. "Oh, historical research mostly," John said easily. "Location and documentation of ancient sacred sites. Preservation of ancient music. Very dull and boring, really."

Jared thought of Meghan's perfect voice lilting into old ballads. And he thought of the siren Song that led him to the rocks. "I'm interested in historical music," Jared said.

"Are you, then?" John flashed a keen look at him. Abruptly he turned to pry their bags from the mangled trunk. The metal hood squealed open at an odd angle. Meghan, meanwhile, had wandered a few feet across the stone-paved courtyard and was looking this way and that. Jared joined her.

"I think I'm dreaming," she said.

The castle rose above them, seeming to have grown up from the rock itself. It was like a guidebook photo – ancient stone, with turrets and narrow pointed windows. The entrance-way arched over two huge wooden doors. Cheerful gargoyles perched on corners and laughing lions had been carved into the stone itself.

"As castles go, it's rather small," John said, casting an amused eye at Meghan. "But we have all the important features."

"Like what?" Meghan demanded.

"Oh, drafty halls, narrow twisty stairways, fireplaces that need a tree trunk to fill them up properly, and of course a dungeon."

Meghan frowned at him uncertainly. "You're making fun of me."

"Not at all," John said. "Although I confess, my grandfather did convert the dungeon into a wine cellar and storage rooms. Not much call for torture chambers any more."

Jared grinned and John winked.

"Give me a break," Meghan muttered.

"Let's get the bags, kids," their mom said.

They hefted out their suitcases. John lifted Deirdre's with the same ease Jared had noticed before.

"Is Mrs. Jenkins still here?" Deirdre asked as they walked toward the front door.

John nodded. "And Peter. We lost Aaron a few months ago."

"Aaron?" Deirdre stopped then touched his arm. "I'm sorry, John."

"Yes, well, here we are." He twisted the big iron handle and the door swung open. The entry hall was huge, paved with the same grey-white stones, roofed with huge beams and hung with old tapestries that had faded to dull beige. A plump little woman with improbable strawberry blonde hair, dressed in tight jeans, high blocky sandals and an embroidered shirt, clattered into the hall.

"You're here!" she exclaimed with an unmistakable Texas drawl. She threw her arms around Deirdre. "Honey, we have missed you!" She turned to Meghan and Jared. "And these are the babies. Oh my darlings, you are so big and beautiful and handsome!"

Both Jared and Meghan found themselves grinning foolishly under the welcome. Jared had a fleeting thought that the woman was crazy, but her greeting was so warm, he didn't really care. No one else had ever been so happy to see him.

"Now, you won't remember me," Mrs. Jenkins went on, "but we used to be the best of friends when you were no more than three..."

"Gayle," Deirdre interrupted, flushing a little. "Please remember our agreement."

"I remember, honey," Mrs. Jenkins said. "Why don't you all come up with me and we'll get you settled into your rooms."

But before they could take more than a couple of steps up the broad staircase, the front door crashed open. Everyone jumped and turned.

"Deirdre!" a deep voice shouted. "My only true love! You've come back to me!"

Meghan giggled. Deirdre dropped her bags, ran across the hall and warmly hugged the newcomer. "Ian," she cried. "I didn't expect to see you so soon!"

"My dear, when you call, what can I do but drop everything and come!" Ian returned her hug carelessly and surveyed the assembled company. "My, but the infants do grow, don't they?" Jared felt the hairs on his neck prickle with embarrassment. "Just got here? You didn't get caught in that storm, John?"

His brother nodded. "Yes, it was a near thing. It was *Them* of course."

The smile disappeared from Ian's face. "I saw the clouds ahead of me and so I did break a few speed restrictions."

"Will you be staying until the singing?" John asked.

"I have some commitments." Ian shrugged. "And you do have Deirdre plus the children back."

"Now, wait one minute," Deirdre said sharply. "I told you John, we would have nothing to do with the singing..."

"Which you all can discuss later," Mrs. Jenkins interrupted firmly. "The children and Deirdre need to get settled. Old arguments can keep a little longer. Let's go, kids."

"This argument will be settled now," Deirdre said. "You two go along with Mrs. Jenkins."

"What's going on?" Meghan demanded. "What's all this singing stuff?"

"Just an old pagan ritual they keep alive around here," Ian said. His eyes gleamed as though he found it very amusing. "The locals think it keeps away the bogeyman."

"Is that your research?" Jared asked John. "Rituals like that?"

His mother's eyes flashed. "Upstairs, kids," she commanded.

"Just when things were getting interesting," Meghan whispered as they followed Mrs. Jenkins up the stone staircase. The steps had hollows worn from centuries of feet, and the ceiling above was vaulted like a church. They followed her down narrow corridors where the coolness of the plaster under Jared's trailing fingers spoke of ancient stone underneath. Occasionally, he noticed a streak of pale light – a kind of luminescence that crossed the floors at odd angles and disappeared into the walls.

Meghan and Jared stopped a moment to peer out one of the arched windows, set so deep in thick stone that to really see out, they had to crawl over the stonework that passed for a ledge. Each window was like a small, light-filled cave.

Below lay a patchwork of green fields, some polka-dotted with black and white cattle, some with woolly puffs of sheep. A quiet signal had been given, for the cows were ambling in a long line toward distant stone barns. A black and white dog placidly escorted them. All the fields were marked out by stone fences that Jared guessed had been built over generations. As he looked he saw the same lines of barely visible light spreading from Apple Tor into the distance. He smiled with involuntary pleasure.

"Come along, you two," Mrs. Jenkins urged. "With Ian come, I have another room to make up."

The twins slid out of the window cave. "Are you the housekeeper?" Meghan asked cautiously.

Mrs. Jenkins laughed. "I suppose you could say that. I came over here seventeen years ago and I liked it so much I stayed. I do most of the cooking and organizing, so I expect that makes me the housekeeper. We get help up from the village for the cleaning and day work, but it's a real informal kind of household – except for the spring singing." Mrs. Jenkins hurried ahead, her sandals clopping on the stone floor.

Meghan sprinted to catch up. "Exactly what is this spring singing that Mom and everyone are so worked up about?"

Mrs. Jenkins hesitated just a fraction of a second. "Oh, this house is full of music – old, historical music. And every spring we have kind of a...party. And singers come from all over the world...those that are interested in our kind of music. This year is a special year, kind of an anniversary, so we're expecting an especially big crowd."

"Mom doesn't seem to think much of it," Meghan probed. Jared elbowed her, but she ignored him. "And neither does Ian."

"Your mom had a very bad experience here. But Ian..." Mrs. Jenkins lips tightened. "Even though he was born to it, he doesn't take the work we do seriously."

She pushed open a short, wide door. Beyond it, the narrow corridor suddenly opened into a wide hallway with light streaming in through a tall leaded glass window at the end. The floor was wooden and the doors on either side of the hall didn't look quite so old.

"This is the new part of the castle." Mrs. Jenkins opened the first door along the corridor. It led to a large room, quite modern, decorated mostly in greens. "This is yours, Jared, honey. Meghan, sweetie, you have the room right next door." She pointed to an oak door set in the wall of Jared's room.

"Cool," Meghan said. "But, where's the bathroom?"

"Right across the hall. Follow me." Mrs. Jenkins led her off.

Jared stood just inside his room for a moment or two. Despite the sound of Meghan's and Mrs. Jenkins chatter, he felt as though the silence of the castle's years was flowing over him, welcoming him. He wrinkled his nose and breathed deeply. In this room there were no other people smells, no stink of disinfectant. He dropped his bags on the rug, noticing with pleasure that the overall green was patterned with wild roses. The same faint lines of light crossed his rug and headed to the thick wall. One of the lines was whitish and the other had a hint of blue to it. Curious, Jared knelt and ran his hand over each. A sense of warmth crept up his arm. He tried standing on the streaks. When he stood on the pale light, he felt a swelling warmth rising up his neck and into his head. It was like breathing a fresh breeze while raising bare arms to a spring sun. He stood for a moment, enjoying the sense of well-being. Then he stepped on the bluish line. The awareness of growth and warmth was the same, but this time the feeling spread from his feet, as though he were a great tree whose roots searched through rich soil. He felt bound to earth and sky, free to exist in light and air. He shook his head and grinned. Never in his life had he felt so good.

The window had been opened, so he left the rug and went to look out. Here the sill was only about a foot and a half deep, and the window was much wider. Boosting himself up, he sat leaning his back against the cool stone, staring out at the countryside. His eyes wandered down steep green slopes, over old village homes and outward toward rolling hills and moors. Here and there, groupings of tall, standing stones seemed to ring the castle. With pleasure, he saw the lines radiating from his room stretched out across the green fields, part of a network of pale light that shone from the castle. The setting sun cast more golden light everywhere.

"Brilliant," he whispered. He had never seen anything, anywhere that was so beautiful. It was as if the years of city grime rolled off his soul and he breathed deeply.

The undulating land was mostly a rich green, with some outcroppings of whitish stone. But to the north, the hills cut away in a jagged cliff. Jared shivered as he stared at it. It looked liked a hungry mouth, ready to devour the peace of the green hills.

"Admiring the scenery?" John's voice at his elbow made him jump.

"Sort of...I mean, yes. But those cliffs over there – what are they? They look...dangerous."

John frowned. "Dangerous? Yes, the Dark Peaks are dangerous. The winds howl across those black cliffs like demons riding out of hell. Climbers have been blown from the rock face itself. Many people have died there over the years."

"Why is it different than here? Even the rock's a different color?"

"Those hills are made of gritstone," John answered, "not the limestone of our White Peaks. There are villages back of the edges, too. Some are poor, sad places. The Dark Peak is harsh."

John lapsed into a silence that seemed to reach like a streak of light across the land toward the rearing crags. Or maybe the darkness crept toward them. Uncomfortably, Jared searched for something to break the silence.

"This is a great room," he tried. "In the hotels, I mostly get cots and sofa beds."

John smiled. "I hope the bed is more comfortable than that. Please tell me if it isn't."

"Sure."

Silence fell between them again. Jared let his eyes trace the patterns of light. He wondered if John had seen them. The man's eyes didn't seem to stray to them as Jared's did.

"Well," John said at last. "I'll show you all around tomorrow if you like. Please don't go outside the castle gates alone. There are some dangerous bits on the hillside – caves beneath the turf where the limestone is so old and rotted away, your weight could send you crashing through."

"Okay." Jared hesitated. "If it's not too much trouble, I'd really like to see or hear some of your work. We've traveled a lot and I'm really interested in old music."

Something glinted in John's eyes. "Yes, well, if your mother approves."

"Why wouldn't she?"

"Dinner is in about thirty minutes in the small dining room." John abruptly turned to go. At the door, he turned around again. "I'm delighted you're here. I was...very fond of you and your sister when you were babies. It's good to see you again."

He left before Jared could say anything in response. He leaned back in the window embrasure again. Despite how good it made him feel, there was something really weird about this castle, Jared decided.

The door in the wall crashed open and Meghan tripped in. "This place is so cool," Meghan sighed. "I have my own room. Do you even remember, Jardy, when we ever had our own rooms before?"

Jared grinned and shook his head. "Rich is good."

Meghan laughed and plopped down on his bed. "John came in and told me how thrilled he is that we're here. Stage one of buttering up Mom."

"He sounded like he meant it," Jared protested. He swung around so that his legs dangled into the room and his back was to the window.

Meghan made a rude sound. "Maybe he does mean it right now, but he won't in a couple of days. Everybody knows that teenagers make adults miserable and they don't want us around."

"How can we really know what John is going to feel about us?" Jared argued. "I don't think we're that bad. This could be good... really good for our family."

Meghan sat up and looked at him wonderingly. "You really like this place, don't you?"

"Don't you?"

She shrugged. "I can do scenery and history for about two days. Then I want some life. Mrs. Jenkins told me they have trouble getting an internet signal and there isn't even a *radio* in our rooms. The only good thing about this set-up is Ian."

Jared was startled. "What's so great about him?"

Meghan smiled, eyes glinting. "He produces for the BBC, remember, so he *has* to be on the lookout for new talent."

"Yeah, like Mom would let you."

Meghan's eyes flashed. "Like she could stop me!"

There was no point in arguing because there was no way his twin would listen. "I have to get changed," Jared said.

When his sister had flounced out, Jared hunted for a hiding place for his rocks. Under the bed was way too obvious; the deep drawers in the bureau didn't seem very smart either. Finally, for the time being, he settled on shoving his backpack into the far corner of the big oak wardrobe. He hoped the shadows would be enough to conceal it from anyone cleaning or poking around.

He refused to question why he felt he needed to hide the rocks, even here.

Jared had just enough time to take a quick shower and change his clothes before a distant gong sounded through the house. Meghan, anger apparently forgotten, came dashing into his room again. "Did you hear that?" she demanded, eyes dancing. "A dinner gong! Jared, this place is so medieval I can't believe it!"

"Warming up to it, are you?" Jared grinned. "So maybe at dinner we throw chicken bones over our shoulders to the dogs."

"What are you talking about?"

He laughed. "I forgot – you don't do history."

Warriors of the Peaks

Cullogh rubs another streak of blue warrior paint across his chest. Far off, through the Peak's creeping mist he pictures the Roman army preparing for battle too. They would be readying their iron swords and spears, so much stronger and sharper than those of the British tribesmen.

Cullogh squares his shoulders. No matter. With a scrap of cloth, he wraps a twig to his spear's shaft. Only yesterday morning, Nesta, the chief's daughter cut it from the sacred apple tree on the White Peak.

He sighs wearily. Last night, despite Cullogh's furious protest, the Druid priest finally convinced the clan that the gods would only give victory for a great price. The tribesmen listened grimly when the Druid named the sacrifice...but they are desperate, so they agreed. All but Cullogh and his brother Brach.

Cullogh keeps his back to the Dark Peak, to the place where the Druid threw Nesta from the cliff onto the rocks below. Cullogh can still hear the scream that escaped from her lips.

If she had to die, and he doesn't believe she did, it should have been a clean, ritual death on the White Peaks.

The Druid, Cullogh thinks, wanted revenge on Nesta for preferring Cullogh to him. It has nothing to do with the gods. So now Nesta is dead and the Roman legions beyond the moor are still strong.

"Will they come to us?" Brach asks. "Or will we attack them?" His young brother tests once again the heft of his war spear. This will be his first real battle.

The wrongness of Nesta's death has sealed the evil they feel is coming. Gripping his spear, Cullogh stands and faces into the fog. Despite the Druid, he and all the clan will fight for their home.

It is then that Cullogh sees her through the creeping mist. A hoarse cry escapes his lips. Nesta beckons to him. He grabs his weapons and runs toward her.

He sees them – the Romans! Using the blanketing cover of fog, they have crept up on the tribesmen. Cullogh shouts warning, already knowing it is too late. He slashes at the soldier bearing down on him, sees the man fall. The Roman commander on the fire-red horse shouts to his men. The soldiers surge up the hill in waves upon waves.

Nesta raises her fist, urging the warriors forward, toward the White Peak. Cullogh fights. They all fight, shouting their war cries until the call echoes from the cliffs. Cullogh sees Brach go down with a spear through his chest. He fights grimly on.

And then, as he lies dying, a sword cut through his belly and a spear thrust through his shoulder, Nesta comes to him.

"Did I fight bravely, my heart?" The words bubble through the blood in his mouth. She nods and smiles. Then, as befits a chief's daughter, she picks up a spear and gestures again to the White Peak.

Cullogh feels himself rise up beside her. The Romans will not take their sacred home. He picks up his own spear and follows her through the mist. Beside him come Brach and his spear brothers. Without regret, they leave their bodies to lay quietly in the barrows on the moors, but spears ready, they ring the Peak, generation upon generation.

Chapter 14

The Horsemen

The castle may have been ancient, but the dinner served that night was thoroughly modern and better than anything Jared ever remembered eating before. The meal was spread out on a glossy table that could have comfortably seated twelve. John sat at the head with their mom on his right hand and Mrs. Jenkins beaming on his left. Ian sat beside her; Meghan grabbed the seat beside Ian.

"It's just so good having you all here," Mrs. Jenkins said. "Now dig in and pass the dishes around. We eat boarding house style here."

Jared doubted that any boarding house would offer a platter of lobsters in garlic butter, along with prime rib roast, some kind of meat and vegetable pie, and bowls and bowls of vegetables and salads.

"Oh, Gayle," Deirdre exclaimed as she lifted the lid off one of the bowls, "all my favorites. How could you remember them?"

Mrs. Jenkins' smile grew even wider and she busied herself with passing another dish on to John. "This is just such a special dinner, having you back at last, darling. And the babies too," she paused to bestow a grin on the twins opposite. Meghan grinned back through a large mouthful of lobster. "You won't remember but I baked what used to be your favorite – apple crisp made with our own good apples and heaps and heaps of clotted cream."

Jared eyed his loaded plate. If he ate all this, would he have room for dessert? It was worth a try. He dug in.

Meghan turned to Ian. "Will you tell me about the shows you're producing?" she asked. "Do you do many musicals? I'm a singer, too, you know."

The man smiled down at her. "Then you'll have to sing for me, won't you?"

A current of air ruffled the candles as the door to the room opened. A tall, rawboned man with eyebrows as tufty as a hedge came in.

"Apologies for being late." His eyes locked on the twin's mother. "So, Deirdre, you've come at last." His voice was gruff. "You've been missed. Aaron would have been very glad to see you."

Their mother's face flamed and she looked as if the man had hit her.

"Peter," John warned.

"It's all right, John," Deirdre said. "I'm sorry about your brother, Peter. You know I was fond of him."

"They're coming, you know," he said. "We've been trying all these years to hold them back, but you saw what happened this afternoon. You saw..."

"Peter, hold your tongue," John commanded.

But the damage seemed to have been done. Deirdre pushed away from the table and hurried from the room.

"Brilliant, as usual," Ian snapped at Peter. The man only glowered at him.

John rubbed a weary hand over his forehead.

"Peter," Mrs. Jenkins said tartly, "you are four kinds of fool."

Jared and Meghan watched without understanding. Suddenly, the food didn't taste so good any more. Together they stood up.

"Excuse us," Meghan said with dignity.

They went after their mother. In the hall outside, they realized they had no idea where in this huge place she might be.

"Who does that creep think he is?" Meghan fumed. "This place is more and more like a Saturday afternoon flick. They probably have ghosts. I just hope we can talk Ian into giving Mom or me some work so that we can get out of here fast."

The hallway was brightly lit, but beyond, the ancient passages stretched into deep shadow. It looked like walking down any one of them would whirl them right into ancient times and muttering secrets. Jared shuddered but followed his sister.

They found their mother three doors down the corridor sitting on a fur rug before a blazing fire in a stone hearth big enough to hold a sofa. She had her arms around the thick ruff of a black and white dog with a greying muzzle. She was sobbing as they never had heard her cry before.

"Oh, Kip!" she was saying over and over again. The dog was doing its best to wash every tear away with a long pink tongue.

"Mom," Meghan cried. "What's wrong?"

Deirdre lifted her swollen face. "It's my dog. It's Kip. He was hardly more than a puppy when I left and now he's old. I missed nearly his whole life because I went away. I had to, Kip. You know I had to."

The dog nuzzled her and made soft, eager sounds while it licked her face and neck.

After a moment or two Deirdre stopped crying and simply hugged the dog. Then she straightened up. "I must be a sorry mess," she murmured. "I'm going to clean up."

Dog at her heels, she left the room. Meghan and Jared just stood there, completely bewildered.

"I don't get any of this." Meghan went to the fireplace and heaved in a log. The sparks and embers flew up in a shower of light and dark. She stood there, fists clenched. "Jared," she said finally, "how come Mom has a dog here?"

"How should I know?" Jared looked around. All this stone and timber and even the paintings in here were almost as old as the hills. Nothing made sense.

Meghan whirled around. "You do know. Same as me. This castle is what we've been running from all these years. And that weird guy, John."

"I don't think he's weird," Jared insisted.

"No? Like our drive here was so normal?"

Jared bit his lip. Like him, John had seen the horseman, but Meghan and his mom hadn't. Knowing the man also saw the unexplainable terrors that he did, made Jared desperate to defend him. "Bad driving isn't going to make Mom move all over the world and never stay in one place," Jared said finally.

"That's right," Meghan agreed. "So what's the secret? What's so terrible that she would leave everything, even her dog, and take us and run? If it isn't John, then what?"

Jared leaned against the fireplace and ran his hand though his hair. "I don't know," he muttered. "But Meghan, we've been broke so many times before. What finally made her come back?"

*   *   *

The night closed around him. Jared lay in the great four poster, wondering if kings and princes had lain alone in beds like this. The ancient stones and land made the lives that had gone before seem pulsingly real. He wondered if the long dead had been as scared as he was.

It wasn't just the dark, which was more thick and shadowed than a city back alley. It was the silence that was so crammed with sounds. He could hear some kind of bird screaming a hunting call through his open window, the moaning complaints of far off cattle and sheep, the rising sigh of wind around corners. He could hear his own breathing as well, overlaid by the beating of his heart.

He didn't remember ever sleeping alone before. Mrs. Jenkins said that he and Meghan had both had cribs in the nursery at the end of the hall when they were babies, but was vague about how long that had lasted.

"Time just flows together when you're my age, honey," she declared and patted his head as though he were still that baby. Jared was sure she was lying. He was equally sure it had to do with whatever agreement their mom had made before bringing them back here.

The room seemed liked a box that was holding him fast. A strong box.... Jared's mind wandered to the idea of a safe hidden within the walls of the castle. The rocks were the treasure stored in the safe...and outside the shadows were gathering.

Drowsily, Jared heard the Song rising gently on the wind. For now, cradled in this place of ancient stone, he and his family were safe.

240   Susan Brown

The Path to the Dark Peak

Through his dreams Jared hears shouts and clanging weapons...cries of dying men...and then hoof beats thudding on the ground. Two horses rear before him. He steps back and stumbles. Kronos rides a horse as red as embers; Rhea is astride a mare as grey as ancient bones. They pause on the path just beyond the standing stones that circle the castle. Jared hears the yowling of the red-eared dogs that race at the horses' heels.

The riders' eyes turn on him. Jared feels them pinion him, reach for him. He is on a rocky path, desperately climbing upwards, his backpack weighing down his shoulders. Wind roars and tosses around him. The dogs are hunting again – hunting him! Ahead, tortured monuments of rock lean against the deep shadows of night.

Where is he?

The hounds bay below. Jared climbs, panting, blind with night and terror. Horses' hooves thunder behind. They are going to catch him. He reaches the top, staggers and falls, his knees painfully striking the rough ground. Behind, a laugh howls into the night and the dogs yammer in blood lust. He lurches to his feet.

A pair of dogs with gleaming white ruffs and glossy black fur, charge toward him. He cries out, holds up his arms to fend them off, but they swerve past in a frenzy of sound and speed, and hurl themselves on the night dogs. The scream of a horse tears the air as it stumbles and falls into the whirling melee.

The two dogs fight against five. The bigger one goes down and the night hounds dive for his throat. He howls in pain and fear. The smaller dog leaps the red-eared dogs' backs, twists in mid air and lands facing them. Head down, tail straight, she snarls into their faces.

Jared snatches up a rock and hurls it at the leader of the night dogs. It smashes into the creature's head; yelping, it retreats. The others mill and growl.

Kronos walks his horse forward.

"Call off your dogs, Jared." His voice is like smooth steel. "Give me the rocks."

Unable to speak, Jared shakes his head.

Kronos laughs. "There's no point in fighting. I am the god of time. The wheel will turn, the tree will die, this universe will end...and I shall win."

Rhea remounts her horse and walks up beside Kronos. "Husband, he is too stupid to even know who you are." She laughs and it sounds to Jared as if the noise flies into the wind and echoes across the entire sky.

"Give me the stones, Jared, and perhaps you and your sister will be allowed to live." He smiles then and holds out his hand. The spidery emblem glints in Jared's eyes.

Unable to stop himself, Jared slides the backpack from his shoulders. No....his mind cries. He can't help himself. Fumbling, he undoes the pack's strap. The rocks huddle inside. He can hear them howling and keening. The Song is broken, in pieces. He reaches for a rock to give to Kronos.

The black and white dogs strike. The small one yanks the strap from Jared's hand. The larger springs at Kronos' horse.

Kronos slashes at the dog with his riding crop. The dog falls back.

The smaller dog tugs fiercely at the backpack. Jared's hand jerks and closes over a rock. Pain tears across his mind, waking him. The rocks tumble to the ground, a rough circle.

"No!" Kronos shouts.

Panting, Jared drops the bloody black rock into its place. The Singing rises, gathered into circling, exploding light...

Jared throws his empty pack at Kronos. It passes through air. The riders are gone. The smaller dog leaps up and licks his face. The moors become ghostlike and fade.

Chapter 15

The Wheel Is Turning

Jared's eyes flew open. He was not on the Dark Peak, but in his castle bedroom with the grey light of dawn edging in the open window. And a dog was licking his face.

Jared yelped, tossed himself back in the bed, and tangled in the heavy blankets. Caught, he stared at two brown eyes, staring back. The dog sat alertly, perfectly at home, plumy white-tipped tail slowly brushing the sheets.

Once again, her white muzzle, freckled with black, nosed him. A pink tongue flicked across his mouth in a wet kiss. The dog turned around once, and with a huffing breath of content, flopped down beside him, her back to his chest, her head on his pillow.

"Make yourself at home," Jared whispered.

She was the smaller dog from his nightmare. But how...? He must have opened his eyes during the dream, seen the dog in his room, and then incorporated her in his imaginings. Jared grinned. Not a bad way to get rescued from a nightmare like that one.

Freeing his hand from the blankets, he gently touched the white streak that gathered just above the dog's nose and rose in a graceful curve between her eyes, ending at the top of her glossy black head. Her muzzle, feet, ruff, chest, and tail tip glistened white. The rest of her was pure black. Jared guessed that standing, her head would reach the top of his thigh. Everything about her was gleaming and graceful. She was the prettiest dog he had ever seen.

He flattened his hand to stroke her whole head. "Hi there," he said softly. "What's your name? Do you know Kip?"

The dog lifted her head, looked at him from wide eyes and panted as if she was thoroughly enjoying the conversation.

Encouraged, Jared unwound himself from the rest of the blankets and sat cross-legged. The dog rolled over and sat alertly, still smiling. He hadn't realized before that a dog could smile.

"Hey girl, who's dog are you?"

It seemed silly to expect an answer, but somehow he did. The dog put a paw on his knee, then abruptly twisted and leapt off the bed. She trotted out the door and disappeared.

Disappointed, Jared flopped back against the pillow. A few minutes later, the door opened and Meghan peeked in.

"Jar, are you awake?" she whispered.

He sat up again. "Yeah, what's up?"

Meghan came into the room, turned around and whispered, "C'mon boy." She grinned back at her twin. "Look who came to visit me."

She climbed up on the bed beside her brother, and repeated, "C'mon boy. Come here." A second later another dog trotted through the door. With cold shock, Jared recognized the second dog in his dream – the one that had leapt at Kronos' horse.

Get a grip, he told himself. This dog must have wandered into his room with the other one. It too, was black and white, but with more white in its ruff and chest. It had light brown eyebrows and socks above its white feet.

"You wouldn't believe it, Jar," Meghan was saying, "I was having this horrific dream where rabid dogs and a woman on a grey horse were chasing me through London. Then this dog jumped out at the horse and saved me. I woke up, and here was this beautiful puppy, licking my face. He snuggled right up to me as if he belonged. Isn't that cool?"

"Yeah," Jared forced out. "I had a nightmare too. And there were a couple of dogs who saved me."

"That's really weird," Meghan agreed. "Maybe it's some kind of twin thing. You know – a shared nightmare because of this creepy old castle."

Jared felt himself relaxing. He and Meghan had always had similar thoughts and ideas. Why not dreams, too?

"Probably. And there was all that stuff about Mom's dog."

Just then, the dog leapt nimbly up onto the bed and Meghan promptly threw her arms around his neck, burying her face in his silky ruff. "Isn't he gorgeous?" she cooed.

Jared wished the dog who'd visited him had stayed. "I had a dog in here too," he said, "but she left."

"It wasn't this one?"

Jared shook his head. "No. She was smaller and all black and white. No brown. Did you see her?"

"Nope, just this beautiful boy." Meghan yawned and glanced at her watch. "It's only six o'clock. I'm going back to bed." She headed toward her room; the dog jumped off the bed and followed at her heels.

Jared leaned back against the pillows, hands clasped behind his head. He wished that the dog had stayed with him. He'd never had any kind of a pet. For a moment he let himself imagine what it would be like to stay here, to be able to go out onto green hills with a dog trotting alongside him. All his life he'd looked out on grimy streets and gone to sleep with traffic sounds echoing through crowded rooms. The only dogs he'd seen were the scrawny, sad-eyed animals some of the street people kept, or the even skinnier and sadder strays.

Meghan had thrown her arms around her dog, but he'd done no more than pat his. Maybe that was why the dog had left.

Jared hurried out of bed and pulled on his clothes. More than anything he wanted to find that dog. He wanted to put his arms around it, feel its fur on his face, and have it follow at his heels. He refused to think about how dumb he was being. In two weeks they'd be gone. You can't have a dog for just two weeks.

The sun cast long, thin rectangles of light along the corridor. Almost at a run, Jared hurried toward the main staircase. He wanted to call the dog, but didn't even know her name.

Downstairs in the main hall, he looked around. She could have gone down any of the corridors or into any of the rooms that opened off one another. He tried whistling softly. The sound echoed from the high vaulted roof.

Nothing.

"Okay, Jared, if you were a dog, where would you go?" His stomach rumbled. "Kitchen! I'd go to the kitchen!"

His sense of direction was pretty good – he only made one wrong turn. Then the rich smell of brewing coffee led him right there.

The low ceilinged kitchen was obviously astir already. Mrs. Jenkins, a white apron tied around her turquoise pants suit was tending a pan full of sizzling bacon. Peter and John were seated on benches at a long wooden table, large mugs of milky tea steaming before them.

"...never come so close before..." Jared heard Peter say. The man stopped talking and took a long drink of tea when he caught sight of the boy.

John swiveled around and smiled. "Early riser, are you?"

Jared nodded shyly. "Sometimes."

"Then country life will suit you. Do you drink tea or coffee?"

"Now, don't you be giving the boy coffee," Mrs. Jenkins scolded. "What about some nice cocoa?"

Jared grinned. "I'd rather have coffee with milk and sugar, if that's okay."

"It'll stunt your growth," Mrs. Jenkins told him, "but honey, nobody around this place listens to me."

"I don't see how we can help it," John murmured.

Mrs. Jenkins laughed, poured some coffee and handed it to Jared. "Cream and sugar are on the table. You just help yourself."

Jared sat down beside Peter, who silently passed him the cream and sugar.

"A dog came into my room this morning," Jared said as he stirred the coffee. "I was wondering what her name is, and if she's around here somewhere."

"We have a half dozen or so dogs," John told him. "They help on the farm and keep out intruders."

"She's black and white and about this high," Jared held his hand at a level just below the table.

"The dogs are border collies mostly," Peter grunted. "Happen they're all black and white and about that high."

"Well, the one that went into Meghan's room was bigger and had some brown on him too," Jared retorted.

"That would be Billy," John said slowly. "You both had dogs visit you?"

"Yeah." Jared wanted to tell about his dream, but decided it would make him sound like a baby...or a lunatic. "The dog startled me," he said instead. "But I was just getting to know her and she left again."

"They didn't rouse me," Peter said. "If it had been Them, the dogs would have woken us."

"They can't get in here," Mrs. Jenkins face looked sharp. "The castle has stood for centuries!"

"The wheel is turning," John rubbed his forehead as though he suddenly was old or sick. Jared choked on his coffee.

That was what Kronos had said in his nightmare. *The wheel is turning!* What wheel?

"We have two weeks still," Peter said gruffly. "Plenty of time."

Jared gripped his mug tightly. "Time for what?" he demanded.

With a loud clatter, Mrs. Jenkins dropped a plate of bacon on the table. "Time to get ready for the singing festival, of course. Folks will begin arriving any time now. By the way, John, I'll need to hire extra help to get things ready for the guests."

"Yes, of course. Whatever you think best," John replied.

Jared stared at them. They had turned the conversation aside. Whatever was happening, they didn't want him to know. With a crushing sense of embarrassment, he remembered he was only a visitor. His family probably wouldn't even be here for the festival they were talking about. And if he found the dog, he would have to leave her, too. Jared took a gulp from his steaming mug.

"Coffee on?" Deirdre asked as she came into the room. Kip followed at her heels.

John sat back and summoned a smile. "You get up early now?"

"Not by choice." Deirdre grimaced and slid into a place beside John. "I'd forgotten how loud rural silence is. I thought all country people did healthy things like early to bed, early to rise. Was there some kind of masquerade going on too? I could swear I saw a bunch of people dressed like Roman soldiers and British tribesman waving spears around. And who was that yahoo galloping around here last night with those yammering dogs?"

The silence thickened in the room.

"What?" Deirdre demanded.

"There was no horseman," Peter said sharply. "You were dreaming, Deirdre. They cannot come here. Not to the White Peak!"

254   Susan Brown

The Battle

In the time before time, when earth was a chaos of fire, wind and waves, twelve immortal Titans ruled. They were proud, quarrelsome and cruel.

The Titans produced many children who were even more wild and uncontrolled than their parents. Kronos, chief among the Titans, had six children. A prophecy warned that he could be defeated only by his own child. Determined never to give up his power, Kronos swallowed each of his offspring as it was born. His wife, Rhea went to her mother and father, the earth and sky for advice. They told her to prepare a cave for the birth of her next child. They also told her to command nymphs to guard the infant god.

She did as they advised. When the time came for the birth of her child, she hid in the cave until the baby was born. Then she left him in the care of nymphs and the goat, Amalthea, and returned home. She showed a wrapped stone to her husband, Kronos, telling him it was their child. Unaware his doom approached, Kronos swallowed the stone.

Meanwhile, the child, Zeus, became strong from goat's milk and honey. When he grew up, he went to his father in disguise and tricked him into drinking a magic potion. Immediately Kronos vomited up all of Zeus' brothers and sisters.

As foretold in the prophecy, Zeus and his siblings made war on the Titans. During the terrible battles that followed, they tore the land with flaming rock, howling winds and endless storms. All earth's creatures cried out to the Creator for relief. But there was none.

The war of the immortals raged on until at last the young gods won. Zeus imprisoned the Titans in Tartarus, the region beyond hell.

In time, Zeus and the gods of Olympus returned to the stars and forgot earth. Kronos, the god of time itself, waited until the stones of his prison wore away. Then he and Rhea and the ten others returned to earth. But it had changed.

People had flourished and become strong. And so the Titans declared war on humankind.

Chapter 16

Tell Me His Name

Deirdre's eyes flashed. "I was dreaming, Peter? Fully clothed, looking out my window before I even began to get ready for bed? Standing there, wide awake, I dream of battles, galloping horses and howling dogs?"

"I did rounds," Peter insisted. "I would have seen or heard."

"Only if you did them after two a.m.," Deirdre retorted. "I stayed up reading."

"Here's your coffee," Mrs. Jenkins interrupted. "And the bacon and eggs are ripe for eating. I won't have this meal ruined by arguing, Peter."

She put more platters and a rack of toast on the table. Peter hunched over and glared at his tea for several moments while the others silently filled their plates. Then he lifted his head.

"You tell me what I don't want to hear, Deirdre," he said gruffly. "I apologize for doubting you. And for what I said last night. We were friends once."

Impulsively Deirdre stretched her hand across the table and laid it on his. "I hope we can still be friends. I had my children, Peter. You know I had to do what I did."

The man's face shifted into what Jared guessed passed for a smile. "I know you did what you thought right. We won't agree on that one, though."

Deirdre nodded and removed her hand. Jared didn't understand what they meant but the tension seemed to have been eased. Mrs. Jenkins chattered about hiring a couple of new girls for the extra housework. Deirdre offered to help where she could.

"Where are the dogs?" Jared asked. "I'd like to see if I can find the one that visited me."

"They're working dogs," Peter said. "They can't be playing and fetching sticks and all to amuse you."

Jared felt himself flush. "I'd like to see her work then," he said.

"I'll help you find her." John stood up. "It must be Nugget, Mattie or Chance." He smiled down at Deirdre. "Kip sired Mattie, Chance and Billy. There's another litter coming in about a week too, by Kip's granddaughter. You'll like that, won't you, Deirdre?"

He sounded anxious to Jared, like it was terribly important to him that Deirdre be pleased. She smiled at him over the rim of her coffee cup.

Together Jared and John went out the low back door into a wide kitchen garden. John led him past what looked to be an ancient stable, then through another stout gate in the outer wall of the castle. The brilliant green fields spread down the hill and in every direction. The village nestled at the bottom of the hill and snuggled up its sides like toys in a tumble of green blankets, stitched together by low stone walls and pale streaks of light.

Jared tried not to look toward the bleak and ravaged hills that rose on the far side of the valley. He knew that that was where he had been attacked by Kronos' hell hounds.

But it was impossible – a dream. A shiver ran over him. More than ever he wanted the black and white dog to come back.

"...the border collies help us to look after the sheep and cattle," John was saying. Jared forced himself to listen. "One good dog can do the herding work of five men."

"What about trespassers?" Jared asked. "You said earlier that they keep away trespassers. Who are they?"

"Oh...undesirables," John began. Then abruptly he stopped, and looked down at Jared. "I promised your mother not to discuss certain things with you. But I won't lie to you either. There are dangers here that the dogs help us with."

"Like horsemen in the night," Jared said.

John's face was hard and cold. He nodded, a jerk of his chin down and up. That was all.

Jared's shoulders shook and he felt the strength going from his legs, like his whole body was made of mud, not bones or muscle. His lungs had gone funny – no matter how hard he breathed he couldn't feel the air. The echo of bleating sheep and lowing cattle seemed to swirl and echo like a side show horror house...

Jared plunked down on the grass, eyes closed, breathing hard, his hand curled around the first rock in his jacket pocket. A soft, hot tongue swished across his cheek and he was looking into the eyes of his dog again. He threw his arms around her neck and clung to her, face buried in her thick, sweet fur. Strength flowed back into him.

"Mattie is the best of them all," John said. "I'm glad she's for you, son."

Mattie wiggled out of Jared's grasp and leapt backwards, barking invitation and joy. Jared scrambled to his feet.

"But we're just here for a visit. We'll be gone in a couple of weeks."

"Maybe," John said. "Still, it would please me to have you stay a lengthy time. A very lengthy time."

Jared turned his eyes to the dog, panting gently, waiting for him. Like the whole castle and these hills had been waiting for him.

"Would you like to see our orchard?" John asked. "Legend has it that our orchard is the home of the first apple tree planted in Britain. That all the others are the offspring of our tree."

"Right." Jared laughed. "And the tree is still here to prove it." He dropped his hand on Mattie's sun-warmed head. This could be Eden itself as far as he was concerned.

John chuckled. "I make no claims," he replied. "But there is one tree that is older than all the rest, and we have no record of when it was planted, as we do for the others. Mrs. Jenkins watches over these trees like they were her children."

The orchard lay behind a high stone wall on a sun flooded hill behind the castle. Jared nearly caught his breath at the sweetness of the pink-white blossoms that misted the branches of every tree. He wandered silently with John while Mattie danced and scooped up sticks from the long grass.

"Here is the great-grandmother of our trees." John gestured toward the center of the orchard.

The tree was gnarled and twisted, yet its smaller branches reached gracefully to the sky. The bark seemed to have been rubbed silvery smooth by hands that could not help but reach out and touch it.

As Jared's fingers traced over the creases and cracks in the bark, it was as though he held one of the rocks. He sensed the being of the tree – ancient branches weaving a dance with the wind; ancient roots anchoring to the wisdom of the earth.

Jared frowned. Beneath his feet, the slow pull of earth power felt browned and rotting somehow. He shifted position. He must be imagining it. Looking up, he saw that some of the highest blossoms had a tinge of brown on the edges.

But what did he know about trees? Maybe the blossoms were nearly ready to fall as the apples started to form. And the tree was old, older than anything he knew of. As old as his rocks, he thought with surprise. Perhaps it was dying.

He patted the tree and silently wished it well.

John smiled. "There's a fine walking path through the gate over this way. You'll get a glorious look at the Peaks."

Jared followed as he strode off. Mattie barked and galloped ahead, then turned and woofed encouragement to Jared. He ran to catch up.

The rest of the morning was pure joy. John and Jared rambled the fields and the paths over the hills and down the valleys. They strode through sways of bracken fern, through patches of thistle and heather. All the while, bird calls like whistled snatches of the Song, echoed through the air. At one point a fox paused atop a rock and looked them over before disappearing into a hole in a stone fence. John pointed out wildflowers, shrubs and birds in response to Jared's eager questions.

The whole way, Mattie accompanied them, sometimes at their heels, sometimes dashing ahead or to the side on ventures of her own, but always darting back before they lost sight of one another. The castle, Jared soon saw, was the center of a large working farm. John pointed out their flocks of curly-horned Swaledale sheep and herds of Fresian cattle that he and Peter were breeding to improve the quality of the stock.

Before long, they stopped on a slope and John gestured to a long, undulating hill. "That's the Sleeper," he said.

"Is that a legend?"

"Yes. He was an immortal but gave up life to save our people. The gods tried to destroy him, but, the legend says, Gaia, the Earth Mother took him into her body where he sleeps."

"Is he ever supposed to wake up?" Jared asked.

"Of course," John replied. "When the earth herself is threatened."

Jared laughed wryly. "Now would be a good time. With global warming and all the weird weather and the wars all over the place, the earth seems to be in a real mess." He looked around at the soaring blue sky and rich green that covered the hills. "Except here," he said. "Everything here seems perfect."

Jared tried to imagine what it would be like to be born and grow up in one place – to belong to a countryside like the one before him. "You've always lived here?" he asked John.

"Yes, except for school and some traveling," the older man replied. "My family seems to stay hereabouts. Except for Ian – country life doesn't have much appeal for him. Since he left university, he's been in London at the BBC. That was how I met your mother, through some work she did for him."

Jared felt a stir of excitement. "Was that before or after we were born?"

John frowned. "Before."

"But we were at the Castle when we were little. Did you know our father?" Jared couldn't keep the rise of excitement out of his voice.

"Yes." John walked swiftly on ahead. Jared darted forward and caught him by the sleeve.

"Who is he," Jared demanded. "Please tell me his name. I...we...keep trying to find out but Mom won't tell us anything."

John pulled away his arm. "I can't," he said.

* * *

The Castle seemed to have erupted into activity while Jared hiked with John. A vacuum cleaner roared from distant rooms; buckets of water sloshed in teenage girls' fists and the smell of wood polish floated above it all.

"Now honey," Mrs. Jenkins was directing a flushed girl, "just take that mop and swish it over those flagstones like it was your dance partner."

The girl giggled, picked up a mop and bucket and hurried into the far passage.

"Well, I see you found your dog, darlin'. Make sure her paws are clean before you go traipsing over my rugs. Folks will start arriving for the singing any day now and I want the castle to sparkle."

Mattie pressed against Jared's legs, looking around his knees at the hubbub. Jared wished he too had someone to hide behind. "Where's Meghan?"

"Dusting the spare rooms in the east wing," Mrs. Jenkins replied. "I promised to take her shopping in Sheffield tomorrow in return for her help."

Jared made his escape up the broad staircase. A blast of music led him to his sister. In a bedroom off a new-looking passageway, she was enthusiastically singing, dancing and flicking a cloth over the wooden surfaces. Clouds of dust motes shimmied in the sunlight streaming through tall windows.

Jared called, then switched off the music.

"What?" Meghan demanded. "Oh, Jared, Mrs. Jenkins loaned me this CD player. It's old but it's a really good one. And we're going shopping tomorrow...."

"John knows about our father," Jared interrupted.

Meghan stopped cold. "And?"

"He won't tell me anything. But he said he knew Mom before and after we were born."

Meghan plunked down in an overstuffed chair. "So? That just means Mom didn't tell him who our father was. That *is* her pattern, you know."

"He might have been lying..." Jared hesitated. "Maybe John is our father."

Meghan rolled her eyes. "Maybe. Or what about Ian? Or some guy she met somewhere?" Meghan switched on the music and cranked up the volume. "I don't know and I don't care." Without another glance at her brother she began cleaning the room again.

Jared went back to his own room, Mattie trotting ahead. Inside, Jared closed the door tightly. He took the bag of rocks from its hiding place behind the wardrobe and sat in the center of the roses woven into the green rug. With the sun shining like a spotlight through the window, Jared deliberately took the rocks out one by one. As always, the obsidian managed to slice through his skin, leaving a slash of hot pain at the tip of his finger. He sucked on it briefly, too intent on what he was doing to care. It was the price of the rocks.

He knew the order as if the rocks had been labeled. Each seemed to fit into its place in the circle as though they had always lain like that. Jared's hand holding the First Rock hovered over the circle. What if he sat inside? Would that huge power become part of him?

Before he could worry himself out of it, Jared widened the ring of stones and sat in the center. Mattie paced and whined anxiously. Jared ignored her. Sitting cross-legged, back stiffened, he placed the first stone into its place at the head of the circle.

Tintagel Castle

Jared stands alone on a small beach in the center of a storm. Wind lashes spray upward from the heaving sea. The gusts beat so he can hardly stand. The roar of surf and weather deafen him. He is surrounded by night so thick it appears like black shadowed on black. No houses...streetlights...just the roar of crashing waves and taste of salt crusting his lips.

Where is he? Where has the power of the stones catapulted him...and when? Can he get back? He stands paralyzed, blown by the elements, terrified that a misstep will plunge him to his death. Where is he?

"Think, Jared," he orders himself, but the wind blows away his words.

He wraps his arms around his body – useless against cold and wet. He has to get out of the storm...or die here on the raging beach. Cliffs rise in dark shadows above his head. Maybe he can find shelter at their base. But it is so dark he can't see his footing. Stumbling over rocks and seaweed drifts, he ploughs ahead.

He holds out his hands until his fingertips jam into stone. Runoff pours down the rock face, drenching him further. How long until morning? Can he survive this place?

Jared raises his head. A light glimmers deep within the rock. A cave. Gasping, he struggles toward it, nearly falling inside. Within the flickering shadows, he sees two men sitting together by the light of a fire built against a small boulder. An unlit lantern sits beside them.

"Help me...please..."

They do not raise their heads or look toward him. In despair, Jared realizes that they can neither see nor hear him. He is in the middle of magic, but it is different than other times – he can feel everything but is still as invisible as a ghost.

He edges to the fire, desperate for heat, but keeps a frightened eye on the men, in case he suddenly becomes visible. Nothing. Just as he settles against the boulder trying to soak in the fire's warmth, one of the men stands restlessly. His richly colored cloak falls back showing rough cloth and a leather jerkin. The other man's face is hidden by a cowl as he stares into the flames.

"It must be near time. Or has your magic failed, Merlin?"

Jared sucks in his breath. Merlin! The magician who worked miracles at King Arthur's side! Jared feels a thrill of excitement. The rocks have sent him to the time of King Arthur. Could the man before him be Arthur?

"My magic has not failed. If the time is not right, your venture will not succeed, King Uther."

Uther? Arthur's father was Uther Pendragon...

"What of the storm? Did you conjure it? It's wild even for Cornwall." Brows drawn together, Uther peers out at the howling dark beyond the mouth of the cave.

Merlin stirs the embers with a stick. "I did not conjure it," he says. He opens his hand and stares down at a stone with a hole through the center. Uther turns back and watches him, frowning.

"Are you scrying still? Are you unsure of your magic?"

Merlin closes his fist over the stone and puts it away under his robes. Restlessly, Uther strides to the mouth of the cave and Merlin stares after him. In the light Jared sees the sorcerer is barely middle aged, not the old man of the stories he has read. "I am sure of my magic," he says in a low voice, "but I am not sure of what other forces are at work tonight. Still...."

Uther paces back. "Is it the right time yet, magician? You have promised to give me the form of Gorlois so that I can take his place with his wife Ygraine. I am not a patient man." His hand clasps the hilt of his knife. Merlin hesitates, and then shrugs his shoulders.

"There is no other time," he says. He raises his head and speaks more loudly. "I will bring forth the breath of the dragon. The old knowledge claims it will allow a man to change his face from sunset to sunrise. All will be as you wish. You will do better to sit or even lie down."

"I'll sit," Uther says. He settles opposite the fire, so close that Jared is afraid to move. Still the men seem to be unaware of him.

They sit in silence except for the roar of weather outside. Merlin sets a round metal dish on the embers. It seems to be iron, decorated with etchings of fighting dragons breathing fire. From under his cloak the magician takes several small packets with symbols written across them. He lays them in a row on the ground in front of him.

"Should we pray?" Uther says uneasily.

Jared sees the twitch of Merlin's mouth. "It is always good to pray."

Methodically, he sprinkles powder from each packet onto the heating metal. Then he speaks softly, a monotone. Jared leans forward to hear. With a chill, he recognizes the words are part of the Song.

At first nothing seems to happen, and then slowly smoke curls upward into the dim cave. Some of the smoke is white, some blood red. The two colors twine together but do not mix. Jared scoots back as far as he can to keep himself from breathing the fumes. He feels a cleft in the rock and wedges himself in farther.

The dragon smoke swirls around Uther's face. The king cries out and slumps backward, his head almost at Jared's feet. As Jared watches in disbelief, Uther's face blurs and reforms to the face of a stranger.

Merlin watches in grim satisfaction. Jared looks toward the cave mouth. Mist, the color of old bruises, gathers at the entrance to the cave. It oozes forward and curls around Merlin. Jared pushes farther back into the cleft rock. The magician frowns, sighs deeply and then appears to slip into a trance. A man walks into the cave from the beach. Jared sucks in his breath. The stranger's clothes are dry, but outside the rain still sheets across the night. His face is the same as the new face that Uther wears. Is he the true Gorlois...or another apparition?

The man touches Merlin's shoulder. "Now it is time, magician. Take me to the beautiful Ygraine."

Merlin shakes his head as though trying to clear it and slowly gets to his feet. "Yes, it is time," he says thickly. As he lights the lantern, he does not even glance at Uther still lying by the fire.

Merlin leading, they go out into the storm. Jared edges past Uther and follows them. The rain has dropped off, but thunder cracks open the night. More by the light of flashes than by that of the lantern, they climb a steep path winding up the cliffside. Jared sees it is one face of a vast escarpment that juts out into the tossing ocean. Before long, Jared's clothes are wet again and rain plasters his hair to his face. He doesn't dare look down as the path inches above hurling breakers. At last they reach a causeway that leads narrowly to a castle crouched over the thrashing sea. It appears locked and barred against night and enemies.

Gorlois pounds on the small wooden door beside the main gate. "Open to your lord!" He shouts.

An old, shivering gatekeeper slides open the bolts. "My lord duke," he quavers. "We did not know...did not expect..." He ducks his head in respect.

Gorlois pushes inside. Merlin, head down in his cowl, and then Jared darting after, pass through the thick walls into the courtyard. A few torches and lanterns burn feebly against the storm. At the top of a far stone stair, a door opens. A beautiful woman, rich brown hair hanging loose, is silhouetted against the inside light.

"Husband?" She looks startled. "...but the battle? Is it won?"

Gorlois goes up the stairs two at a time and puts his arm about her waist. Jared trots after but hesitates at the foot of the stairs. Merlin stays where he is.

"Would a battle keep me from the beautiful Ygraine?" Gorlois sweeps her into the room and the door slams shut.

Unsure what to do, Jared goes back to Merlin. The magician is looking up at the night. "I do not like this storm," he says. "But the time is now..." He sighs and turns to the gatekeeper.

"Is there somewhere I can await Duke Gorlois, out of the rain?"

The gatekeeper looks at them, puzzled, then jerks his head toward some low buildings. "The stable be dry," he mutters.

"I thank you," Merlin replies, his voice low.

In the stable, the horses are nervous, fretting and tossing their heads, as Jared and Merlin settle in the hay. He must have slept, Jared thinks, because the night sky is lightening through heavy greenish clouds. They hear a stir in the courtyard, and yawning, Jared follows Merlin outside. Gorlois is running briskly down the stairs just as a soldier calls down from the battlements.

"A messenger...a messenger from our army! Open the gate!"

As the gatekeeper opens the main gates, Gorlois, laughing, pushes open the small side door. The three slip out and onto the path into the greying early dawn. Without speaking they make their way down the slippery trail to the beach and cave. The storm is passing. On the horizon, streaks of light break through and shine over heaving seas.

Merlin leans wearily against the rock and looks outward, watching the sunrise. Jared follows Gorlois into the cave.

The man bends over Uther and grasps him roughly by the arm. "Wake fool...but carry with you a memory of your stolen night with Ygraine..." He waves his hand over Uther's face.

Jared drives a fist against his mouth to keep from crying out. A golden distorted spider seems to crawl from Gorlois' hand. Tendrils of mist curl around Uther's face. The king smiles and straightens as a shaft of morning sun strikes through the entrance, highlighting his features. Uther's face blurs and returns to its original form.

As though he does not see the man who took his place, he stands and struts to the cave's entrance. Jared watches as he claps Merlin on the shoulder. "I owe you a great debt, magician."

"One you will repay," Merlin replies, "as we agreed."

"Yes, yes. If there is a child, I will give him to you for rearing. But that is in the future, man. We must rejoin my army...."

A soft laugh sounds behind Jared. He turns and looks full into the face of Gorlois. But as sunlight strikes it, this face is shifting, changing into...Kronos!

Jared screams and falls back...twisting...spinning through time, carried by the magic of the Song.

Chapter 17

The Chamber

Jared threw himself backwards knocking the stones askew. The black stone skittered the farthest, into the shadows under the bed. Jared lay on the floor panting, feeling the blood pound through his arms, legs, and beating heart. Knowing he was back in his own times and place – away from Kronos. The stones had sent him face to face with the immortal. He half crawled to the First Rock, and closed his hand around it.

Mattie whimpered and her tongue touched his cheek. Footsteps pounded outside his room.

The door crashed open. John, Mrs. Jenkins, Peter, Ian and followed last by his mother and Meghan, ran into the room and then simply stood in a semi-circle, staring at him. Mattie retreated to a corner, whining softly.

Jared propped himself up, hiding the First Stone beneath his body.

"Jared!" his mother cried. "Are you okay... are you hurt?"

"Yeah," Jared said, knowing he was breathing too heavily. "Just...um...something weird...."

She slumped down on his bed. "No! I won't have it, John. You promised!"

"I didn't do this, Deirdre!" John crouched down beside Jared. His hand reached out to touch the agate, then he drew it back. "Are... are you all right?" Instead of grasping the stone, his fingers touched Jared's brow.

Jared nodded and stood up, slipping the First Rock unobtrusively into his pocket.

"He brought them..." Mrs. Jenkins murmured. "He brought the stones. Who would have...?"

"They have to be hidden," Peter interrupted, "put in a place of safe keeping. That's why they've been coming closer. They must know about this."

"What do you mean," Jared interrupted. "These are my rocks. I've collected them from all over the world." He hated the tremor that vibrated in his voice.

"John, we must get these to the stronghold," Peter said urgently. He hesitated then picked up the stone with the running horse. The tension left his face, and a hint of a relieved smile twitched his lips. "It's all right."

"No it isn't!" Jared shouted, grabbing for the stone. "That's my rock! You can't take it." Peter stepped back easily, holding him away.

Meghan thrust her face into Peter's. "That belongs to my brother, and you can bet we'd sell it before we give it to you!"

John caught each twin's arm in a powerful grip. "You children don't understand. You can't understand. These rocks have been hidden – no, *lost* for nearly a thousand years. They are vessels of power. It's a miracle that they've come together now, when our need is so great."

"I'll get something to carry them in," Mrs. Jenkins said and whisked out of the room.

"What need?" Jared demanded.

"We have to get them hidden away," Peter insisted. "Explain to him later, John, if you must. You know that if we heard the Singing, They will have too."

"Too late," Ian said. "They've heard."

He pointed to the open window. Clouds, black as earth, shot with murky green, roiled across the sky. Wind and weather howled like the screams of an animal in pain.

"John, you promised we'd be safe here!" Deirdre cried. "That They couldn't breach the castle walls."

"They've never done so." He released his grip on the twins' arms and rubbed a hand over his face. "Not in a thousand years."

"I know...I know..." She stared out at the storm thundering toward them.

Mrs. Jenkins returned with a tray covered in a white cloth. "Will this do?"

"Yes," John said. "We have to hurry."

John, Peter and Mrs. Jenkins scooped the rocks onto the tray. The edges of the white cloth flapped in the wind as Deirdre and Meghan struggled to shut the window against the gathering storm. The gale arrowed into the room, whipping their hair and carrying away speech.

"Help us!" Meghan screamed over the roar. Jared cast a raging glance at John, then he and Ian leaned against the window too, finally swinging the panes shut and twisting the latches.

John held the tray before him like an alter cloth and the Castle people all hurried from the room.

"Mom!" Jared cried. "My rocks!"

She headed for the door. "John knows what's best. Jared, you don't understand. You can't even imagine who They are – what They can do."

"They're why you left," Meghan stated, her voice flat. "You were part of this whole creepy castle thing, too."

Deirdre paused and nodded wearily. "They were after me and you, too. That's why I left – trying to protect us all."

"Then why did you come back?" Meghan demanded.

Deirdre gestured helplessly. "It's been so many years. I thought They would have lost interest – and we had no more places to go. John wanted us badly, and...and..." She covered her face with her hands.

Meghan rushed over and hugged her mom. "And you wanted to be with someone who loves you best of all," she whispered.

Deirdre smiled and scrubbed at her damp face. "I shouldn't have given in. The war isn't over and I would do anything to keep you safe."

"We weren't safe." Jared's voice sounded odd, even to himself. "In Seattle, they were after me – after my rocks."

"If those rocks are what They want, then John should have them," Deirdre told him. "No one else will know how to use them now."

"Mom," Jared insisted, "the stones found *me*, not John!"

She shook her head. "Jared, you don't understand. You can't possibly."

"I understand that I have to have the rocks!" Jared cried. "Mom, I was chosen!"

Deirdre shook her head once more, and left the room.

Meghan took her brother's hand. "Let them go, Jar. They're bad news. Like this whole place."

"They're not getting my rocks," Jared snapped yanking back his arm.

Meghan sighed and sank down on a chair. "Too late, brother. They've got them."

"Not all of them." Jared dropped to his knees beside the bed, and reached far underneath, groping for the black stone in the shadows. When pain raked his palm, he knew he'd found it. Sucking in his breath, he closed his hand around the black rock, ignoring the anguish.

Standing up again, he displayed it to his sister.

"You're bleeding," she cried, jumping to her feet.

"It doesn't matter," Jared told her. "I've got to hide it. And I have to find out where they've taken the others." Mattie left the corner and pressed against his leg, whining her anxiety.

"I think you should throw it out the window," Meghan said fiercely.

They both looked toward the locked panes. Beyond murky green clouds pressed down on the land.

"For Them?" Jared asked.

Meghan glared, and then with an angry gesture, relented. "Oh all right. I know a place you can hide it – inside the castle wall. I was looking at the farm horses in the stable and I knocked over a trough or something and it banged a stone out of the wall. No one else was around, so I put it back together. You could hide your stupid stone there."

"I knew you'd help me!" Jared told her.

"I'm not sure this is helping," Meghan retorted.

They eased out of the room. No one else was in sight. The wail of the wind drowned out all sound. Billy left Meghan's room and with Mattie, ran down the hall at their heels. They made their way to the main level and cautiously entered the kitchen. Empty. Gesturing for her brother to follow, Meghan dashed out the kitchen door, across the courtyard and to the old stables at the back. A couple of huge horses whickered and snuffled at their hay. Meghan led her brother into a roomy stall and around the flanks of the dappled horse that occupied it. The dogs sat outside the stall, looking like they were on the watch. With his nerves strung tight, Jared found it comforting – at least they were unquestioningly on his side.

"Here." Meghan pulled a stone out of the old wall, leaving a ragged cavity. Jared wedged in the black rock and Meghan shoved the stone into its original position. There was no sign that anything had been disturbed.

Jared brushed his fingers lightly over the wall. The stone used to build the castle had been quarried from the earth and the earth remembered the Song. The obsidian would be safe here.

"Thanks," he told his sister. "Now I have to find the rest of the rest of my rocks."

"Count me out." Meghan turned on her heel and left, Billy following.

Jared sidestepped to avoid the moving horse, bumping into one of the sides of the stall. The First Rock shifted in his pocket. How could he have forgotten it? He had to hide that too. The opening where he had hidden the black rock was too small to hold another. Desperately he pried at the wall until he found another loose stone.

With the First Rock safely hidden, he left the stall and crouched down by his dog. "Where'd they go, Mattie? Where'd they take my rocks?" he whispered.

Mattie whined sharply and led him from the stable. Following, Jared ran back into the castle kitchen. The room was deserted. Mattie trotted to one side, into the pantry.

"No!" Jared cried. "We aren't getting food!" He tried to grab her collar, but she was too quick, darting away from him into the darkened far end of the room. There, a narrow passage, almost completely hidden by the shelves and shadows, turned at right angles.

Jared let out a soft whistle. The kitchen light didn't reach this far, and reluctant to turn on any lights, he felt his way. The walls here were raw stone – ancient. Gingerly, Jared made his way down the short passage. At the end, nearly invisible in the deep shadows, a solid wooden door stood ajar. Mattie lay down beside it, whimpering softly.

"Oh, good dog!" Jared touched her head, and then, heart beating, pushed the door all the way open. A weak electric light set in the rock revealed another dim passage of arched, ancient stone. Jared hesitated, feeling as though the earth could close in on him. The air smelled cold and damp, like a cave. His head nearly brushed the uneven stone roof and his shoulders had only a few inches of space on either side. Twisting steps led downward. Jared felt the centuries flow before him – he had reached the living heart of the castle.

Leaving his dog behind, Jared plunged down the stairs.

The steps were shallow and uneven. Again and again, he steadied himself against the cold, sweating walls as he felt for his footing. He went down and down. Occasionally, the stairway widened, showing gloomy passageways leading off to one side or the other. Jared realized this part of the castle must tunnel deep into the hill. He wondered how many centuries had passed growing the castle upward from these caves and passageways.

At each crossing, Jared stopped and listened but heard nothing except the echo of his own harsh breathing. He continued down. Now, at last, a light reached upward from below. Abruptly the stairwell opened into a well-lit, roughly rounded room – a limestone cave.

Except for his mother and Meghan, they were all there.

The chamber was bare, but for a big inlaid circle, with a series of lines forming a many pointed star. A ring of twelve limestone blocks, about waist high, stood sentinel at the points of the star, just inside the circle. Jared could see the lines of power radiating outward from the center.

Holding the tray before him, John stood in the center of the star circle, slowly turning so that the tray pointed toward Mrs. Jenkins. She walked clockwise around the perimeter of circle, singing wordlessly in a clear alto. John joined in then with the melody, and Jared recognized the Song.

How could he know this Song?

He started forward, but someone grabbed his shoulder hard. Peter. No matter how desperately he twisted, Jared couldn't pull free. He would have cursed at the man, but he couldn't bring himself to interrupt the Song.

At long last the Song seemed to sigh into another, softer rhythm. John walked to the perimeter. At each standing stone, Mrs. Jenkins took one of the rocks from the tray, and placed it in a slight hollow on top.

One by one the stones were taken from the tray and put in their proper places. The Song was done, but two hollows remained empty. John and Mrs. Jenkins stopped in confusion.

"Where are they?" Peter's hand squeezed Jared's shoulder painfully. It would be purpling to a bruise soon, Jared thought. He glared at the man.

"Jared," John strode over to him. "There are only ten."

"Yeah?" Fighting down his anger, Jared made his face smooth into bewilderment.

"There should be twelve. There must be two more. Where are the other stones, son?" John grasped his arm.

Two bruises.

"I'm not your son!" Jared snapped and finally managed to twist away. "These are the ones in my rock collection. If you want more, find them yourself!"

Raging, he turned and ran back up the uneven stairs, through the kitchen, to the yard and then out of the gate. The smoldering clouds had receded, apparently as quickly as they had appeared. Jared didn't stop running until he threw himself onto the sweet grass of the White Peak. He felt, rather than saw Mattie stand guard over him, her warm, strong body pressed against his side.

The strength of the earth flowed into him. Spoke to him. Jared lifted his face, and his eyes sought out the grim outlines of the Dark Peak. John, Peter and the others had it all wrong. There – that was where the fight should be. And the place for the rocks was on the surface of the earth, not buried in a cave beneath it. The power couldn't be used there, any more than the giant who slept beneath the earth could simply rouse and fight Kronos.

Alone on the windswept hill, Jared faced what he had somehow known since he completed the first circle. He alone was chosen. This was his battle. Jared's breath rasped in ragged fear. No one, not even John, could fight this battle for him.

The Sleeper
and the Song

The Song floats over the hills and Jared sits up. He can hear every note and trill, the words and chorus. It is many songs, blended and intertwined, deepening and resonating through time and stars. It is the Song of creation.

The power and joy of it flow through Jared, spinning him back through time. He is the music; all that he has been drops away. Vaguely, at a distance, he wonders who he was, what his name was. All forgotten, unimportant, in the joy of the Song.

He becomes aware of others in the dance of light and creation. The Song swirls them into being. He sings gleaming stars, exploding volcanoes, skittering bugs, soaring birds, heaving oceans and a fox cub playing in a primordial forest. It is all things glorious.

Then the Song begins to change. The perfect melody doesn't waver, but there are different words twining through the chorus. The harmony becomes discordant. Still he sings, but it becomes harder and harder to remember the words. He sings courage to a starving hunter in a snow storm, comfort to a deer fleeing hopelessly before a forest fire, warning before an avalanche of rocks roars down across a cluster of huts. He stubbornly sings the old words, but new ones begin to drown his voice. Waves of cacophonous sound flood over the Song.

He begins to see the other singers...Kronos, Rhea, and ten more he seems to know and not know. Then these beings create more beings, and the Song becomes harder and harder to hear.

Desperately he sings, but the new songs roar through the universe in fire and wind. Songs of power and anger and greed. Songs of pain and suffering and cruelty.

The joy is nearly gone. Cling to the Song, to the memory of the words, to the tatters of the chorus of joy. Do not forget it in the cold and hunger and pain.

"A gift for your brothers and sisters, nephew." Prometheus' finger touches his hand. Fire, like the cut of the black rock, burns in his palm.

The fire's indescribable pain burns away the howls and screams of the other songs. He remembers the Songs of creation...the Songs of life.

He holds out his burning hand, and over the years people touch the fire and carry sparks away. Men and women, in tatters and bits, remember the Song. But the rage of Kronos and the others scream through their lives, stamping out sparks.

He holds out his hand still, until at last Kronos turns his eyes toward him. The very earth heaves and vomits flame and death. But he sings the Song. Death swirls around him, and he sings. He holds the fire until men and women take twelve flames and hide them away in the earth's ancient stones.

As he dies, he faintly hears the Song in the bones of the mother earth and the stars of father sky. A Song of life, of hope, of rebirth. He lays his ear to the earth and sleeps.

Chapter 18

My Son

Jared put his arm around Mattie and burrowed his face in her thick fur. How could he know about the giant who slept, about the earth that sheltered them all, about Kronos and Rhea and the battle to come? How could he know?

The rocks had done this. They had hypnotized him, dumped ideas into his head. Meghan was right. They *were* bad news. How could he fight immortal beings? How did he know they were immortal?

Jared leapt up and raced for the castle. They had never breached the circle. The earth itself protected the people. But They were creeping in, pushing at the edges, watching for a crack.

Panting with fear, Jared ran faster, across the ragged fields, until the gate stood open before him. Once inside the walls, he collapsed, chest heaving, on the front steps. Mattie crowded against him, warm and solid.

"I think I'm a coward," he whispered. She replied with a swift, wet kiss on his mouth. He sat there, soaking up the sunlight, steadying his nerves. Gradually, he became aware of music flowing from an open casement – piano, followed slowly by a flute.

It was the Song again, set in the rhythms and richness of classical music, but the Song nevertheless. Jared got to his feet and went in.

In the music room off the main hall, John was seated at a grand piano. The notes flowed from beneath his supple fingers. Meghan, more and more confidently, rippled the melody from her flute. Ian stood against the wall, arms folded, watching.

Meghan made a mistake, broke off and laughed. John looked up, smiled, and replayed the notes. For an instant Jared was tempted to sing the ancient words, but didn't. There were too many undercurrents here in the castle. Too much danger to let anyone know what he knew. And blushing, Jared realized he didn't want to try singing in front of them with his recently deepened voice.

"Jared," John said, when he saw the boy. "I have to explain to you…"

Jared shook his head and walked out. There was nothing to explain. He made his way to the kitchen, avoiding Mrs. Jenkins.

The passage at the back of the pantry was hidden by a large cupboard. Jared pushed it aside, and tried the door. He wasn't surprised to find it locked.

*   *   *

For Jared, the next few days passed in a dull haze of worry. The skies remained clear but he felt as edgy as if a thunderstorm boiled outside the castle gates. He avoided John, who seemed to accept the rebuff and stopped trying to start a conversation. When he could, Jared sat at the foot of the ancient apple tree, back to its trunk, fingers twined in the lush grass, and tried to lose himself in the tree's connection to earth and sky. But when he felt the tendrils of himself begin to weave into the spirit of the tree, he felt the rot of creeping evil, and yanked himself back.

Two days later, Pat, his mother's former agent drove up. When she got out, Edward Simon accompanied her. Jared watched his mother hesitate, then throw her arms around Pat.

"Oh Deirdre," Pat cried. "I'm so sorry, but we had to get you home. It's time, you know."

His mother nodded, tears streaking her face. Everyone, even Meghan, spent long hours talking and talking. Jared avoided them all.

Other people began to arrive at the castle – famous musicians, people Jared had seen in the business, people he had never seen before in his life. One afternoon as he was lounging against the sun-warmed wall in the front courtyard, Mattie perked up, danced and whined. An old man with a white beard, accompanied by a border collie, walked slowly up the drive. He supported himself with a staff and paused to look up at the towering walls of the Castle.

Jared felt his heart leap. This was the homeless newspaper seller from Seattle! Before the man noticed him, Jared ran and hid himself in the stable. Throbbing with anger, Jared tried to work out how much of his life had been manipulated by the people who were now gathering at the castle. And why? No one but Meghan had known about the power of the rocks.

And no one but him was called by them. Easing past one of the big horses, Jared laid his hand on the stone concealing the First Rock, drawing comfort from its presence. Drawing strength.

The castle's rooms echoed with voices speaking a dozen languages; songs trilled and boomed and whispered through the walls and passageways. Jared carefully kept out of the way, tried to avoid hearing the stumbling attempts of so many to sing the Song.

John sang it again and again, his voice becoming hoarse with the strain of the demanding notes. Deirdre, it seemed could sing it too, but Jared heard with rising panic, that although the others could sing the chorus, no one else could carry the melody. No one asked him if he could sing.

"Why should I care?" he demanded of Mattie. "Why does it matter if anyone can sing it?"

Had the castle people seen him as the messenger, who having delivered the rocks, had finished his role. It angered him so much that he left any room where a singer was struggling with the melody.

But the Song filled him. In his own bedroom, safely buttressed by the thick stone walls, he stood on the green and rose rug and sang the Song. Mattie was his only audience. His voice had gone clear again, a satisfying baritone like John. He never wavered on the hard notes, but lost himself in the joy of the one great Song.

He was humming it to himself when Meghan came in one morning. She fixed her eyes on him. "How do you know that song," she demanded.

"It's the Song sung by my rocks," Jared said. "So I know it."

"Those creepy rocks that you should have thrown away." Meghan bounced hard onto the bed. "Right. Whatever. No one will teach me. Every stinking person in this castle is singing one song, like their lives depend on it, but no one will teach me the words."

"Get real," Jared retorted. "Everybody is making this huge fuss over you. I figured you had your career signed, sealed and delivered."

"I thought so too," Meghan sighed. "But something's wrong, Jar. It's like even when they talk to me, I'm invisible or can't be trusted or something. You know, when I came into the Blue Parlor this morning, Mrs. Jenkins was practicing the chorus with that scary old woman from India?"

Jared nodded.

"She stopped singing in the middle of the line when she saw me. And even Mom told me she didn't really know the words or the melody. That's a lie, Jar. I heard her singing it with John. She knows every note, every phrase. We're the only people here that no one is teaching the song to."

Jared frowned. "Maybe because we're kids..."

"That's not it," Meghan interrupted. "That twelve-year-old who came from Buenos Aires with her mom is in the music room right now. It's *us*, they don't trust, Jared. They think there's something wrong with us."

"We aren't the enemy," Jared argued. "We don't scare up storms and bash people around."

"Maybe they think we do. Maybe the storms started when we came." Meghan scowled. "I asked mom what the deal was. Her answer is right up there with who our father is. Nothing and nothing and nothing!"

Jared shrugged his shoulders and smiled. "Well, like I said, I know the Song...and I'll teach it to you."

"That's my bro. It's us against them." Meghan grinned and hopped off the bed.

They stood on the rug together, with the dogs listening and thumping their tails. As Jared sang and his twin's voice soared in, it was as if he soared free among the cosmos again, hearing the winds of creation. He felt the sleeping giant stir as the Song soared from the open window and filled the sky.

They had begun the chorus when the door exploded open.

"Stop!" Mrs. Jenkins shouted.

Feeling like he had slammed back to earth, Jared faltered and stopped. Meghan's voice died away too.

The castle people crowded into the room. Jared felt himself wanting to stand protectively in front of his sister.

"How do you know it?" John demanded. "How can you know the Song?"

"Obvious, wouldn't you say," Ian interjected lazily. "Their father taught them!"

"No," Deirdre cried. "No, Ian. You won't say that!"

Jared felt his breath coming fast.

"I'll sing what I want!" Meghan yelled. "And you lied to me, Mom," she turned on their mother.

"Meggie, listen..."

"No," she said. "No! I'm tired of listening. Everything about our life was a lie and I tried so hard to help you."

Jared grabbed Ian's sleeve. "Who is our father?" he demanded. Ian laughed bitterly, shook off his hand, and strode out of the room.

*   *   *

Jared didn't come out of his room that evening. It seemed no one noticed. He stood at his window for a long time, staring at the Dark Peak. As the sun set, there was a tap at the door. His mom came in with a plate of dinner.

"Jared, honey," she whispered. "Are you okay?"

He didn't turn around, didn't answer. When he heard the door close again, he saw Mattie up on her hind legs, sniffing eagerly at the plate on the dresser.

Jared ate some and fed the rest to Mattie. She buried the salad under the rug.

Thinking she might need to go out, Jared left with her and slipped down the long passageways. Everywhere he heard snatches of the Song, and with savage satisfaction, he knew none was exactly right.

For awhile he paced beside the kitchen garden, staring morosely at the sprouting vegetables and herbs, realizing that unless the stuff came wrapped in cellophane, he couldn't even identify the source of his dinner. He had felt so wanted, so at home when they first came to the castle. As though the tangle of his past had begun to unknot. But there were new snarls he had never imagined.

Feeling angry and all at loose ends, Jared went in search of his twin. She wasn't sulking in her bedroom – she was in the music room with everyone else. Watching from the doorway, Jared saw her flit from one recognizably important person to another – as brittle as an ice butterfly. When Ian idly played chords on the grand piano, Meghan lilted across the room and bent over him. She giggled. Jared thought that only he would recognize the false note in his sister's demeanor – she had her own way of dealing with the deceptions practiced on them. Ian leafed through the music, then with a loud introductory flurry, the two of them began a duet of a popular show tune. Conversation stopped. Eyes turned toward the pair, some appreciative, some faintly condemning.

Jared listened for perhaps half the song, then left again. The walls of the castle, the incessant snatches of Song that excluded him, made him restlessly irritated. He had to get away from them. Leaving the main rooms, he headed out the front door, across the courtyard and through the gate to the open lands surrounding them. Out on the hill, he stood listening to calls of the birds and the rustling of sweet grass, letting out his breath slowly as peace begin to slip over him. All of them were singing notes and phrases of the Song. He almost missed the *clip clop* of the horse's hooves. Mattie pressed against Jared's legs, and growled low in her throat.

Kronos looked down at him from the back of his great stallion. "You must decide soon, Jared. You appear so human, but even my enemy knows you aren't what you appear, doesn't he?"

Jared's throat felt frozen. He could never make it back to the safety of the castle before Kronos...did what to him?

"What do you want?" Jared croaked.

Thunder pealed across the countryside. Clouds scudded across the sun. Kronos laughed and leaned over his horse's neck, closer. "Everything, boy. It is my right. I will have it all. You may join me, or you may die...my son..."

His image faded, leaving the hillside empty. Jared sank to his knees, trying not to vomit. Thunder cracked again, and the rain began. It pelted down over him, icy and pure. The wind roared across the valley, shrieking and thrashing through the trees. Wanting to simply sink into the ground, to sleep and be done with all this, Jared didn't move until he felt Mattie trembling violently against him.

That roused him. Gathering what strength he had left, Jared murmured gently to her as he picked her up and held her trembling body close to his chest. She sighed and swiped her tongue across his chin as he slogged up the muddying hill. "It's okay," he whispered. "It's going to be okay."

Rivulets ran everywhere. Clods of grass washed away, exposing grey-white stone.

Rain lashed him and his feet slipped again and again. But he stayed upright and carried Mattie through the Castle gates and into the warmth that lay within.

He found Mrs. Jenkins in the kitchen. "Mattie is wet through," he said.

"Oh my lord," she declared, then awkwardly patted his shoulder, "and honey, you're no better off yourself. You sit yourself down right there. I'll get towels for that poor puppy and some hot cocoa for you."

She draped a thick towel over his shoulders and put a hot mug in his hands. He was trembling so violently that he could hardly hold it. Mrs. Jenkins kept up a flow of chatter while she dried Mattie.

"Where's John?" Jared asked abruptly.

"In the music room, darlin'," she said. "Everybody else has gone on to the big hall for dessert."

Jared nodded his thanks and put down the untouched cocoa. In the vast entry hall, he saw Meghan talking earnestly with Ian. She laughed suddenly, joyfully, and so Jared slipped into the music room before she saw him.

John was alone, moodily picking out the tune of the Song on the piano. He looked up when Jared entered.

Jared crossed the floor to stand in front of him. "I saw Kronos," he said. "He told me I had to choose. He called me his son."

He was fighting down panic, waiting desperately for John to tell him that everything Kronos had said was a lie, that he would wake up from this nightmare and all would be well again. For long moments there was silence.

"Do you know the story of the birth of King Arthur?" John said at last, seeming to be studying the piano keys.

"I...I'm not sure." Jared wanted to scream. He only wanted reassurance, not more history.

"King Uther fell in love with Ygraine who was married to Gorlois, Duke of Cornwall. He convinced Merlin to change his appearance to that of Ygraine's husband. Merlin did. Uther went to Ygraine, appearing as her husband, and fathered Arthur. I have researched, pieced together fact, legend, and my knowledge of the immortals. I think it was not Uther who was Arthur's father, but Kronos. He has done this so many times before over history. Legends, especially Greek legends, are riddled with accounts similar to this."

Jared opened his mouth and shut it again. He knew. The rocks had taken him there... shown this to him.

"And he did it again," John said. "Sixteen years ago. I am your mother's husband. But Kronos...when he took my place, I don't know how identical he made himself to me. I want to believe that he was exactly like me – took my exact genetic pattern. You *are* my son and Meghan *is* my daughter."

"But you aren't sure," Jared managed to say.

"No," John said sadly. "I'm not sure."

The Gift

For ten years, the gods and the Titans battled, not caring about the destruction of other living beings on the earth. At last the gods won, and Zeus banished his father, Kronos, to Tartarus, the region below hell.

The gods lived where all was beautiful and without pain or hunger. It was not so on earth.

One of the immortals left their hall and traveled among the creatures of the earth, and most of all among its people. They gave him many names: Prometheus or Raven or Ainu or Coyote or El or Thor or Lummi or Mercury or a hundred others. He saw the wreckage of earth and had compassion for its people.

He stole fire from the gods and gave it to humankind. With the light in their campfires came light in their minds. They called themselves, The People. As they named and knew themselves, so they struggled to name and know all of their world. From the new knowledge and the old memories they created art and song and writing – a magic of their own. In time, the people became strong enough to forget about the immortals.

But the gods did not forget them. Their own battles forgotten, the gods waged war with their weapons of wind, earth and waves, and above all, of cruelty, greed and anger. They released the four horsemen – Famine, Plague, Drought and War. The horsemen rode among the generations and ate well.

Unable to defeat the immortals, fearing ultimate destruction, the leaders of the people bound the fire of their humanity into the rocks of the earth and hid them.

The immortals wreaked their cruelty where they could, but they waited. Even rocks wear down in time. The Guardians spent their generations protecting the knowledge of the stones and preparing for the time when the stones must be remade.

Chapter 19

Home

Mattie followed faithfully as Jared trod across the flagstones in the great hall. How many centuries had these stones lain here?

Another day had passed. The crowd had settled into the dining room for yet another feast prepared by Mrs. Jenkins. The sun was lowering over the land, casting shadows, not yet fully dark.

Jared couldn't eat. All day, he'd been watching himself for differences. Differences that would come from a father who was not human. Terrified at what he'd find...more terrified that he would live the rest of his life not knowing who he truly was. His dream of ever having a normal life seemed laughable now.

Restless, he headed up one of the oldest stairways in the castle. The narrow stone walls brushed his shoulders and the rough steps twisted in a tight, uneven corkscrew. He hadn't investigated this route yet. Every half-hidden passage and corridor and staircase winding through the ancient castle seemed to lure him on with the hope of answers. And exploring gave him something to do besides rage at the broken Song drifting through every room.

After climbing and climbing the stairs stopped at an arched doorway held with an old iron latch. Jared pulled it open and stepped out onto a weather beaten walkway edging the battlements. Breathing deeply, he gazed out across the rolling landscape. Mattie stood on her hind legs, paws on the low wall and looked out beside him. Below, the village nestled in the mounding green hills, lights shining steadily against the gathering night. Beyond, the Dark Peak waited, cloud-hung, a great mindless beast rousing from slumber.

Before long, he heard steps mounting the steps behind him.

John barely glanced at the vista spread before them. His expression was stony. "We have to have the last two stones," he said. "I know you have them, Jared, or you couldn't have made the circle."

Jared stared out at the hillside. John should have been his father, but Kronos had ruined that too. "The stones are meant for me," he replied finally. "They came to me. I'm the only one who can really use them."

"And what will you use them for?" John demanded. "I am trying to save our world. I've spent my life learning the Song that will remake the stones – keep the old gods from destroying us."

Visions swirled in Jared's mind – the words and suffering of each person who had passed a sacred stone to him. If he couldn't make John understand, he knew there was no hope for any of them. But the magnitude of what he had seen seemed beyond words, beyond his power to explain. Instead he fell back on what he had argued before. "The stones came to me! The Song came to me!" he said. "You have to trust me!"

John gripped the boy's arm. "Then trust *me!* With the stones I can complete the circle. When the sunrise gathering begins in three days, your mother and I will sing north and south, and Ian and Mrs. Jenkins will sing east and west. The chorus will swell with all the other guardians. The stones will be remade – Kronos and all the others will finally be driven back."

Jared could see the gathering now, as if he had attended a thousand. Two men and two women, the two sides of humanity standing as pillars of the four elements, the four winds, and the four seasons of the earth. Singing their fragile humanity into the twelve bones of their mother, the earth. Resisting the fury of the gods. This was how his people would outlast the immortality of the old ones.

"Try to understand, Jared," John pleaded. "We sing every year, but the stones themselves have only been remade five times. Last time, the Guardians had become scattered, and the singing nearly faltered. From the Dark Ages, we have had a millennium of Kronos loose on the earth. In this century, as the stones weakened, we've suffered destruction of every kind – two world wars, plagues of new diseases, devastating weather shifts. Can you imagine what will happen if we can't remake the stones – all the stones!"

Behind him, over the land, Jared heard the melodies of the earth, of the small songs. The words of each Guardian whispered in his mind. He understood now. The Song had to be perfect to remake the stones. A flaw, any flaw, would allow Kronos to rise to full power, to split the world apart.

But there was a huge flaw in John's plan.

"Mrs. Jenkins can't sing the whole Song," Jared said. "I've heard her. She stumbles every time. And what about Ian?"

"They'll learn it by the Singing," John said. His hands tightened on the stone balustrade. "They have to."

"You know they can't!" Jared retorted. "But Meghan and I already know the Song...I think we were born knowing it. We have to be the east-west singers."

Thunder rolled above them. Over the Dark Peaks the skies split with lightning. The lights in the village below suddenly disappeared.

"He's closing in," John said, voice tight. He turned to Jared. "Kronos can bind you – with heritage and with gifts of all the things you've never had. I believe you want to help, but I can't risk the world against the chance you might weaken."

"I won 't weaken," Jared insisted. "He...he has come after me before."

John looked startled, but after a pause reached out and gripped his shoulder. "Kronos offers everything – wealth, friends, parties... even the games and gadgets teenagers all want?" John's eyes searched his face. "If you join Kronos and win you can rule the world, command the elements, have everything you wish for instantly."

Jared laughed. The weight he had carried forever, had fallen from his back. "If I join you," he said, "I can have a home. And that's all I've ever really wanted."

Jared found himself being hugged fiercely. "My son, my son," John said roughly. "*He* couldn't steal you after all."

For a moment Jared clung to his father, then they fell back, faces covered in idiotic grins.

"Well," John said, scrubbing at his wet eyes.

"The rocks," Jared grinned. "And I have to find Meghan."

They went down the ancient staircase and made their way to the music room. Despite the late hour, many of the people were still there. Someone was playing popular music on the piano and a few were singing. Deirdre was among them.

Jared waited for a break, then, "Mom have you seen Meghan?"

Deirdre glanced around. "I guess she went to bed, Jar." She eyed John and her son. "What's up?"

John put his hand on Jared's shoulder. "We've just been chatting."

A flush rose up Deirdre's face and her smile broke like sunrise. "I see."

"How about another song?" Edward Simon interrupted.

"John," Mrs. Jenkins clutched his sleeve. "Could I have a word with you?"

"Well, I..." He caught the shadowed look on her face. "Certainly, Gayle."

"I'm going to find Meghan," Jared said. He slipped out of the room, and with Mattie at his heels ran up the main staircase two steps at a time. Finally, everything would work out. He and Meghan would have a home. The circle would be made whole and Kronos didn't have a chance against this family!

He faltered to a stop. Billy lay outside Meghan's door, head on his paws, whimpering softly.

Jared rapped on the closed door. Nothing. He hesitated, not sure what to do. The two dogs began circling at his feet making soft growling noises in their throats. Jared retraced his steps and went into his own bedroom. For a moment he stood on the thick carpet, considering what to do. Maybe she was just asleep. She hated being woken up. But this was important.

Jared gently opened the door between their rooms. The light had been left on. The room looked ransacked.

The wardrobe doors hung open, drawers were pulled out, the waste basket had been knocked over, and used tissues cascaded onto the carpet. The bed had not been slept in.

Jared froze, only his eyes darting around the room. On the mantle, an envelope was propped against the stone chimney. *Jared* was scrawled across the front.

He grabbed it and ripped it open.

Twelve   315

Jar,

My Big Chance has happened!!
Ian's offered me the lead in a BBC documentary he's producing about traditional singing. It'll be a local village festival thing with the traditional costumes and well dressings and me singing that song everybody around here is so crazy for. I can't take any more of this down home, country house life with everybody oh-so-politely snubbing us. We're leaving before Mom or John get wind and try to stop me.

I took that disgusting black rock with me – I know it's got you mumbo-jumboed so you won't get rid of it. Ian knows some collector who'll pay a mint for it. Look after Billy for me. I'll call you from London.

Meghan

Jared stared unbelieving at the letter. Meghan was gone. Meghan had taken the rock. The set was incomplete. The singers would be incomplete.

Kronos would win.

Jared pounded down the stairs. His first thought was to find John, but he had to make sure Meghan had really taken the Black Rock.

He tore out the back entrance and ran to the stable. Sure enough, the stone hiding the black rock was lying on the floor of the stall. The hole was empty. Frantic, Jared turned back to the place where he'd hidden the First Rock and pried out the stone. The rock was there, gleaming softly in the moonlight. Jared eased it out, slid it into his pocket and ran back toward the Castle, both dogs at his heels. He burst into the kitchen where John and Mrs. Jenkins stood talking in low voices.

"John," he interrupted. "Meghan's gone!"

"Meghan?" His father sounded bewildered.

"No, darlin'," Mrs. Jenkins said in a tight voice. "It's Ian that left a couple of hours ago. Back to London – and at a time like this. And him raised to the work, too...."

"He took Meghan," Jared interrupted. "And one of the rocks. We have to find them!"

John sat heavily down at the long table. "Ian," he said. "My brother..."

"John, we have to find them!" Jared pulled at his arm.

Mrs. Jenkins leaned back against a cupboard as though her knees had gone weak. "Oh no, it can't be Ian..."

"Yes, it can," John said. "How else could Kronos have been tracking Deirdre and the children, getting closer and closer? And Aaron.

How else could he have trapped Aaron? It makes sense – terrible sense. Ian always wanted fame and power and above all, a lot more money than this life can offer."

"Like Meghan," Jared whispered. His sister wanted fame and money and the power that went with it. Meghan wouldn't betray him... Meghan had taken the black rock...

"If Ian's made a deal with Kronos," Jared cried, "we've got to do something – right now. He's got Meghan!"

John roused himself. "I'll get our strongest people together. If Kronos has even one stone, and I step foot outside the castle, he'll kill me. But some of the others could get to London and hunt for Meghan."

"Ian won't hurt her, will he?" Jared forced out.

John squeezed his shoulder. "No. No, of course not."

Only slightly reassured, Jared forced down his panic and followed John to the music room.

"Could I have everyone's attention, please," John called out. As the room became silent, Jared leaned against the wall, his fingers caressing the writing on the First Rock. Briefly John explained to the singers what had happened.

"If They have those two, there's no point risking ourselves," the old man from the bus station argued.

"I'll drive down to London and try to get to Ian's flat," Edward Simon offered. "I'm not powerful enough for Them to bother with."

"My brother Aaron had no power, couldn't even sing," Peter said. "But They killed him anyway. They have no feelings – no sympathy, no mercy, nothing but power, lust and greed."

Deirdre jumped up. "I'm going. If he has Meghan, I won't leave her."

John squeezed her hand. "They'll kill you and you'll have no chance of saving Meghan. Edward will go."

"And I'll go with him." Pat gave Deirdre a hug. "I watched her grow from a baby. No egomaniac immortal's going to mess with one of my clients!"

The group gave a weak laugh. Deirdre sank down on a chair beside the table as though her legs would no longer hold her up. Jared wanted to insist he go too, but knew he wouldn't be allowed to leave the safety of the castle. "What about the rock?" he asked. "Don't we have to get back the rock?"

There was a sudden silence. "We're making plans to remake the missing rock," John said.

"If you give me the other, we have that much greater chance of success."

Jared nodded, but as his fingers touched the cool stone in his pocket, he felt he couldn't give it up. "I've hidden it," he lied. "I'll get it in the morning when it's light."

"In the meantime, I'm off," Edward Simon said. He and Pat strode quickly from the room. John and Peter followed. Deirdre remained at the table, her head sunk in her hands.

Jared awkwardly put his arm around her shoulders. "She'll be okay, Mom," he said. "Meghan is meaner and tougher than anybody. Ian won't have a chance if he tries to double-cross her."

Deirdre gave him a watery smile. "I should have explained everything to you years ago, but how can you tell children that they were fathered by an immortal and you've been careening all over the world to keep him from getting custody."

Jared laughed. "And he never even got us on an Amber alert.'"

They hugged and she gave him a gentle push. "Go to bed, Jar. John knows what he's doing."

Up in his room, Jared realized there was no way he could sleep. Instead he sat on the wide window ledge and stared out at the

Peaks. As always, clouds boiled and lightning crackled the sky. Sometimes he thought it took the shape of a distorted spider. Kronos and Rhea and who knew how many others of the immortals were there, waiting, like hungry spiders in a web. How could Ian have betrayed his family to them?

Jared stayed there all night, thinking and sometimes dozing. His fingers stayed wrapped around the First Rock, a talisman against the evil that was growing.

At dawn, he stretched, stiff and miserable. The sun rose pale and weak, the sky a chilling cast of green. He shivered, clutched the rock and looked toward the road to London. Edward Simon's car was climbing the hill toward them.

Jared flung himself from the room and tore down stairs to meet them at the front door. John, his mother, and Mrs. Jenkins beat him to it. As the door opened, sickly green sunlight oozed across the flagstones, bathing them all in its light. Jared felt a surge of dizziness. Too tired. He clutched the First Stone for strength and felt the numbness ebb away.

"Did you find her?" Deirdre asked.

Edward yawned and stretched. "No," he said, "but Pat and I thought maybe we're going about this the wrong way. We got to Ian's town house all right – left a note tacked to his door asking him to call right away."

"That's all?" Jared demanded.

"Well, I could hardly break down the door, and besides they weren't there anyway," the man smiled cheerfully.

"We thought we'd call the BBC offices a little later this morning, as soon as they're open," Pat added. "See where Ian's planning to shoot this documentary. Meet up with them there."

At his feet, the dogs whined and circled. Jared looked from one to another of the adult faces. John and his mother still frowned slightly, but the others were smiling cheerfully, their faces pale in the wan light.

"What about Kronos?" Jared insisted. "What if he gets her – or the rock?"

"Well, he's got no reason to bother himself about a cute little girl like our Meghan," Mrs. Jenkins said. "It's the stones he wants. Besides, maybe her being related, so to speak, will kind of soften him up."

"I thought he didn't soften up," Jared argued. "I thought the reason we could outlast Them is because they haven't evolved emotions of love and kindness the way we have. Why would he care about Meghan? And what about the rock? We have to have it for the singing."

"Now, Jared, you just don't understand," his mother touched his cheek fondly. "John's got the singing under control. Just one more day and we're going to be free of this monster."

"True enough," John said. "I think we should all take it easy and give Meghan or Ian a chance to call us."

"I'm beat," Edward agreed. "We have almost 24 hours. Plenty of time."

He and Pat left, wandering up the stairs toward the bedrooms. Mrs. Jenkins murmured about fixing breakfast and the others followed her, talking about getting some coffee. Jared stood alone in the hall, stunned. It didn't make sense. They'd all gone crazy.

Morosely he climbed the ancient stairs to the battlements and looked out over the hillside. There were no lights on in the village below, despite the pale morning. The power must be out.

The clouds over the Dark Peaks were lying low. He could pick out the monolithic rocks that jumbled the plain above, and wondered exactly where the immortals lived. Did they haunt those stony wastes like spirits? He knew that they didn't have a body like he did. Bodies break down and die, return to the earth. Zeus and the gods had once imprisoned Kronos and the others in the earth, but they didn't die, didn't become one with the elements of creation. They were the utter antithesis of what it meant to be human or part of the earth.

Troubled by the adults' reactions, Jared wandered downstairs again. In his room, he stretched out on the bed and despite his belief he'd never shut his eyes again, fell into a deep sleep.

The Hall of the Immortals

He stands in a vast hallway of stone and gold that stretches so far he cannot see the distant walls. Kronos, Rhea and ten others lounge in thronelike chairs, gold and jewels shimmering around them. In the center of the room, a fire large enough to fill a hotel lobby, roars and leaps. Surprisingly, it flames above a clear pool of water. A circle of twelve stones seems to be its fuel. The stones crack, pop and then melt at its base. But a moment later they are there again, remade or perhaps never consumed. A hot wind flows from the flames carrying the smell of scorched earth, steam and soot. Jared wrinkles his nose, and turns away.

"Welcome, my son," Kronos drawls. "You have at last journeyed to the house of the gods."

Jared nods at him, feeling neither fear nor pleasure. He wanders over to a window and gazes out into a fantastic garden. It is wild with a jungle of plants – trees, shrubs, flowers, grasses, all more vividly exquisite than any he has ever seen. But he does not like them. They are too bright, too pale, too hot and too cold all at the same time. His eyes are drawn toward a tree, nearly hidden in fog, which seems more like the trees he once knew. As he gazes, the mist clears an instant and he recognizes the brownish-grey bark and soft green leaves of a living tree. He remembers climbing trees in a park, the hand-scraping roughness and green smell of life. It seems surprising that this tree shines silver, and the fruit gleams gold. Yet he knows this tree is very alive. Jared can see now that the rest of the garden has no life. It has been fashioned to outshine life, but it has never breathed nor grown. It is a garden of death.

He looks again at the silver tree, but it has disappeared. He turns back to the great hall.

"Jared..."

Meghan! She lays on a stone slab behind the fire, in front of the immortals. She is as pale as the sick light that shines through the windows. Tears glisten on her cheeks and eyelashes, but Jared can see her try to smile.

"Run, Jared," she whispers. "They'll get you, too,"

Fear sweeps over him. Kronos and Rhea laugh and laugh as he stands there. Quivering. Shriveling in fear and death.

"Jared...run...."

He cries out and tries to run away but his feet are nearly frozen, holding him to the cold stone floor.

The fire is still in front of him and he can't escape it.

"Run, Jared," Meghan breathes.

She is dying, he thinks. If she is dead, he can escape. He wants her dead. He wants to get away from the fear –

326   Susan Brown

it crawls over his skin and gnaws his stomach. He weeps and tries to run again, but the fire is always before him and Kronos' laugh whips and tears him cruelly. The stones are slippery with his own blood...he can see his bones through his rotting flesh...

"Give me the rock!" Kronos commands.

Mad with terror, Jared cries out. At his feet lie the two rocks – the First and the Black Rock.

"Give me your future and I will destroy your fear," Kronos demands.

First Rock. Numbly, Jared reaches for it. As his fingers brush the First Rock, a feeling, like the first birdsong of spring flows through him, breaking apart the terror.

"Take it. Throw it in the fire, and you will be free," Kronos says softly.

The flames lick towards him again, and Jared hears the cries of anguish and death – of his own death. Kronos will free them all from suffering...

"You can be a god. You will never suffer. You will never die. Your sister is the sacrifice that will elevate you."

Jared leans down, clutches the rock and raises his arm to throw....

328   Susan Brown

Chapter 20

Lost Meghan

Jared couldn't move. Something heavy and painful dragged on his arm. He fought, but the ache and weight, spun him away from the house of the gods. His eyes flew open, and he saw Mattie and Billy, their teeth clamped to his arm, floundering in the blankets.

"No!" He sat up and shoved them off the bed. They landed with awkward thumps, twisted and leapt up beside him again.

He was shuddering, sobbing. "Meghan!" he cried. Was she dead? Had he killed her? He hadn't thrown the rock. He hadn't given it to Kronos. The dogs had stopped him.

Trembling so hard, he could barely push back the blankets and pull the socks off his feet. His skin was unbroken, not rotting. On his arm, the dogs' teeth marks were purpling his flesh. This real physical pain was so much less than the pain Kronos had driven through his mind. He was still alive and unharmed! But was his sister? The dogs whimpered.

Jared lurched from bed and stumbled to the window. The sun, still green and sickly, nearly obscured by clouds, was sinking in the sky. The wind was picking up, smelling of rain and thunder to come.

His stomach roiled and his throat was parched. Dogs at his heels, he ran down to the kitchen. Several people were gathered around a spread of food, talking cheerfully, lounging with mugs of tea and coffee. Jared helped himself to a mug and sandwich. A small TV in the corner was turned to the BBC news, although no one seemed to be listening to it, except Mrs. Jenkins.

"India is reeling under the impact of one of the most violent monsoons on record," the announcer was saying. "Relief workers say the devastation is beyond comprehension. Thousands are feared dead as flooded rivers have swept away entire villages." Behind the announcer's immaculate form, bloated bodies lay in muddy, lapping water.

She went on to narrate footage of collapsed buildings from earthquakes in Japan, wailing families standing in tornado tossed rubble in the Midwest of the United States, a seared lava flow victim being loaded into an ambulance in Hawaii.

Jared gulped coffee, trying not to remember the desperate pain of his dream. Pain such as those people were feeling.

The announcer only mentioned the cascading power outages across Great Britain, before the station cut to a scientist talking about the violence of the changing weather patterns.

Like a sleepwalker, Jared turned to John. "Did Meghan or Ian call?"

"Meghan and Ian?" A frown crossed John's face but he shook it off quickly. "No...no...but I expect they're busy."

"We have to find them," Jared insisted. No one paid attention. He tried another tack. "The Gathering! The Singing! It's to be at dawn. There's only 12 hours."

John stretched out his legs. "Yes, yes...I suppose we should organize some kind of car pools to the stone circle."

"Car pools? What about Ian? Who will sing for him? Mom, aren't you worried about Meghan?"

Deirdre smiled. "She's nearly sixteen. And she's with Ian, after all."

"Young folk are always so anxious," Mrs. Jenkins chided. "You want a nice piece of pie, darlin'." She forced a large plate of apple pie into his hands. "These apples of ours give a body strength. Eat the pie, Jared, honey."

"It's good pie," Peter grunted. His gaze swiveled to Jared. "You ought to know better than to be worrying about things that John has under control."

"How?" Jared demanded. "How is it under control?"

John shrugged. "We have ten of the rocks. And Hope isn't lost or else we'd be awfully depressed!" The others laughed as though it were a great joke.

"Hope? Do you know what each rock is?" Jared asked.

"Yes of course – Transformation is the first, then Hope, and Mercy..."

"...Sacrifice, Loyalty and Courage," Peter interjected.

Deirdre smiled at Jared, "And then Compassion, Creativity, Faith and Love of growing things...."

"Don't you forget Reverence for the earth," Mrs. Jenkins interrupted. "That's my personal favorite."

"That's eleven," Jared said softly. He recognized them all now – but the black rock was not among them. "Do you know what the black rock is?"

John stirred uneasily. "It's one of the great rocks."

Peter stirred his coffee. "We're better off without it."

Jared thought of the old man lying in his own blood all those years ago. Of the agonies of meaningless suffering and death. "The black rock holds fear," Jared said. "Fear of evil."

"Oh let's not talk about that awful stuff," Mrs. Jenkins exclaimed. "I still got more of my special pie that needs to be eaten. And Jared, honey, why don't you go find a good book to read. Kind of calm you down."

Jared left. Kronos had the Black Rock, perhaps had destroyed it. There was no fear left in any of the people who had come for the Gathering. Without fear, there was no urgency to saving Meghan – or themselves. The storms, floods and disasters would sweep them away and they would never realize they faced such mortal danger.

All the fear they were missing seemed to be inside himself. But he could still walk, think, plan. The stone in his pocket had saved only him from the mindless placidity of cows in a field.

He would not let Kronos take his sister. But what could he do? How could he find out how to defeat a god? He laughed without humor. He might as well take Mrs. Jenkins suggestion and find a good book to read. Maybe mythology...about the defeat of the gods...

Jared ran into the library.

On John's desk, a book of Greek mythology lay open – the story of how Rhea had tricked Kronos into allowing Zeus to live, and the prophecy that only Kronos' own children had the power to defeat him.

Jared took a deep breath. Mythology was a way for people to explain their world. It wasn't history. It wasn't a promise. But there was truth in it nonetheless. With leaping heart, he accepted that he had been fathered by Kronos. To save Meghan, Jared had to overthrow the immortal. Only the god's own children could defeat him.

Billy whined and circled impatiently by the door.

"We'll find her," Jared said. "I promise."

Checking through shelf after shelf, he found John's section on local books. Choosing a book of hiking trails, he flipped to the right page and traced the path to the Dark Peak. The guidebook warned of its dangers – sudden winds amid the rocks that had blown climbers to their deaths, and mists that had caused hikers to stumble into watery bogs and drown.

Jared tore the map from the guidebook and left the study. The party had moved to the music room where loud choruses of show tunes were being sung. Jared ran toward the front door then skidded to a stop. Mrs. Jenkins barred the way.

"I have to go," he told her.

She smiled. "What? Run all the way to Dark Peak? You wouldn't make it, darlin', and even if you did, you'd be so tired out and late, it wouldn't do you and your sweet little sister any good at all."

"Then what?" Jared demanded.

She laughed suddenly, lines crinkling around her deep green eyes. "Why, honey, I think you'd better drive." She tossed something in the air and Jared caught it instinctively – the key to Edward Simon's car. "And take a few of these good, sweet apples, too," she said. "Help keep up your strength."

Bewildered, he took the paper sack, then he and the dogs tore out the door.

The many-paned windows of the music room faced the courtyard where Simon's car was still parked. In their present mood, Jared was sure no one would notice his movements.

He slipped into the driver's side; the two dogs leapt in with him. Mattie sat up in the front seat. Billy settled in the back. Both looked as though they were standing sentinel – or riding shotgun.

He tossed the apples onto the seat. Fumbling in haste, Jared stuck the key in the ignition. As the engine cranked and squealed. Billy leaned over his shoulder and barked.

"I know. I'm hurrying." Jared touched his foot to the gas and tried again. This time the engine roared. Trying to remember exactly what he had seen drivers do, he eased the car into gear. It lurched forward. He turned the wheel and aimed the car toward the gate. The car jerked crazily from side to side as he got used to steering. It was delicate, responding even to movements he didn't intend. A big streak of black paint was left on the gatepost.

And then they were cruising – fast, too fast – down the hill toward the village.

Jared did his best to maneuver, but more paint streaked signposts and stone walls. If he survived this night, he'd bet Simon would kill him. A middle-aged man and woman were walking down the village's unlit sidewalk. Jared just missed them.

"Watch it, then!" the man shouted after him. Jared hunched over the wheel and kept driving.

All too soon, he left the village and turned onto the narrow highway. Above, thunder and lightning crashed and rolled. Trees bent as blasts of wind buffeted the car. In the flashes of light he saw sheep and cattle huddled against sheds and outcroppings of rock. Houses lit only by candlelight faded against the deep night and searing lightning. Sometimes Jared heard snatches of song, or saw groups of people wandering aimlessly by the farm houses. They had all lost their fear of the dark.

Panting lightly, his hands gripped the wheel until his knuckles whitened. He had enough fear for the whole world.

Too many cars were on the road and he had several close calls. Once Mattie whimpered, then barked defiantly at a truck that barreled down the center. Jared swerved nearly into a ditch. He grabbed the map with one hand and cranked the wheel to avoid a motorcycle with the other. Following the map, he headed down the road to Edale and in panting relief turned into a car park by the pub. He would have to cover the rest of the distance on foot.

Even though wind howled and rain lashed out, the narrow streets were full of people who should long since have gone to bed. A few were dancing to soundless music. Mattie and Billy kept close as Jared trudged up the lane to the path to the moors. A group of teenagers laughingly smashed windows. A policeman strolled by and laughed too.

The scant light from the village faded. Beneath his feet, the gravel path crunched. He passed through a stile and mounted slippery steps to a wooden foot bridge. The water was hidden in gloom below, but Jared could hear the sullen roar. On the other side, they passed through another gate, then scrambled up ancient stone steps into a pasture full of sheep. The animals watched without moving as Jared and the dogs ran along the path's smooth-laid field stones. Once Jared slipped on slick rock and crashed to the ground. The dogs snuffled and circled in their anxiety. He forced himself to his feet, and they went on.

Thunder growled on the Peak. The slope rose hard and steep, jumbled with rock and snagged by twisting gorse and heather. Higher and higher the hill rose – to the Dark Peak. Sudden flashes of lightning exposed vast, tortured outcroppings crowning the summit.

He left the pasture. The trail became rough and twisty. Continual flashes of lightning streaked across the landscape. The torrent of water on Jared's left shone the color of old blood. He hunched his shoulders and kept walking. In the far distance, towering over the moor at the top of the Peak, he could see a greenish light pulsing over the black land. It was Kronos' Hall.

Jared struck out across the treacherous ground, forcing his way through heather and brush. The dogs coursed ahead sniffing and testing for the clearest path. Even with their help, Jared skidded on slick mud and twisted his ankle on rough outcroppings. Wind howled endlessly.

In the throbbing light, Jared saw the dogs stop short, raise their heads, and then in whining agitation circle a stony mound. He stumbled forward. Arched unnaturally over a jumble of rocks, lay a broken body. It was Ian.

Jared screamed. Ian's eyes rolled open. Head lolling, he tried to focus his eyes.

"Betrayed me...." Ian whispered hoarsely. "Rule the world with him...I betrayed John... Kronos betrayed me...." He laughed and cried at the same time.

"Where is Meghan?" Jared cried.

"Help me, Jared," he groaned. "Save me... broke my back...left me here...Get help..."

Jared leaned over his uncle and grabbed the cold lump of his hand. Surges of remembered pain racked him.... He shook himself from the oozing fear. "Meghan," he insisted. "Where is she, Ian? Please!"

"Too late for her.... Help me, Jared...before he kills you too..."

The wind dropped. The mists rose and curled around them like caressing fingers. Ian sobbed in the sudden stillness, his body dreadfully still and only his face convulsing. " She's gone...get help for me..."

Meghan dead....

"No! She's my twin! If she were dead, I'd know it. You're lying!" With a sob, Jared dropped Ian's hand and stumbled back. Lightning lit Ian's dead-white face and scoured the crags above. "I'm sorry...I'm sorry..."

The dogs growled low in her throats, and heads down like hunters, they moved up the slope. Cold mist licked up around them. Jared ran after them. He didn't look back when Ian cried out again.

For another hour he fought lashing rain and wind, but at last he reached the top. Stretching across the horizon, wind-carved stone stood sentinel. Fog rose thickly from peat bogs. The gale ceased suddenly, leaving his ears ringing from remembered cacophony. Jared wiped his sleeve across his dripping face and set out toward the distorted, castle-shaped rocks.

The silence was absolute now, broken only by the scrabbling of their feet over sudden outcrops and his own labored breathing. Occasionally Jared heard a soft whimper from the dogs, but they never slackened their pace.

Ahead, darkness lay within darkness. Jared struggled toward it. The dogs led him through a shallow stream, and then between two great misshapen stones. Before him stood a door made of iron, framed by uneven stones and timbered lintels.

The dogs fell back. Mattie whimpered softly at his feet. Billy pressed close against his calf and cried.

Jared touched their warm heads. "We'll find her, Billy."

The iron door swung back. Jared and the dogs passed through.

It was the hall of his dream, but richer, more ornate. Tapestries hung on the walls. Red-eared dogs lolled about on the flagstones, panting softly. Jared didn't look too closely at the bones between their paws. In the center of the room, the great fire burned, living flames writhing above a still pool.

Through the leaping flames he saw Kronos and Rhea sitting on huge stone thrones. They were flanked by other stone chairs, mistily occupied. Jared couldn't make them out. The fire flickered over the throne's polished rock, gilding it with light, shimmering like gold and jewels.

The flames parted a moment and Jared cried out. Between Kronos and Rhea sat

Meghan, still in her jeans and favorite sweater, gazing without expression or even a flicker of movement. Clenched in her bleeding hands, she held the Black Rock.

The Quest for the Iron Cauldron

At the command of the chief of the old gods, the nine maidens of Caer Feddwid in Annwn spoke their spells, brewed their charms, and walked widdershins around their iron cauldron. They bound the magic with four unanswerable riddles:

From what direction does the wind blow?
Where does the ocean begin?
Is fire but a single spark?
Who feeds the earth?

When the last word was spoken, the cauldron slowly filled, simmering and bubbling. Across the world, fires raged, winds blew, and tides threatened to drown the land.

The blossoms on the apple trees of Avalon withered and dropped with no fruit swelling after. In Camelot, the king lay dying. Arthur tossed in dreams of fog-ridden death and no doctor-brewed potion could rouse him. The land rotted from within, and the king and land are one.

Merlin peered through his hollow scrying stone into the past, the present, and the future. He saw all things, including the birth and death of the King. He gazed past the world as far as the green island, along the river of night and into the pearl-edged cauldron in the fortress of Caer Feddwid. He saw the land's plenty simmering in the iron cauldron. Sadly, he went at once to the king and told him what he had seen and what must be done, even to death. Arthur knew that Merlin spoke the truth.

Arthur let out a great cry of despair, for he saw that his doom was upon him. But he struggled up from his bed, took his sword Excalibur and with the best of his knights set sail for the green island in the west.

On the first night wind blew like iron fists. Waves lashed into mountains. Lightning shattered their masts. Before daybreak, the first ship was lost and all the brave warriors with her.

On the second night, a bitter fog oozed over the heaving water. The captains and warriors heard the thunder of waves on rocks, but could not tell from where. Two burning lanterns appeared in the night. The men shouted their deliverance and the captains steered for a harbor. But there was none. The second ship dashed itself on the shore and all the men were lost – all but Taleisin. The young bard was imprisoned in Caer Feddwid, held with a blue-grey chain, and doomed to sing his songs and laments to the gods until the breaking of the cauldron.

Only Arthur's flagship, the Prydwen sailed ahead. On the third night, two lights appeared again, but having learned bitter caution, the ship steered carefully. Two huge iron doors set in the cliff, stood open. This was the entrance to Annwn.

Without sail or oars they drifted through still, black water. Rock breathed so close, that the broken mast scraped above. For nine days, the current carried the ship deeper and deeper into the earth, until at last it came to rest in a rocky harbor. Before them rose Caer Feddwid, the Hall of the Immortals. It stood tall and four cornered, light glancing off it like sun on whirling glass.

The walls were manned by six thousand warriors. Here is where Arthur, greatest of the kings of Britain, fought his last battle. He wielded Excalibur for three days and three nights. He killed hundreds of his enemies, but each sunrise they were reborn from the magic of the cauldron. He fought on until all but seven of his men lay broken and bleeding around him. It was then that the Prince of Annwn threw a silver lance that shattered the King's armor and pierced his chest.

With the king's own life blood running from him, the seven knights fought their way to the Prydwen and sailed back through the cavern of black water until they reached open sea again. In sorrow they steered the crippled boat to Britain and carried Arthur to the island of Avalon. There he died.

His body was buried deep in the earth in a coffin made from the trunk of a hollow oak. To hide him from the eyes of the gods, his grieving people laid a lead cross over the grave and a stone over that. As the king's blood seeped into the ground, the goodness came back into the land and it was made whole again.

As was foretold, Arthur's blood bound him to the land forever. When there is need enough, the land will give back that life. The cauldron will be broken and King Arthur will fight the old gods once again.

Chapter 21

The Singing

"Meghan!" Jared screamed. Nothing. Desperate he tried to run around the fire, but the thrones were always on the far side.

"What have you done to her?" he shouted at Kronos. He rushed around the other side. But like a crazy dream, no matter how he ran, he could not go around the circle.

The creature laughed. "Oh, being part human, I thought she should be the keeper of one of humanity's treasures – waiting patiently until you came, Jared."

"What did you do?"

"She refused to give the rock to me – and I offered her so much wealth and fame too. So I allowed her to hold the rock...and to become the holder of all the visions within it. Ever heard the expression, 'paralyzed by fear'? If she hadn't had rather unusual parentage, she would have died from it."

The hall thundered with his laughter.

"Oh, Meghan..." Jared tried again to race around the pool of fire. Heat licked at him. Meghan, blood dripping from her fingers, sat frozen, still separated by the wall of flame.

But he could see the Black Rock clearly. The stench of its hideous fear spewed toward him. He faltered back two, then three steps. He could feel it oozing toward him. His own small fears – *the childish terror of being alone in the echoing hotel room, the airplane sheering to one side and nearly crashing, the old man lying in blood in South Africa.* Behind the small fears lay an avalanche of despair. A thousand thousand mothers and fathers weeping for dying children...flesh rotting from bomb-torn limbs...hunger clawing and burrowing into a million bellies.

Kronos and Rhea laughed.

Behind the waves of suffering, Jared heard hoof beats – not the heart rhythm of the Song, but discordant pounding of harmony gone wrong. The Four Horsemen, famine, plague, war and death left their tracks in the Black Rock. Kronos' power thundered from the ageless sky as his riders ravaged the generations.

Meghan was slung over their saddles.

He had to run, escape...

Meghan...

"Let her go, Kronos – she's your daughter! Have pity on her!"

"Have pity, Kronos," jeered Rhea.

"I am not human," he told Jared. "I have neither love nor pity in me. A fire does not care whether it warms or burns; the wind does not worry if it fills a sail or rips apart a trailer park; water has no desire to sustain life or drown it; earth is indifferent to whether it grows food or crushes villages. I am of the elements. I am a god!"

"Not my god," Jared shouted.

Kronos raised one finger. Swirling before him Jared saw the distorted spider. It was telling him something, reminding him... the juggling sticks he had once had – taken from him, like everything else, everything. No money, no home, no friends.

"A god takes everything he wants, " Kronos said. "It is our nature. Sit by my side, my son, and you will never suffer again."

"Kill him and be done with it," Rhea interrupted. "These offspring of yours are too human and weak to live."

"Be silent." He smiled at Jared who stood unable to move. "I give you, my last son, a last choice. Throw the stone of Transformation into the eternal flames. Destroy it and I will destroy fear – and all your suffering. Become a god sitting by my side, or you will surely die."

The immortal leaned forward holding out his hand. Jared's hand began to move toward the god's, but then, he plunged it into his pocket, grabbing tight to the First Rock.

"If being immortal means being like you, I'd rather die," Jared shouted.

He ran forward, directly into the flame. Don't let me die, he silently begged the Rock. I have to reach Meghan...

His feet moved in slow motion. He felt, his shoes and socks burn away, and screamed. He looked down into the pool beneath his bare toes. The emptiness before creation reflected back. The crackling of flame sounded the great Song; the circle of rocks sang the Song and the wind carried it to eternity. It was carrying him, too.

Not without Meghan...

Jared threw himself forward – out of the flames, against Meghan sitting on the dead throne. Jared tore the Black Rock from his sister's hands.

The terror and pain knocked him to the ground. The First Rock rolled from his slack fingers under Meghan's throne. It didn't matter. There was nothing in the universe but misery and suffering. Time crawled by. He felt his own death a hundred hundred times. He wept with loss and despair.

Distantly he heard his sister's voice. "Jar!"

She was here too...there was no help for them...all was lost.

"Give me the Black Rock!" Kronos shouted.

Jared couldn't move. His flesh was dropping from his bones. Vaguely he heard Meghan again. His sister...she mustn't suffer like this. He tried to raise his head, move a skeletal arm. He held his hand out to her.

Then miraculously, through the bitter fog of despair, he felt her touch. He closed his fingers around hers. A new feeling pulsed through his fingertips, coursed up the veins of his arm, reached to his heart. Never letting go of his hand, she reached under the dead throne.

"Take this, Jared," she whispered. He looked at his right hand. The First Rock shimmered brightly. Slowly he stood up.

Kronos surged from his glittering throne toward the twins. Jared struck out blindly. His right fist, holding tight to the First Rock, smashed Kronos directly in the mouth.

Howling wind filled the Hall. The rocks in the ceiling above them loosened and cracked. The fire roared higher; the pool flowed outwards. Jared threw his arms around his sister, shielding her from flames and falling stone. The dogs pressed against them.

The Song swelled and Jared flew again among the stars. Then the world seemed to explode.

He, Meghan and the dogs lay on open heath. The great Hall was gone.

"Meghan!" Jared crawled to his twin.

She took a long sobbing breath and got to her knees.

"Oh Jar," she whispered. "He said I would be famous and rich and everyone would idolize me. And I could see it and feel it just like I was there. It was everything I'd ever dreamed about. But he wanted your rock. I promised I wouldn't let you down, Jared, and I didn't. I held onto it...I didn't let go."

He held her as she wept. The dogs circled and burrowed their soft furry faces against her, wiping her tears with their kisses until she shakily laughed and pushed them away.

The stars were beginning to fade above them. Jared picked up the two stones. They felt lighter, less charged with power.

"We have to go to the Singing," Jared told her. "We have to finish this. Can you make it?"

"Oh, yes. I have a score to settle." Meghan got unsteadily to her feet.

Half running, half supporting each other, the twins scrambled back to the trail. The winds and mist eddied around them. Jared steered a wide circle around the rocks where Ian's body lay. The sky was still dark, but Jared detected the sun's glow edging up on the horizon.

It was not yet dawn when they reached the car park, but perilously close to it.

"You know how to drive?" Meghan demanded.

"New talent," Jared shot back. Over the squeal of mishandled gears, the dogs panted softly in the back. With a smile, Meghan leaned wearily against the seat, then squirmed forward.

"What's this?" She held up the paper sack.

"Apples," Jared replied. "Mrs. Jenkins sent them – to keep up our strength."

This seemed hysterically funny all of a sudden. Laughing and trying to steer one-handed, Jared took an apple and bit in. The second the juice flowed over his tongue, he felt strength flowing back into his body – the strength of the ancient tree.

"Good apples," he said.

"Mmph," Meghan mumbled through a mouthful.

Jared shot down the deserted roads. Power had come back on in the villages, lighting the roads as dawn approached.

"Where are we going?" Meghan asked.

"Arbor Low," Jared replied. "That's where the stones will be reconsecrated and remade."

He didn't voice his fear that John and the others might not have roused from their stupor in time to reach the making place. They needed four singers. Not two.

He drove desperately, disregarding all safety. Meghan braced herself against the dashboard but said nothing.

"There," she pointed to the small sign indicating the turn-off. Jared wheeled the car onto the narrow lane.

Dawn had come but it was nearly obscured by the rolling clouds.

"Kronos and Rhea." Megan pointed. Her hand shook slightly. "I love a family get-together."

Jared smiled and steered down the track to the farm house. Dodging cars left every which way, he parked as close as he could get. They flung open the doors and raced toward the field where they could see the great stones lying silent in the grass.

Hoof beats. Rhea's horse reared and pawed the air in front of them. Jared held the two stones aloft. With a curse, Rhea let them pass.

The hill surrounding the stone circle was ringed with people, all bravely singing against crashing thunder and howling wind. Meghan and Jared ran toward the processional entrance.

Soaring into the sky, two voices sang the Song – John and their mother. Mrs. Jenkin's voice was a near inaudible quaver. There was no fourth part.

The twins burst into the center. Ten stones gleamed sickly on the fallen offering stones in the center of the stone circle. John stood to the north, Deirdre to the south. On her knees, Mrs. Jenkins still sang in the east.

Cursing like the release of all hell, Kronos rode his red stallion into the ditch surrounding the circle. Rearing and pawing, the horse scattered the people before it. Seeing Jared and Meghan, the immortal's face distorted in rage. He spurred his horse toward their mother.

"No!" Jared screamed.

Deirdre saw him coming. But instead of running, she raised her arms and sang, pure melody soaring above the chaos of thunder and screams of the chorus. The horse reared, but Kronos drove him on.

"Mom!" Meghan cried.

Two black and white streaks shot across the ground. The dogs closed like a vise on the stallion's hocks. Kronos slashed down at them. With a howl of pain, Mattie spun across the grass. Snarling, Billy leaped for the horse's legs and slashed the tendons. The horse screamed, fell, then faded away.

Jared ran to the center of the circle and laid Transformation and Fear in their places. Mattie lay, eyes open, whimpering softly.

"Jared, help us," wept Mrs. Jenkins.

Meghan ran to her. Two singers helped the woman stagger from the spot. Meghan began to sing, counterpoint to the melody that Deirdre and John still carried. Barely able to see for tears, Jared stumbled to the west point of the circle. Thunder and wind roared; lightning struck again and again in the field beyond. Beneath their feet the earth heaved and rolled.

Jared began to sing. The Song rose to the sky and once again he soared in the joy of creation. The lines that joined all life strengthened and shot down into the rich earth. The cacophony of the immortals faded beneath the great hymn of joy and reverence for life. The thrashing earth settled and calmed.

The sun had fully arisen as the Song wound down to its last glorious refrain. In the center of the circle, the stones shone with pure white light. Jared felt lines of power and water stretching out through the earth, farther and farther, creating channels of sacred peace for the earth. He felt joy and the clean rightness of it.

But then his eyes fell on Mattie, where she lay bleeding on the grass. Ignoring the cheering around him, barely able to walk from exhaustion, Jared stumbled to his dog.

Her white chest was red with blood and her eyes seemed dim. Still she whimpered and edged her nose into his hand. Jared held her and cried. His family and the others gathered round.

"Put her in the circle," Meghan sank to her knees beside him.

"The circle is for humankind, not animals," Peter said gruffly.

"There wouldn't *be* humankind without her," Meghan hissed at him. "Come on!" Staggering in tiredness, she tried to lift the dog.

"Let me," John said. His arms gently scooped up the animal and carried her to the center of the offering stones. He laid her on the soft turf in their center. Jared followed, letting his hand rest gently on Mattie's head, humming the chorus of the Song as though it were a lullaby. From above his head and beneath his feet, he felt the power from the consecrated rocks gathering and flowing outwards like a flower blooming across the earth.

Above, the last of the clouds cleared and the sun shone brilliantly. Raising his eyes, Jared saw Kronos, remounted on his fiery horse watching from the distant hills. The lines of power stretched from the stone circle reaching toward the god.

"Till, we meet again, my son," echoed in a gust of cool winds.

Jared's mouth hardened. "I don't think so, Kronos."

The immortal faded into the bright sunlight and disappeared.

Jared felt a shudder under his hand. "Mattie," he whispered. The dog lurched to her feet, stood a moment, shook herself and leapt joyfully into his arms. He lay on his back, with the dog standing gleefully on his chest and slopping her tongue over his face.

"Ow, no, Mattie. Yuck! You have dog breath!"

*   *   *

They barely remembered the ride back to the Castle. Jared had a vague impression of John stripping off his shreds of outer clothing and putting him in bed. Bewilderingly, it was still morning when he woke up.

"It's tomorrow morning," his mom explained from the window seat where she perched. She crossed the room and kissed his forehead. He put his arms round her and hugged hard. "Man, it's good to be home," he whispered.

She hugged back and grinned at him. "Yes, it is. At last."

She left then to go make him breakfast. Meghan, she told him, had woken up a couple of hours before. John and the others had gone to fetch Ian's body from the mountain.

Mattie came bouncing in, tail wagging. Jared allowed a couple of wet kisses before dragging himself out of bed and into the shower. Clean felt very good.

After breakfast, Jared found his twin up on the battlements gazing out at the soft green hills and the village nestling in their folds.

"You okay?" he asked.

She nodded. "I thrive on supernatural, near death experiences. I even prefer them before breakfast."

He punched her lightly in the arm. She smacked him back and grinned.

"I've been thinking about what would have happened if I'd sold the stone to Malik for a hundred bucks," she said. "It would have been the end of humanity as we know it."

"You sound like a science fiction movie."

"It feels like one. That would have meant that the human race only cost a hundred bucks."

Jared leaned on the battlements beside her. "You didn't sell out."

"I wanted to."

"But you didn't."

Meghan considered it. "Yes, when the chips are down, I am terrific," she agreed.

They laughed. Jared turned as he heard footsteps behind them. John came out on the battlement. His face was tired, the lines more deeply drawn around his mouth. Did he know that Jared had left his dying brother on the Dark Peak?

"I'm sorry about Ian," Jared said awkwardly.

Meghan bit her lip and said nothing.

"Yes." John leaned on the low wall beside them. "I'm sorry, too," he replied. Silence lay heavily between them. "We were never close, even as boys. I was the oldest. He called me the Holy Chosen. He wanted to inherit Apple Tor Castle – not its responsibilities. Only the money and the land."

"You don't know how hard it is," Meghan said, "to grow up seeing all the good stuff in the world, and know that none of it is yours."

"If that is what you believe is the good stuff." John rubbed his hand along the weathered stone. "You have your mother's insight – and temper. Jared, now, seems a little slower – a bit like me, perhaps."

Jared felt his breath suspend. Meghan rolled her eyes. "Like father, like son."

"John," Jared suddenly blurted out. "Ian wasn't dead. He was hurt dreadfully. He begged me to get help, but I left him because Kronos had Meghan. I had to tell you, before..."

"Before what," John asked at last.

"Nothing," Jared flushed and turned back to stare over the valley.

"You two are so pathetic," Meghan interrupted. "He means before you two settle on him living here at the Castle forever and being your prodigal son and all that stuff."

"Meghan!"

John smiled and held out his hand to Jared. "I want you to stay. And you are my son." He held out his other hand to Meghan. She stared at him, then suddenly flung herself between his two arms, onto his chest. He held her closely. Jared stood watching, feeling cold and envious.

Meghan raised her wet face, grabbed her brother's sleeve and yanked him closer. "Hug," she commanded.

And they did.

Epilogue

Two weeks later, Meghan found Jared in his favorite spot in the window embrasure. Mattie slept at his feet.

"I'm leaving," Meghan told him.

"What?" Jared swiveled in the window seat, scattering his textbooks. "We've finally got a home. We started school today – a real school, like we always dreamed about."

Meghan perched up close beside him. "Like you always dreamed about," she said. "This domestic scene, in the country no less, is not my dream."

"Fame and fortune?" Jared asked. Meghan nodded.

"I need to sing more than one song." She leaned against the stone wall. "And Kronos did show me how it could be."

"You refused him!"

"Unlike Ian, I refused to sell out my brother to get what I want," she retorted.

"There's no rule that I can't get there by my own talent."

Jared looked out over the hills again. "When do you want us to leave?" He was glad his voice didn't shake.

Meghan drove a friendly punch into his arm. "What do you mean, us? I'm flying solo on this one. Mom is making calls for me and John said he'd drive me up to London. Ian's town house belonged to the family, not to him. I can stay there."

"By yourself?"

Meghan giggled. "No. Mrs. Jenkins is coming too. Did you know she was Mom's voice teacher? That's how she ended up here. But she says now the crisis is over, she's had it with being a housekeeper. She's coming too and we're going for the big time."

"Wow! And I'm not jealous at all." Jared grinned.

Her face suddenly went sad. "I'll miss you."

"Yeah. But I don't plan to stay in the dungeon. I'll come and see your big openings."

"You'd better." She hugged him quickly, then blushed. "Okay then, I've got to pack. We're leaving first thing tomorrow."

She went to her own room, Billy at her heels. Mattie leaped up on the window sill and sat beside him. Books forgotten, Jared gazed out at the Dark Peak. Kronos was still up there. The battle wouldn't end.

Mattie huffed, and like a cat curled contentedly against him. Jared picked up his math book. Gods and the fate of humankind would have to wait. He had homework to do.

Thank you for reading
Twelve

If you enjoyed this, please leave a review
on Amazon.com (even a sentence helps!) so that
other readers can more easily find *Twleve*.

You can find more exciting books by
Susan Brown at www.susanbrownwrites.com

And keep reading for excerpts from
other books by Susan Brown.

Enjoy!

And now a Sneak Peek at

Dragons of Frost and Fire
"I know she's still alive!"

A year ago her mother disappeared in an Alaskan blizzard, but Kit Soriano refuses to give up. Against all logic, propelled by recurring dreams of ice-white dragons and a magical silver knife, Kit journeys to the wilderness town of Silver Claw where her mother vanished. She's clearly not welcome, but her knife throbs with heat and her dreams show the impossible – mythical dragons are guarding her sleeping mother.

The Nightmare and the Unicorn

A Nightmare is hunting Sky Whitmore. Nothing stands between the teenager and the man's malignant evil except the family legend of unicorn magic.

She may be desperate, but Sky doesn't believe in unicorns. Still, when she forms a bond with a mysterious stallion, the unicorn enchantment awakens. With nothing but this uncertain magic, Sky and her magnificent white horse must face and defeat the Nightmare.

DRAGONS OF
FROST AND FIRE

DRAGONS OF EARTH,
WATER, FIRE AND AIR

BY

SUSAN BROWN

ONE

The floatplane touched down on Silver Lake, spewing sheets of water into the air. Pressing her icy hands against the passenger window, Kit Soriano tried to force back a shudder. This far north, the Rocky Mountains peaks thrust into the sky like teeth – old teeth, cruel teeth, with glacial lips pulled back into a snarl.

"Silver Claw," the pilot called over his shoulder. "Last stop of humanity."

David Soriano peered out his own window, then reached his hand across the seat to grip his daughter's cold fingers. Silently they stared at this terrible place where they had come to find answers. Beyond the narrow beach, a few weather-beaten buildings made up the town. Past that, mountainous ice caps blended into clouds in every direction. At the north end of the lake, a glacier hundreds of feet high lay between the mountains like a mythic sleeping monster. Aqua and blue ice shone translucent in the sunlight.

"This is what mom tried to describe...." Kit gripped the dragon-shaped knife hidden in her pocket – she was going to need every ounce of magic her mother had said it possessed. There was nothing else left for her to believe in.

The pilot eased the plane to the dock and cut the engine. Kit's ears still thrummed with the vibrations, when a series of rumbles and cracks rolled across the lake and through the skin of the plane. An ice monolith slowly split from the glacier and crashed into the water. Spray shot a hundred feet into the air. Shock waves raced across the lake, rocking the plane.

When Kit gasped and clutched the armrests, the pilot laughed. "That's Silver Snake Glacier." He pointed to the ice cliff. "In spring it breaks up some – calving, it's called. But you've never heard anything like the roars and howls that come from that ice snake in winter. I was holed up here one year when an early blizzard rolled in. I swear I thought the noise alone would kill me."

Kit forced herself to stare impassively at the forbidding Alaskan landscape. "I'm not afraid of noise." She would not, would not let this place defeat her.

The pilot shrugged. "Hope you're not planning to stay too long," he warned. "Once winter gets her talons into this country, it can cost you your life to go outside of town."

"We'll be back in New York by winter," her father said. "We're only staying a couple of weeks."

Until we find her, Kit vowed.

The pilot heaved himself out of his chair, wrestled with the door, and showed them how to scramble down to the pontoon and then jump onto the dock. Kit shivered. Even though it was mid-August, the Alaskan air was cold through her fleece vest. She warmed up a little as they unloaded their gear.

A dozen of the town's residents drifted down to the dock, but Kit kept her eyes off the kids. Those kids had lured her mother to Silver Claw – nearly a quarter of them were albino, a genetic mutation. Dr. Nora Reits had been a genetics researcher. Nearly a year ago, she had disappeared without a trace in an early fall storm in Silver Claw.

Kit again touched the silver pocketknife nestled in her pocket. Magic find her, she prayed silently. Warmth tingled against her skin – the connection was still strong. Relieved, Kit turned her energy to separating their gear from the supplies ordered by the residents.

A lot of folks were on the dock now. In spite of herself, Kit sneaked a look under her lashes. The albino kids had snow-white hair and glacier blue eyes. Unlike some albino people, their sparkling glances showed good eyesight and they glowed with health.

"Dr. Soriano?" A big man with red hair stuck out his hand to Kit's father. "I'm Pat Kelly, mayor of this place. I wish I could welcome you here under better circumstances."

Dr. Soriano shook hands with the mayor. "We appreciate your willingness to let us get some closure on my wife's disappearance."

The mayor nodded. "I understand your feelings. We lost one of our own boys in that blizzard. This is a hard land – beautiful, but hard."

"Yes," Dr. Soriano said gazing at the ring of jagged peaks. "But I'm hoping the clinic will be a useful return for your hospitality."

"My mother-in-law will keep you busy, even if no one else does," Pat replied with an easy smile. "It's a long flight to Anchorage when the problems are the aches and pains old folks feel every time the weather changes."

As Kit reached up to grab the rest of their bags, she drew a deep breath. After all the setbacks and problems, she could hardly believe they were really here.

It had taken her father weeks to work out their journey. Getting to Silver Claw would be no problem – a regular flight from New York City to Anchorage and then they could book seats on the floatplane that delivered supplies to the town every couple of weeks. But inquiries about where to stay had been discouraging. There was apparently no reliable Internet connection that far north, and so all communication was by snail mail. A letter from the town council, signed Mary McGough, Secretary, had been brusque. The council regretted there was no hotel in Silver Claw.

Dr. Soriano's lips had thinned as he read the letter aloud to Kit.

"Isn't she the person Mom rented a room and office from? Wasn't it above a store or something?" Kit had asked.

"Yup," her dad said. "Let's try this one more time." That evening, he wrote back politely requesting that he and his daughter rent the room that his wife had previously occupied.

Three weeks later a second response from the town secretary stated that she was using the space Dr. Reits had rented for storage and so it was no longer available.

"I don't think they want us," Dr. Soriano had told his daughter over macaroni and cheese.

"I don't care. You promised me..." Kit looked challengingly into his eyes.

"And I keep my promises," he'd said. "Have some salad. It's only a little brown."

After dinner, while Kit had loaded the dishwasher and then tackled physics homework, he had written a third letter to the town council.

Dear Members of the Council,

I am hoping that we will still be able to work out the details of my daughter's and my visit. We are coming to Silver Claw. As east coast city people, we don't have a lot of experience with wilderness camping, but we will come with tents and backpacks and set up on the glacier itself, if necessary.

However, I have a proposal for you. I am a medical doctor and I'm willing to operate a free clinic for the residents of the area in return for accommodation and supplies while my daughter and I are in town.

We will be arriving on August 12th, with or without a place to stay.

Sincerely,
David Soriano, M.D.

The next response came from Pat Kelly instead of the secretary and it was a lot friendlier. A new cabin had been built for his family and he was willing to let Kit and her dad use it for a couple of weeks. He sympathized with the Soriano's need to see the town where Dr. Reits had spent her last few weeks. The residents of the town would be pleased to welcome them.

Kit and her dad flew from New York on August 11th, spent the night in Anchorage and the next morning boarded the small floatplane.

After all her thinking and worrying, it seemed to Kit that she was in a dream as she stood at the edge of the dock and gazed across the wild landscape. The glacier glinted, shifting colors like a living, crystal animal.

Mayor Kelly turned from Dr. Soriano to the people standing on the dock behind him. "Here, you kids give a hand. Kirsi...Dai...grab some of the bags."

Two of the older albino teenagers, a girl and boy, left the group. Both were tall and strong, their white-blonde hair ruffling in the steady breeze. They radiated health and were incredibly good looking. Mesmerized, Kit realized with a small shock that they were better than good looking – they were the most beautiful teens she had ever seen. They were graceful, perfectly proportioned, and there wasn't even a zit to be seen. Kit thought she could hate them just for that.

As Kirsi leaned down to pick up luggage, she turned cold blue eyes toward Kit. "You shouldn't have come here," she hissed. "You soft city people don't belong." She hoisted the heavy pack over her shoulder with ease and strode away without a backward glance.

The breeze off the lake quickened. Kit shivered.

"You'll get used to the temperatures," Dai said beside her. He appeared about seventeen, a year older than she was. Up close, Kit thought his looks alone could warm her up.

Kit made a grab for her peace of mind and shrugged. "I'm not afraid of the cold."

"That's good because sometimes we get a lot of it. I'm Dai Phillips." He stuck out his hand to shake.

Kit hesitated a split second, then shook his hand. It was so very warm and firm. A responding flash of heat shot through her. This was not normal for her at all.

"I'm Kit." At home the kids either didn't touch or did hand slaps and fist bumps. Nobody under forty shook hands.

Patrick Kelly picked up one of Dr. Soriano's medical cases. "We do appreciate your willingness to run a health clinic even for two weeks, Doc," he said. "Hey there, Jancy. You, Mikey. Help the doctor with his bags." Two red-haired children each picked up a suitcase. "Dai, are you going to stand around all day or are you going to help that little girl out?"

Hot color flushed Dai's face. "Yes, Uncle Pat," he said under his breath. He reached for a duffel. "This yours, Kit?"

"I'll get it," she said. "I packed it. I can carry it." She hoisted it up and over her thin shoulder. "And I'm sixteen...not a little girl." She knew she looked too young and fragile to be in the wilderness. But she also knew that her slender bones were connected to tough muscle.

"Okay," Dai said. "But it's a bit of a hike to the cabin and I'm used to the path."

"Whatever." Kit slid the bag back to the dock, refusing to allow even a flicker of relief to cross her face. She'd jammed it with everything she thought might be useful – survival gear, guidebooks, contour maps, compass, and a Swiss Army knife.

Dai's deep blue eyes searched her own.

"What?" Kit demanded. His intense gaze unnerved her.

Dai leaned over and lifted the bag like it weighed six ounces instead of sixty pounds. "It's good you've come to us – you're the kind that's called."

"Called? Called what?"

"Called by the mountains and wilderness. By the heart that beats up there." Again, his eyes pierced her own. "Your mother was the same. You both belong here. I feel it."

Kit felt a lump rise sharply in her throat so she turned away and stared at the town as though fascinated by the worn clapboard structures. Kirsi stood at the top of the path, arms folded, looking stonily down at the people on the dock. Kit stared back defiantly.

"My mother didn't belong here and I don't either," she turned and told Dai. "I'm going to find out what happened to her and then you'll never see me again."

She picked up a bag and marched up the path toward Kirsi. Other men and children took the rest of the luggage. The remainder of the people finished unloading boxes of supplies from the plane and began hauling them up the hill toward town. Dai strode after her, whistling off-key. Kit glanced back at him. She had never seen anyone so vibrantly alive. And he had talked about her mother. Had he gotten to know her? Would he have information that would lead Kit to her?

Abruptly she slowed down, matching her steps to his. But with a cool glance, he trudged faster away from her, still whistling. Kit's eyes narrowed, but she followed without comment. In a moment she had reached Kirsi. The girl looked her over like she was a dead fish washed onto the shore.

"Stay away from Dai. He has no use for your kind," Kirsi mocked.

"What kind is that, Kirsi?" Kit demanded.

The girl's lips curled into a sneer. "A weak outlander. You'll be very sorry you ever came here." She shoved past Kit, knocking her off balance.

Regaining her footing, Kit glared after her. "I think you will be surprised." She made no effort to catch up, waiting instead for her dad and the others.

"The house is this way, Doctor." Mayor Kelly gestured along an overgrown dirt road that edged the lake. "The clinic building is in town, but this cabin has an incredible view of Silver Snake."

The cabin sat on a rounded hill overlooking the lake. The building was made of shaped logs, with a fresh look about them. Shuttered windows along the sides were wide and evenly spaced. A long porch was angled to face the glacier.

Everyone trooped through the screen door, but Kit dropped her bag and leaned on the railing, looking towards mountains and ice. Behind her, voices filled the cabin. But out here, the stillness folded into a sense of being on the edge of another world. Kit breathed deeply, tasting the tang of wilderness, and another acrid scent – sweet and bitter mingled. She tossed her head to let the clean air wash over her. After the long despair, she was coming alive again. Kit remembered how her mother had described this place in her letters....

Silver Snake Glacier drapes the mountains like a huge sleeping animal. It really seems alive, shifting with every color that ever existed. I hope you get to see it some day – it must be one of the wonders of the world! I am going to hike up there and see if I can fathom its secrets. Something that otherworldly must have secrets, Kit. Devin tells me the glacier is riddled with crevasses and caves – a beautiful but deadly creature, I guess. It wakes when the winter storms howl over the mountains....

Dai came out on the porch and stood beside her. Despite herself, Kit was too aware of the warmth he radiated. Of those broad shoulders and lithe build. She'd never been this aware of the boys at home. Pheromones. He must be radiating mutated pheromones and she was feeling every one of them.

Another crack shattered the quiet of the town.

"Loud, isn't it?" Kit said turning to him. She froze. His eyes were a deeper blue. She'd swear they had darkened. Ridiculous. Even weird eyes, genetically mutated eyes, shouldn't change color. It had to be a trick of the light.

"This is a great time of year to be in Silver Claw." Dai's expression once again lightened to an easy smile. "There's hiking, hunting and fishing during the day and bonfires and get-togethers at night. Mary McGough at the general store gets in movies now and then."

"Sounds terrific," Kit said, "But I already have plans." She forced herself to turn away from those hot, mesmerizing eyes and look back at the cold waters of the lake. Her mother had said native legends put some kind of mythic beast in those cold depths.

Then Dai's hand, hot and strong, gripped her arm. "There are no other plans in Silver Claw," Dai told her. "You'll be smart to listen to me." The warning in his voice was unmistakable.

"Or what?" Kit challenged. How friendly or how dangerous was this guy? He was like fire and ice. Already this place was freaking her out, all beauty and danger.

His eyes shifted even darker, making that weird sense of warmth flare through her again. She didn't know whether he would have answered or not because they were interrupted by the door swinging open. The moment bled away.

"Kit," her dad called. "Which bedroom do you want?"

"Excuse me," Kit stepped past Dai and followed her father.

Inside, several men and women had settled on the sofas and chairs. Dai came in after her and crossed over to Kirsi who leaned against the far wall. As they stood talking in quiet voices and sometimes glancing in her direction, Kit felt another surge of anger. Were they talking about her? And why should she care?

In the meantime, two women were opening and shutting the cupboard doors in the kitchen area, calling on Dr. Soriano to admire how thoroughly they had stocked up for him.

"My wife is bringing some lasagna over," the mayor said. "A bit of a welcome to let you get yourself unpacked and settled tonight."

"Dr. Soriano," Dai struck in, "my mother said I'm to ask you for dinner tomorrow at seven, if you don't have other plans.... " He glanced mockingly at Kit.

"Great," Dr. Soriano said. "That's very kind. We'll be there. Now Kit, what about that bedroom?"

Three bedrooms opened off the kitchen-dining-living area, so Kit chose one where the window faced the glacier. While her dad chatted with the people who had helped bring their belongings up, Kit hauled in her bags. Methodically, she unpacked her clothing and filled the drawers of the wooden dresser. She left all her survival gear in the duffel bag, zipped it up, and pushed it far under the bed.

"Kit!" her dad called. "The most marvelous dinner is being spread out here for us!"

The main room was packed with big, loud strangers. It seemed like everyone who had come down to the dock had migrated up to the cabin and brought a few friends along. Did any of those open, friendly faces hide the secret of her mother's disappearance? She wanted to shout at them, demand they tell her what they knew, but instead she forced herself to paste on a fake smile.

"Please, you must stay," her father was urging.

With only a brief show of reluctance, everyone dug into the lasagna, salad, bread and meat that all seemed to have magically appeared. Kit picked among the dishes and settled in the remotest corner of the sofa. Dai left Kirsi and perched on the arm beside her.

Ignoring him, Kit took a bite of the dark meat. Flavor exploded in her senses.

"Backstrap," Dai said. "The tenderest and tastiest part of a moose."

Kit put her fork down but chewed on. It was good – different from anything else she'd tasted. "Great!" she mumbled through her full mouth.

"You're honored," Dai said. "That's probably the last of Uncle Pat's winter store. He's the best hunter in town, but we try to only hunt moose in the fall and winter."

Kit cut another piece of meat and popped it in her mouth. "The only moose I ever saw for real was in a zoo. It was big and sad looking so it seems cruel to hunt them."

"We have to eat and there aren't many fast food restaurants in the wilderness," Dai replied. "Besides, those hamburgers don't come from carrots."

Kit took a big bite of her bread to avoid answering. She knew he was right, but she didn't want to acknowledge that the rules were different here in Silver Claw. With mountains, lakes and glaciers surrounding them, they hunted to eat. They killed to survive.

A burst of laughter filled the cabin. She tried another bite of backstrap. It tasted fine on her tongue. Kit looked around at all the handsome, strong faces. She would learn what they knew, she vowed. And if they had secrets, she would find them.

Despite their protests about letting the Sorianos unpack, the townspeople didn't leave for hours. By the time Kit could finally get to bed, she was too wound up to sleep.

Outside, twilight had eased over the land, casting the mountains into dark relief. The luminous hands on her watch read 11:03 but the sky still shone dusky blue. Kit sat on her bed, wrapped in a quilt, looking out toward Silver Snake Glacier.

It drew her, called her, just as Dai had said it would. Her mom's letters had described the hours she spent hiking by the glacier. She'd written that the sight and sound of the ancient ice relieved her frustrations when the townspeople refused to cooperate with her research.

And that's how I'll start, Kit decided; she would go to the places her mother had described, try to find some kind of clue her mother may have left behind. Looking out the open window at the immense distances and peaks, Kit wondered with a sinking heart whether she would be able to find the places from the descriptions in the letters. In New York, hemmed in by buildings and streetlights, she had not been able to grasp the vastness of the landscape.

Her father came in, set a lantern on the table beside her bed and sat down.

"They seem like nice people around here," he said at last.

Kit rolled her eyes. "That's what Mom said...until they found out what she was doing."

Her hand slipped under her pillow to touch the knife and the packet of letters. In the last one, Nora Reits had written in an excited scrawl from her office over the general store. She had said she would try to slip the letter into the outgoing mail sack before the floatplane arrived. This flight, she was sure, would bring lab results for the blood samples she had coaxed from one albino boy. Kit got the letter two days after her mother disappeared.

"Kit, it was a simple hiking accident," her dad said. "You know she hiked up there alone, even though the weather was threatening."

"Then why did the lab results disappear?" Kit demanded. "And the searchers didn't find a body. They're keeping her somewhere. I know it! My knife...."

"Kit, don't start about that knife again." Her father rubbed his hand over his face; his eyes were exhausted. Kit fell silent.

If only he would believe what Kit knew against all reason was true. Her mother was alive.

Another crack reverberated through the air. The lantern flickered. Somewhere, out there, Kit knew her mother was alive.

The Nightmare and the Unicorn

by

Susan Brown

Chapter 1

A flash of lightning and crack of thunder caused Sky to jerk against the car's worn seatbelt. Shaking with exhaustion and repressed anger, she looked over at her mom. Lindey peered anxiously through the sheeting rain, gripping the steering wheel until her knuckles whitened. She glanced at her daughter and forced a smile.

"Almost there..." her voice trailed off. "Can you feel it Sky?" Lindey's voice shook with longing. "Can you feel the magic? The legend says it comes from the horses..."

"All I'm feeling is tired." Sky pushed back the hair that had fallen forward over her face with the last lurch of the car. "We've been on the road for two days. You know what he'll do if he catches us....and you want to talk fairy tales."

"They're not fairy tales," Lindey insisted. "It's real. It happened."

"Yeah. Sure." Sky didn't care. Not when they were running for their lives. Not when she knew what the Nightmare would do if he caught them. Another one of her mother's desperate plans. But this time Sky had insurance against the Nightmare safely tucked in her jacket pocket. Would it be enough? Another flash of lightning and crack of thunder made her wince and press back against the seat.

"I know you think it's crazy," her mom persisted. "But you've got to know why our family has horse magic."

Sky stared out the window – too tired and too terrified to argue with her mother. Maybe if she just let her talk, they could get her back to sense. Back to the reason they had taken this insane journey.

Her mom's voice went singsong from the thousandth repetition. "The Whitmore women have horse magic. It's all because my great-grandmother saved a unicorn."

"Unicorn. Right," Sky muttered. Reluctantly, she felt slightly soothed by the words. This was the story she'd believed in when she was a kid. The one that backed up the big, stupid promise that everything would be okay. The one she had tried so hard to believe. The one that had trapped them.

Lindey's voice rose over the growl of the motor and the roar of wind. "Nearly a hundred years ago, there was this herd of wild horses – beautiful, strong. But the ranchers wanted them slaughtered to free up grazing land for cattle. My great-grandmother was fourteen, just like you, Sky, but she stopped the kill by running into the middle of the herd. And just like a miracle, the horses quieted.

"Then, one by one, the horses stepped back and the unicorn came. It was his herd she'd saved. He touched her with his silver horn. He...he promised..." Her mom's voice shook. "He promised he would come if she needed help." Lindey paused, face shadowed then illuminated as lightning exploded across the night. "No matter how much I needed it, Sky, I never saw a unicorn. But the women in our family are all horsewomen."

"I've never been on a horse," Sky said wearily.

"Yeah, but it's in your blood, and I promise Aunt Judy'll get you on a horse." Her mom looked worriedly down the dark road as their headlights flashed against the white pasture fences and the wall of rain.

Sky leaned forward to stare out too, hoping to get a glimpse of some horses – real ones, not her mom's crazy story about a unicorn galloping in the Pacific Northwest fog. Throughout the endless scramble to pay rent, keep a job, build a life for the two of them, her mom had never stopped talking about the horses. About the yellow farmhouse where she had grown up. About her Aunt Judy who had long ago taught her to train horses. About the home where they would finally be safe from the Nightmare.

Suddenly Lindey cranked the wheel. Sky's shoulder banged against the passenger door as the car abruptly turned into a gravel driveway almost hidden by thick shrubs.

"Those bushes weren't so big before," her mom said apologetically.

Sky rubbed her shoulder and stared at the house. It was just the way her mom had described it – square, butter-yellow, steep red roof over its second story, big and evenly spaced windows on the ground floor, and a wide covered porch at the back. Light shone warmly through uncurtained windows on the lower floor.

Sky leaned toward the light as the car rumbled over the driveway. On either side, pale roses glimmered through the dripping shrubs – more splashes of light against the night. A big yard, shadowed by more shrubs, stretched into the night with a big shed at the end.

The car lurched and stopped. Lindey switched off the ignition and for a moment they sat silently, staring at the farmhouse they had driven so long to reach.

"Remember, Sky," her mom said, "don't say anything about..."

"Not like I'll forget," Sky snapped, "but are you sure? Can you trust her? If Aunt Judy knew what happened...?"

Her mom gripped Sky's arm tightly, fear stiffening her fingers.

"I'm not sure about anything," she whispered. "I ran away and abandoned all this ages ago. But coming back, in spite of my mistakes, is the best chance we have. Don't say anything! Please! Promise me."

"I told you. I've promised." Sky pulled back her arm.

"Well then, let's do it." Her mom shoved open the rusted car door.

Yanking on the broken passenger door's handle until it opened, Sky stepped out, stumbling from cramped muscles and exhaustion. But she didn't make a sound as she swung her backpack over one thin shoulder and marched through the rain up to the covered porch. Carrying her own pack, her mom followed.

"Ready?" Not waiting for her daughter's nod, Lindey rapped on the wood frame. "Hope she's home...."

Sky noticed her mom was breathing hard, short breaths through flared nostrils; she had run her fingers through her hair so often, it had tangled like someone lost in tonight's storm. The bruises on her cheek and jaw shaded to murky green in the porch light. Sky looked away from her mom's tired face and tried to peer through the door's glass panes. A moment later, a light warmed the kitchen and a woman strode forward. A black dog, the size of a small cow, woofed beside her.

"Who's there?" the woman demanded, staring out into the half-light.

"Aunt Judy, it's me – Lindey. Your niece."

"Lindey? *Lindey!*"

The door swung open. A middle-aged woman in jeans and a faded sweatshirt with graying, frizzy hair pulled into a ponytail, gripped the collar of the dog with one hand and held out the other in welcome. The dog strained against her hand, broke loose and galumphed to Sky, plopping on his wiggling rear as he thrust his muzzle into her stomach in greeting.

"He's harmless." Aunt Judy held out her arms and, with a swallowed sob, Sky's mom stepped into the offered hug.

Sky looked straight into the dog's great brown eyes and sank to her knees. The dog laid his mammoth head on her shoulder in welcome, slobbering on her jacket.

"Hello," Sky whispered. Obligingly, the dog snuffled her ear and swashed a great wet tongue over her chin and cheek.

"Moose! Stop that!" Aunt Judy stepped back, keeping one arm around her niece's waist as she spoke to Sky. "He looks like a monster, but I swear he won't hurt you. I have an absolute rule that monsters are never allowed on my property."

"We've made friends." Sky stood and dropped her hand to the shoulder of the panting beast now leaning against her so hard she had to brace her feet to stay upright.

"He's a good judge of character." Aunt Judy's eyes swung back to her niece. "Lindey, you've waited so long. Fourteen years!" She looked hard at Sky. "So, this is your little girl? I thought you were in California, living the dream – cooking for some big hotel?"

Lindey's smile wavered. "I was. But you know what the times are. I got laid off. So here we are."

Aunt Judy peered at her. "That's quite a bruise on your face."

Lindey leaned over to scratch Moose's head. "I tripped and fell – hit my face on a railing."

"Uh huh. And I'm queen of Kalamazoo." Aunt Judy's expression was stern, but she stepped aside and gestured them in. "Come in and sit down. Can I make you a sandwich?" Her attention turned back Sky who was still standing close beside the dog. "And what's your name? I remember it's something unusual. Hippy sounding."

Lindey forced a laugh. "Even you are way too young for the hippy generation, Aunt Judy. Her name's Skylark...but she goes by Sky."

"And how old are you, Sky?"

"Fourteen," Lindey said, "but she's mature for her age."

Aunt Judy looked over the straight, thin girl before her. "You don't look fourteen."

With a nearly suppressed jab of irritation, Sky met her eyes steadily. "How old are you?"

"Fifty-three."

"You look fifty-three. One day you'll probably look sixty-three, but it won't change when you were born."

"Sky!" Lindey interrupted, pulling her daughter close.

Aunt Judy's cool grey eyes met the steely blue ones. "No, I guess it won't. Do you always say what you think?"

Sky twisted away from her mom and stood straight again.

"I'm sorry, Aunt Judy." Lindey grimaced and turned to her aunt. "We've driven all the way from California without hardly stopping. Can we sit down a bit?"

"Of course." With a slightly lurching step, Aunt Judy led them toward a living room that was furnished simply with a blanket-covered recliner, coffee table, and sofa, and cluttered with bookshelves, framed art, and overgrown plants. A big TV droned on one wall. Aunt Judy motioned them to the blue and brown, striped sofa, moved a pile of books from the cushions to the coffee table, and switched off the set.

"Get comfortable," Aunt Judy said. "So Lindey, after hardly a word in years, why are you here?"

Sky watched as her mom smiled her best smile and relaxed her shoulders. But she twisted her fingers and her skin flushed against the smudgy circles under her eyes.

"Aunt Judy," she began, "I'm desperate. I...we need a place to stay for a few days. My money's gone, but I've got a job – a good job – lined up...I just won't get paid for a week or two. And...I can't take Sky to a shelter or leave her in the car. Please...will you help us?"

Sky's eyes widened a bit at the lie. She and her mom had been in shelters before and slept in the car a couple of times too. But the Nightmare had always found them and made them come back. Sky felt her own fingers curling into fists. Her Mom had told her that this time they would keep going until they got away from him – that they would never go back to the Nightmare's world again. That he wouldn't be able to trace the old wreck of a car she'd bought. That they could live in the safety of the yellow farmhouse. But starting with a string of lies seemed like a stupid idea.

"Explain," Judy said.

"Sky, do you need to go to the bathroom or anything?" Lindey prompted.

Reluctantly recognizing her mom's cue, Sky nodded and stood up. Aunt Judy pointed to the hallway and said, "At the end."

Sky went, made noise closing the door, and slipped back to the edge of the hallway. Her heart was pounding but she kept her breath soft. Since the Nightmare had stolen their lives, she'd made it a rule to always listen.

"There isn't much to explain," Lindey murmured. "You know what it's like trying to get a job these days. I jumped at the chance of this one in Seattle. Closer to home. But I don't have any money, so I'm hoping that you would help us out for a few days."

"What about the money you inherited from your mother?" Aunt Judy's voice was razor sharp. Sky could picture her mom smiling the right smile, and then dropping her eyes. Even now, after everything, her mom wasn't much of a liar. Sky willed her mom to get it right. They didn't have anywhere else to go. She'd promised they would be safe. That Aunt Judy could protect them – even from the Nightmare. Sky no longer trusted that anyone could protect them. Her fingers slid over the lump in her pocket, reassuring herself that her insurance was still there. Fiercely, she told herself again that nothing could drag her back. Nothing.

"This isn't the first time I've been out of work...and a child costs a lot. Maybe I made some bad decisions."

That's for sure, Sky thought.

"Drugs?" Aunt Judy demanded.

"No!" Lindey's voice was vehement. "Never. I hate drugs. I know what they do."

There was silence. Sky eased back to the bathroom and flushed the toilet. She turned on the tap and then slid back to her listening post.

"I won't give you money," Aunt Judy said.

"And I didn't ask for any," Lindey retorted. "But Aunt Judy...I could use a place for us to stay for a few days. And you're the only family we've got." Sky heard the catch in her mom's voice. "I wanted Sky to see where I grew up, the place I loved before I made all those dumb mistakes...." Her voice trailed off but there was no answering sound from Aunt Judy. "Does...is Neil McClelland still raising thoroughbreds?"

"Yes," Aunt Judy said. "Winners, too." She paused. "His breeding and training programs are flawless," she said grudgingly. "His horses are some of the best in the country and they've made him rich. Are you thinking you can whisper his horses again? After everything?"

Silence. Bitterly, Sky pictured her mom's bowed head, her helpless tears.

Judy spoke again, but her voice suddenly sounded troubled. "He's got a new horse...a beautiful creature. But utterly, completely wild. Neil can't do a thing with him." Sky had to strain now to hear her aunt's voice. "There's something about that stallion that's calling for horse magic, Lindey. Did you lose your magic when you ran away from here? Have you...can you?"

Sky pressed closer to the wall. A thrill, unexpected and intense, caught her breath. She tried to push it away, but her childhood dreams had always been about horses, about the beautiful creatures her mom said she'd loved and trained. In the darkest of times, Sky imagined herself riding bareback through flower-laden fields or standing perfectly balanced, arms outspread, her body swaying easily to the perfect rhythm of a perfect horse. Free...

Lindey's sob broke open Sky's dreams. "No..." her mom said. "My gift is gone. I looked for a job at a stable in LA but the horses can't hear me any more. You were right, Aunt Judy. When I ran away, my magic died."

"I'm sorrier than I can say," Aunt Judy said softly.

"But I can still muck out a stable." There was a thin edge of longing in her mom's voice.

"I don't keep horses any more," Aunt Judy said bluntly. "Six years ago, I took a bad fall, broke my leg and hip." Silence stretched out. "You know Neil won't welcome you."

Sky heard her mother's weary assent.

"I've never met anyone who could make as many mistakes as you, Lindey," Aunt Judy said. "But I still see the goodness in you. The two of you can stay."

"Thanks...thanks, Aunt Judy."

So relieved she had to force back tears, Sky went back into the bathroom, turned off the tap, and returned to the living room. Her mom was leaning back into the sofa cushions in exhaustion, but her face twitched into a small smile. "Hey kiddo," she said, pulling her into a hug as though she were four, not fourteen. "How about we stay here for a few days?"

Resting her head against her mom's shoulder for a moment, Sky looked at Aunt Judy, assessing. Aunt Judy returned the gaze, also assessing. *She isn't sure she likes us...me...*

Sky realized. She gave an inward shrug. *We'll fix our lives without the old woman's help. Somehow.*

Moose huffed and collapsed into a pile at her feet, his head resting on her knees. Sky dug her fingers into his soft fur and suddenly felt her eyes droop in the exhaustion she couldn't fight off any longer. Later, after she had chewed through half a sandwich and gulped a mug of hot sweet tea, she stumbled after Aunt Judy upstairs to a small bedroom. Stripped to her underwear, Sky crawled under a pink flowered quilt, letting her hand trail over the side to rest on Moose's massive head. *Sleep... finally sleep....*

*   *   *

The next morning, the sun was barely up when a noise woke Sky. Completely still in the unfamiliar room, Sky searched her memory for where she was. *Aunt Judy's house.* A second sharp bang. Sky yanked herself out of bed, and, hands pressed against the glass, watched through the window. Below, her mom's car choked and revved. Sky tried to slow her breathing as the memories flooded her mind.

The plan. *The plan to escape the Nightmare.* Sky shivered. He must not find them again.

Never. Bitterly, she remembered her mom's statements that Aunt Judy's "magic" was enough to ward off the Nightmare's horror. How could her mother believe in fairy tales after what they'd suffered?

When the car turned onto the road and grumbled away out of sight, Sky got back into bed and pulled the quilt up over her head. She made her breath stop coming in harsh gasps, until eventually she drifted back to sleep.

Her old dream came again. She rode a white horse, standing, arms outstretched, rising and falling, light as a moonbeam in the rhythm of pounding hooves and glistening magic.

You can find Dragons of Frost and Fire and
The Nightmare and the Unicorn and
Susan's other great books on Amazon.com or at
www.susanbrownwrites.com

About Award-Winning Author, Susan Brown

What if? What if the extraordinary erupts into an ordinary life? Adventure, mystery, and magic fuel Susan Brown's imagination and writing, propelling her towards more and more stories for book-lovers who also live in wonder.

Susan lives with her border collie rescue dogs amid wild woods and overgrown gardens in Snohomish, Washington. From there she supervises her three daughters, assorted sons-in-law and two grandsons. It's a great way to be a writer!

Find more information, free stories, and news about upcoming books at:
http://www.susanbrownwrites.com

Susan Brown is also a founding member of the Writers Cooperative of the Pacific Northwest.
http://www.writers-coop.com